CLASSIC AT BAY

Recent Titles by Amy Myers from Severn House

The Jack Colby, Car Detective, Series
CLASSIC IN THE BARN
CLASSIC CALLS THE SHOTS
CLASSIC IN THE CLOUDS
CLASSIC MISTAKE
CLASSIC IN THE PITS
CLASSIC CASHES IN
CLASSIC IN THE DOCK
CLASSIC AT BAY

The Marsh and Daughter Mysteries

THE WICKENHAM MURDERS
MURDER IN FRIDAY STREET
MURDER IN HELL'S CORNER
MURDER AND THE GOLDEN GOBLET
MURDER IN THE MIST
MURDER TAKES THE STAGE
MURDER ON THE OLD ROAD
MURDER IN ABBOT'S FOLLY

CLASSIC AT BAY

A case for Jack Colby, Car Detective

Amy Myers

This first world edition published 2016
in Great Britain and the USA by
SEVERN HOUSE PUBLISHERS LTD of
19 Cedar Road, Sutton, Surrey, England, SM2 5DA.
Trade paperback edition first published
in Great Britain and the USA 2016 by
SEVERN HOUSE PUBLISHERS LTD

British Library Cataloguing in Publication Data
A CIP catalogue record for this title is available from the British Library.

ISBN-13: 978-0-7278-8608-8 (cased)
ISBN-13: 978-1-84751-711-1 (trade paper)
ISBN-13: 978-1-78010-772-1 (e-book)

All Severn House titles are printed on acid-free paper.

Severn House Publishers support the Forest Stewardship Council™ [FSC™],
the leading international forest certification organisation.
All our titles that are printed on FSC certified paper carry the FSC logo.

Typeset by Palimpsest Book Production Ltd.,
Falkirk, Stirlingshire, Scotland.
Printed and bound in Great Britain by
TJ International, Padstow, Cornwall.

Author's Note

Jack Colby has been working for the fictitious Kent Car Crime Unit for several years now, and *Classic at Bay* is his eighth recorded case. He operates at Frogs Hill near Pluckley, the former being fictitious, of course, but the latter very much the opposite. The Three Parrots club and some other locations mentioned in the story are also fictitious, but the general area of the North Downs and Greensand Ridge remain as glorious today as they were thousands of years ago.

My thanks go to my husband, James, who both encouraged me along the way in writing this novel and runs Jack Colby's blog for him (www. jackcolby.co.uk). I would also like to thank Adrian Turner and William Pettett for their help, and I remember with affection the late Peter Gladstone Smith, whose book *The Crime Explosion* was helpful in setting the scene for sixties Soho.

The bedrock for the publication, however, is my incomparable agent Sara Keane of Keane Kataria Literary Agency, together with the wonderful team at Severn House, including Piers Tilbury, whose cover designs flag Jack's cases off the starting grid so splendidly.

Jack Colby's list of those involved in his latest case:

Jack Colby: myself, the proud owner of Frogs Hill farmhouse and classic car restoration business

Louise: my partner in love

Len Vickers: irreplaceable crusty car mechanic in charge of the Pits, the barn we use for car restoration

Zoe Grant: Len's equally irreplaceable number two

Rob Lane: her come-and-go partner in love (not too sure about the love angle)

Dave Jennings: head of the Kent Car Crime Unit for whom I work (on and off)

DCI Brandon: of the Kent Police and Serious Crime Directorate

Adora Ferne: cabaret star of the fifties and sixties

Danny Carter: manager of her Jaguar collection

Diane Carter and Sam: Danny's estranged wife and son

Sir Rex Hargreaves: former husband of Adora Ferne and Three Parrots club member

Simon Hargreaves: son of Rex Hargreaves and Adora Ferne

Alice and Michael Hargreaves: Simon's daughter and son

Charlie Dane: former husband of Adora Ferne and son of the owner of the Three Parrots club

Melinda Dane Wilson: daughter of Charlie Dane and Adora Ferne

Harry Gale: former husband of Adora Ferne and hopeful prospective husband

Noel Brandon-Wright: former member of the Three Parrots club, now in a care home

Gabriel Allyn (now Earl of Storrington): former member of the Three Parrots club

Valentine Paston: former member of the Three Parrots club, now in a care home

Montague Greene: actor and former member of the Three Parrots club

Fred Fox: former gardener to and 'admirer' of Adora Ferne

Blake Bishop: former 'admirer' of Adora Ferne

Alan Reeve: former 'admirer' of Adora Ferne

Doubler: king of the Kent car crime underworld

ONE

'Don't go there!'

'Why not?' I had seen no earthly reason why Louise should warn me against driving over to Sussex to Downe Place. After all, it was in the interests of a paid commission to buy a classic Jaguar that personally I would drool over. So why should my beloved partner be so aghast at the idea?

I was beginning to realize I should have paid more attention, however. Louise hadn't been the only one to warn me. Zoe had backed her up.

'Forget it,' she had snorted. Zoe is number two to Len Vickers who runs the Pits – that's our name for the converted barn at Frogs Hill Farm in Kent, where our classic car restorations are carried out in loving detail. The business is owned by yours truly, Jack Colby, but it's easy to get the wrong impression, such is the single-minded devotion paid by Len and Zoe to their work.

'Why?' I had asked these two female pillars of my existence mildly as they exchanged meaningful looks.

'Adora Ferne.'

They had spoken in unison and so solemnly that I'd laughed and driven on my merry way. After all, I wasn't dealing with that notorious lady herself but with Danny Carter, the manager of Miss Ferne's car collection and an entirely different proposition. He was not quite so enticing perhaps, but certainly down to earth where my commission was concerned. My task would be to persuade the Right Honourable Earl of Storrington to sell his classic and rare 1937 SS 100 2.5 litre Jaguar sports car to my client. Price no object. 'Run it by me first,' Carter had said, 'but there's no ceiling. We've got to get it. It's the thirteenth car.'

Mine not to reason why, but to charge right ahead. Easy, I had thought. Now, at Downe Place, I could see there was a problem.

'My answer is no,' His Lordship told me courteously – almost anxiously, as though he were genuinely sorry to disappoint me. With a venerable classic car owner such as he to deal with courtesy was to be expected, especially as he must be nearly eighty, but there was an extra element here that seemed strange. For a start, if he was adamantly against selling the car, why had he agreed to see me?

'I can understand that,' I replied sympathetically – and honestly. The SS 100 Jaguar is a very special car, the most stylish of the pre-war models and, judging by the earl's dwelling at Riverdowne, a hamlet near the small town of Storrington, the cash value of the car – great though it was – could hardly be a factor. Besides that, the sordid matter of money had not even arisen between us.

I had another try. 'Although the buyer wishes to remain anonymous, there's a very good price on offer.'

'Of that I have no doubt,' he replied, 'but my answer is, and always will be, no. You may tell Mr Carter that.' A pause. 'And Miss Ferne,' he added.

It was not entirely to my surprise that he either knew or had guessed correctly who was behind the offer, and I wasn't going to fence with him. It was time to build a bridge. I longed to ask whether he knew Miss Ferne but that wouldn't be my best route. Cars would be, however. 'Do you have other classic Jaguars, Lord Storrington?'

'I do not.'

The attempted bridge had been quietly rejected. I'd come all this way and hadn't even seen the car. True, when I had asked Danny Carter why I couldn't simply ring the earl, I'd been told I would be paid both expenses and time, but even so, failure is never pleasant. We were taking coffee and some very tasty biscuits in what must once have been a splendidly impressive withdrawing room in a splendidly impressive Jacobean mansion. It was still impressive, but had been adapted for comfort, and this room was a relaxed mix of antique furniture and paintings, bookcases, a small writing desk and family photographs. In one corner stood a grand piano – an old Steinway at first guess.

Pleasant though this was, I was stumped. Should I gracefully retreat since it seemed clear that His Lordship was not going to change his mind? On the other hand, I reasoned, I had nothing to lose by prowling round this impenetrable fortress of a man, who didn't seem antagonistic towards me personally, only to my mission. That, at least, was a relief.

Impenetrable or not, his eyes were the gentlest I could remember seeing for a long while. Although he wasn't a tall man, his slim, wiry figure and composure gave him a commanding presence. I had checked him out online and learned with great interest that in his younger days he was judged to be a fine poet. He had published two volumes of his work under the name of Gabriel Allyn: *Private View* and *Shout at the Sunset*. He was then a viscount as his father was the current earl, but his rank did not seem to be something on which he had traded. Most references were to Gabriel Allyn and those under his current title were mundane. I could trace nothing under the name of Allyn later than the mid-sixties, however, and I wondered what might have happened to stop the poetry. Perhaps nothing, save added responsibilities, and yet it seemed to me that the man before me would have taken those in his stride and, even if his poetry had taken a different turn, it would not have died.

I decided to try one last shot. 'Was the SS 100 your first car?'

'Not quite.'

'First cars have emotional value all one's life. I can understand—'

'I doubt that,' he interrupted quietly.

The stone wall was firmly in place and it was clear I would get no further, even though His Lordship was eyeing me with a slight air of amusement. When I had arrived and pulled the bell rope at the front door of his home, he had opened the door himself, otherwise I would have wondered whether he was surreptitiously ringing bells for a butler to escort me off the premises. Instead there was an unexpected olive branch.

'Would you care to see the car?' he enquired.

He was indeed gracious in victory, and I warmed to him. 'I would, very much.'

That was the understatement of the year on my part. Although there had been tentative forays into the field, the SS 100 was the SS Cars Ltd's first triumphant production for the sports car world of the future. Correction, the SS 90 – ten miles an hour slower – had been its predecessor, but the 100 had trodden so smartly on its heels with all the small flaws ironed out and other refinements that it was reckoned the first major achievement. The year was 1937, and although Jaguar had not yet become the company name it was catching on as the name of the cars themselves. William Lyons, later knighted for his transformation of the British car scene, was hovering on the threshold of his and the company's future starred careers.

Not only, I reasoned happily, would I get to see this fantastic rarity, but I might get an inkling of why the earl was quite so opposed to selling it. It could be that I was overestimating the strength of his opposition and he was playing a waiting game so I would up the price before I had even mentioned one. Somehow I did not think so, however.

The earl escorted me along a corridor that reeked of past centuries and ancestors, but our destination proved to be a very modern rear door to a paved terrace overlooking the gardens beyond, clad in all their late April, spring finery. No gardens for us, however. We were heading past them to a group of outbuildings to one side of the mansion, obviously the former stables.

I was right. The stables and tack rooms set around the courtyard now accommodated a Land Rover, an old Bentley and a small BMW where once perhaps two carriages and half-a-dozen horses might have lived. There was no sign of the SS 100, but I was conducted to a red-brick building standing by itself beyond the courtyard with access through it. It had small windows along one side (too small for burglars lusting after any charms within). We went in the stately way through the door, however.

And there was Danny Carter's thirteenth car.

Why the emphasis on that number? I wondered. Carter had seemed to attach a lot of importance to it, but the look on his face had invited no questions and I had asked none. I'd presumed that it was some whimsy about the number thirteen. Now, faced with this wondrous sight, I wished I'd pressed him, especially in view of the earl's refusal to part with it. No reason I shouldn't ask now, however – with care.

Before me was a beauty with attitude for all it was nearly eighty years old. Glowing in its British racing car green, it was in perfect condition, looking as though one had only to open the door and slide in to drive into dreamland. Its forerunner, the SS 90, had disparagingly been dubbed by some 'the poor man's Bentley'. No such disparagement for the SS 100 when its position was consolidated by victories in the Monte Carlo Rally, club races and the International Alpine trials. Jaguar cars were here to stay.

'Did you drive it a lot?' I asked.

He laughed. 'When this car left the factory I was only just born. When I bought it second-hand I was twenty-two and so was the car. At that time the enthusiasm for what we now call classic cars had not yet spread. To us they were merely used cars, no matter how splendid they looked. In 1958 I was far from rich and bought it because I liked the look of it and I liked its age. I drove it' – he hesitated – 'very often.'

'And since then?'

'Not at all, save to keep it in good health.'

He offered no explanation of why this should be, and I decided to save my ammunition a while longer and take the mundane approach. 'It's for your family to treasure,' I said. I'd read that he was a widower, but that he had children.

'I doubt they will. My son has no eye for cars. Nor my daughters.'

With anybody else I would suspect he was putting me off, but the earl struck me as speaking nothing but the truth. His refusal to sell was therefore even more mysterious. I had to press on, however, if I was to honour my commission.

'You're resolved not to sell the car and it is indeed a beauty. So why,' I asked, preparing to be rebuffed, 'did you agree to see me?'

A long pause now. 'You come from Kent, Mr Colby. That confirmed for me who your hopeful buyer is.'

At least he'd replied. 'That makes a difference? Would you sell it to someone else?' I asked.

'Please tell Miss Ferne that I will never sell this car to her *or* anyone else. Not now, nor after my death. I am leaving instructions for it to be destroyed.' He spoke in such a matter-of-fact way that I was jerked into protest.

'*Destroy* it?' That would be sheer vandalism. How could *anyone* do that, let alone this otherwise reasonable and intelligent man? 'Could you not bequeath it to a museum?'

'Not even that.'

I had to suppress my rising anger. 'Then *why* agree to see me and why have you kept the car for so long?'

As he did not reply, I shot an arrow into the dark. 'You do realize it's the thirteenth car?' It was a savage attack and it hit a target.

He winced. 'All the more reason for my refusing to sell it,' he nevertheless replied.

I was none the wiser but even more convinced that this car had a story behind it. Whether that story was a happy or unhappy one was not clear. What seemed to be clear was that the notorious Adora Ferne must be part of it.

I had never met Adora Ferne and perhaps her name was not as widely known as once it was, as she would be in her eighties. To me she was famous for being notorious and yet I didn't know a great deal about her. I knew she had been the queen of singers on the London nightclub scene in the late nineteen fifties and sixties, considered the British Edith Piaf with her own take on songs such as 'Milord' and 'La Vie en Rose', but with an astonishing range of voice and repertoire that took in 'Hit the Road, Jack' and 'Are you Lonesome Tonight', plus many of her own hits. She was also an exotic dancer and beloved of the gossip columns.

Quite why her name was so tinged with notoriety rather than fame I did not know. Nor had the Internet much to offer on that subject, save that she was chiefly associated with the Three Parrots, a club that closed down in 1964 for unknown reasons – possibly drugs, as these were the mainstay of London's gangland in the mid- to late sixties, and clubs were familiar trading places. The days of gang leaders Billy Hill and Jack Spot had passed but the Richardsons and Krays were flexing their muscles.

Today, for classic car lovers such as myself, she was known as the centre of a different legend, the owner of a small collection of classic Jaguars that would make many an eye water. It wasn't open to the public but she often appeared at car shows in one or other of these beauties. Occasionally too she was seen in one of the cars at Danny Carter's side as he drove her sedately through the country-side. 'That's Adora Ferne,' the whisper went round at car shows, yet she lived quietly now, from what I could gather, and her past history was largely forgotten. To most people she was merely an old lady being driven around in her old car by an equally ageing driver. Danny must be at least twenty years her junior, but his grumpy expression didn't make for a youthful appearance. I knew nothing more about him until he had turned up at the Pits out of the blue with his commission.

'Why me?' I had asked.

He had shrugged. 'Why not? You want the job?'

A rhetorical question. With an SS 100 at the end of it and a mortgage payment due shortly, of course I did.

I was convinced that I'd played a minor part in an ongoing story and I wanted to know more. Rumours had circulated in the car world every now and then that each of Adora Ferne's Jaguars represented a different husband or lover in her life, although no doubt the true story had become embellished over time with a lack of evidence only adding to it. All the same, it was an enticing thought, especially now that I had met the Earl of Storrington, former poet. Question marks were sprouting in my mind like overnight bristles begging for a quick shave.

The earl had apologised for having brought me on a fool's errand but still offered no explanation. When I had thanked him for showing me the car, he had replied, 'At least I could do that.'

All I had to do was report my failure to Danny Carter. OK, my commission had been a washout but I was determined to see Adora Ferne's Jaguar collection. I decided the way forward for that would be to break the news to Danny Carter in person.

As luck would have it, Louise had just left Frogs Hill and would be away for the next week so I couldn't discuss the plan with her. As she is a well-known actor on stage and screen, absence is unfortunately no rare occurrence. In the past this had led to our separation, but now we have an understanding and, if I smart from time to time, I flatter myself I hide it well. Absence doesn't make my heart grow fonder, though. That wouldn't be possible as it's at top-level fondness already.

I could see Zoe working in the Pits as I drove into Frogs Hill. Silence reigned while she and Len worked on a 1952 Sunbeam-Talbot. In fact, all I could see of Zoe was her red hair sticking out from under a baseball cap. In age I sit comfortably between them as Zoe's still in her twenties whereas Len can cap that by an extra forty years. I think one of them glanced up as I entered, but even when I spoke neither stopped work for anything as trivial as listening to their employer.

'You were right,' I announced, tired of waiting for their attention. No gasps of astonishment. 'I knew that already,' Zoe said.

'Rum chap that Danny Carter,' Len commented, giving the distributor cap a flick of his beloved rag.

'Have you seen Adora Ferne's collection?' I asked curiously.

'Nope. Like to, though,' Len said. He's crusty and doesn't waste words, so this was high praise indeed.

'What's so odd about Danny?' I asked. I'd met him, of course, but to me he seemed nothing more sinister than a grumpy man in his sixties.

'He's been looking after this so-called collection for years. What for, if no one ever visits it?'

'Perhaps he lives in the grounds and does it in lieu of rent?' I suggested. 'Has he got a family?'

'Not around, if so. Heard about a son once.'

'What's odd then?' I persisted.

Realizing he wasn't going to get rid of me, Len straightened up and actually considered the matter. 'Doesn't mix.'

That was rich, coming from Len, the arch loner. 'What's wrong with that?' I was beginning to feel I was driving up a blind alley.

Len treated the remark with the scorn that it perhaps deserved. 'He's got his own agenda, that one.'

'For what?' I ploughed on, regardless of my lack of progress.

'Dunno.' Even Len realized this might not satisfy me, and Zoe giggled. 'Control,' he muttered. 'Knows it all, not like all the idiots around him. That's Danny Carter for you.'

Then Zoe took the stand. 'No one controls Adora Ferne,' she objected.

'You've met her?' I asked.

'No, but that's what they say,' she was forced to admit.

'They?'

'Rob does, anyway.'

Rob does? In Zoe's view that means it's true. Rob Lane is her boyfriend, though of what status I am never sure. She ring-fences him. Rob is as unlike Zoe as it's possible to be. He's from a wealthy farming family background but too lazy to do any farming himself. Zoe is industrious and far from wealthy. Rob has an eye for the main chance; Zoe puts cars before money. I can never tell whether she puts them before love or not. She's a feisty lady and is ready to defend her beloved against all odds, so I don't push it.

She seemed to be blushing, however, clearly sorry that she had mentioned his name. 'He's met her.'

'How did he do that?' I asked.

'Through her granddaughter, Alice,' she muttered, 'who according to Rob is the greatest dancer in the world and the prettiest, daintiest little thing that ever sweet-talked herself into whatever she wanted.' A touch of sarcasm here? I wondered. 'And she doesn't know a bonnet from a boot,' Zoe ended savagely.

Len and I were speechless. Never had Zoe exhibited such emotion over anyone or anything – well, not for a long time. I gulped and returned to the matter in hand. 'Why did you warn me not to get mixed up with Adora and Danny?'

'Both weirdos.' Len had become interested now.

'Alice too?' I asked Zoe.

'Never had the honour of meeting her, but she has to be. The whole family is out in orbit.'

'Which consists of whom, besides Adora?' I couldn't define why I was so interested at first. Then I realized if there was a story involving Adora and the Earl of Storrington, that could be relevant. But relevant to what? I had no ongoing commission.

'Melinda something, Adora's daughter. Also Adora's grand-daughter, Alice, Alice's brother, Michael, and Adora's son, their dad Simon, live in Crockendene Cottage in the grounds. Danny's got a cottage too, but Melinda lives in the main farmhouse so she can watch her mother like a hawk.'

'Does Adora need watching?' I was getting even more interested in this woman. After all, I might meet her with any luck. 'No husband around?'

'She's had at least three of them, maybe four,' Zoe told me, 'plus Rob says a string of gentlemen friends that made it to the bed but not the golden ring.'

'So perhaps the rumours about the cars stemming from her ex-lovers are true?'

'Could be. Rob thinks she demanded one from each of them when they split up.'

I grappled with the practicalities of this nonchalant statement. 'They just handed them over?'

'Wouldn't know. They seem to have done.'

'All,' I said thoughtfully, 'except Gabriel Allyn, now Earl of Storrington, who has the thirteenth car.' I couldn't wait to meet this remarkable lady, although caution suggested that Danny should come first.

* * *

There are lanes in Kent that look so inconsequential that the immediate assumption is that they lead nowhere in particular. However, if you choose to follow them you might come across a paradise of unexpected pleasure – or alternatively they might lead to the local rubbish landfill sites. Oakfield Lane was one such road and it was new to me. It was not far from Ashford and on a high ridge of the North Downs, which over the years have been crossed by smugglers, Templars, invaders and countless pilgrims on their way to Canterbury, and still carry the atmosphere that they left behind. Adora Ferne lived near a stretch of the North Downs Way, the track that prehistoric traders would have beaten to the Channel ports. The whole area is riddled with hints of our past of several thousand years ago.

In today's world, however, my satnav appeared to be stumped on how to reach Crockendene Farm, so I relied on my faithful Ordnance Survey map and, sure enough, once past a bluebell wood just coming into bloom, several fields of sheep and a lonely apple orchard, I found the turning that possessed a signpost half hidden in budding spring greenery and pointing the way to my destination.

As I drove along a bumpy potholed track, I was relieved that I had not brought my stately four-seater Gordon Keeble classic sports car but my daily driver, Polo. The Gordon Keeble lives in the old barn behind Frogs Hill farmhouse and has two trusty companions, a 1938 Lagonda and an old Packard. Each with its own personality, the three of them live together in quiet harmony.

Ahead of me now, I could see Crockendene Farm. Some farm! It was a handsome early-nineteenth-century red-brick mansion with a large courtyard before it. The portico to the house looked too imposing to be my destination, but as I entered the courtyard I saw a sign reading Reception with an arrow to the left, indicating that the collection might lie that way.

The reception lay in a large modern building with an office at the near end. The rest of the building, large though it was, did not seem to be spacious enough to display the Jaguar collection. The office proved to be a spic-and-span room with practical working surfaces and what looked like the latest computer technology. The only thing it lacked at first sight was a receptionist. Then a high-backed chair swivelled round and there was Danny Carter. He was a short man in perhaps his mid-sixties and thickset, with what seemed a perpetual scowl above a not-too-well-shaven chin.

'What are you here for?' he growled in welcome.

I arranged my face to convey complete surprise. 'To report on the commission you gave me.'

'Next time give us a bell first.'

'I will,' I assured him cordially, though he might be disappointed over there being a next time. 'Bad news, I'm afraid. I got nowhere with the Earl of Storrington. He refuses to sell to me, to you or anyone else.' I held back on the earl's arrangements for the car after his death.

Danny didn't look too amazed at this, to my initial relief. Then I began to wonder *why* he wasn't surprised.

'Bill me,' he ordered.

'I will.' I paused. 'Could I see the collection while I'm here?'

He looked at me as if I'd asked to raid the place. 'No one sees the Lair without madam's agreement.'

'The Lair?'

'The Jags,' he snarled.

'Why the Lair then? Jaguars don't use lairs. They're lone hunters.'

'None of your business.'

'True. I'll ask madam if I can see them.'

'*I'll* ask her.'

Danny reluctantly produced an efficient-looking gadget, punched in numbers as viciously as though they were on my face and had a brief conversation with someone – hopefully Adora Ferne herself. The conversation included the news of my failure to buy the SS 100, which I assumed would blow my chances. I was pleasantly surprised, therefore, when Danny announced reluctantly: 'Madam will interview you first.'

To be interviewed to see cars? Ah, well. This was a first. 'I'll go over now.'

He glared at me. 'No, you won't. I'll take you.'

I was duly marched across the courtyard to the majestic farmhouse, feeling like a naughty schoolboy on his way to the head. We made an odd couple, Danny stalwart but a mere five foot nothing, myself almost as stalwart but more than a foot taller. I didn't give a damn. I was going to meet Adora Ferne.

The woman who opened the door could not be Adora Ferne, however. She was in her forties and as unremarkable as Adora Ferne must be the opposite. That might be an unfair judgement as first impressions can be wrong and she hardly looked formidable. She was sturdily built, clad in smart trousers, a cardigan and T-shirt. Their muddy colour combined with her short brown hair and anxious face suggested that her role – if indeed this was the daughter, Melinda – did not permit competition with the famous Adora Ferne.

'Here's Jack Colby, Mrs Melinda,' Danny announced, handing me over like a parcel to higher authority.

'Thank you, Danny.' Her coldness and lack of interest did not indicate a happy household.

Boundaries had clearly been established between them, and I was left with Melinda as Danny sullenly walked away.

Mrs Dane Wilson (her formal name, she told me) led me with protocol so strict that this might have been Buckingham Palace, not an old farmhouse – large though it was and indicating wealth. The austere corridor gave way to a room full of light overlooking a rear garden. There was music blaring out – not background classical melodies but pop music from the sixties. I followed Melinda in, peering round to spot Adora Ferne. I could see no sign of her at first – because it didn't occur to me to peer behind the door we had just entered.

'I like doing this,' explained the extraordinary woman who slid gracefully out of her hiding place. 'I can tell all sorts of things from the way someone comes into the room. Especially men. I can tell all sorts of things from their buttocks.'

'Mother!' Melinda said in a tone that suggested remonstrations would be of no use.

'I'll entertain Mr Colby alone, darling,' said Adora, while my mind was still reeling at this introductory theory. 'His backside suggests he is quite acceptable.'

For what? I wondered somewhat nervously, while she gave me such a charming and intimate smile that I automatically shared the joke with her. I was still grappling for a hold on the situation. Almost visibly gnashing her teeth, Melinda departed, her heavy footsteps dying away along the corridor conveying her reproach. I was alone with Adora Ferne, who had moved over to the CD player.

She was tall, extremely thin and wearing bright, extraordinary clothes like a Spanish dancer, with a wide, long bright red skirt, purple top, flamboyant patterned shawl and beads everywhere. Her hair was piled haphazardly on top of her head and was held ineffectually in place with a diamond clip. Real? I wondered.

'Do you like Elvis? Well, no matter. We'll dance anyway,' she informed me.

In a trice she threw herself into my arms so that I had no excuse not to obey her instructions to dance, her lithe, energetic body hurling itself against me.

'Dear me, Mr Colby,' came her voice just below my chin, 'you're out of practice. Shall we tango?' she laughed, her eyes twinkling.

'I'd like that,' I replied obediently. I wouldn't. I'm hopeless at most ballroom dances, especially the tango. I did my best to shoot my head and shoulders sharply in different directions, my chin pointing upwards, but she gave up on me. Instead I watched her, fascinated by the sensuous movements that must once have seduced any man she chose. The technique was still there, and the power, but fortunately I could tell it was not at full strength any more. Just as well. I couldn't provide her with another Jaguar.

'So,' she said eventually, coming to a standstill before me, 'we have established that you are no dancer and I'm told you cannot fulfil straightforward commissions to buy cars. What *are* you good at, Mr Colby?' It was just as well she was laughing. The velvety, throaty voice purred insinuatingly at me.

I wasn't going to fall for it; this was her method of gaining control. It was time to establish my own persona. First, a touch of formality would not go amiss; otherwise the story of the Jaguars was going to be entirely one-sided. Fish caught in a net do not have much say in what's going on and I preferred to judge the story objectively. Why did I want to? I'd had one fruitless journey and a lot of guarded comments thrown at me, and finding out the reason why was a compelling plan – even if I had to risk being led into a labyrinth with no knowledge of what might lie ahead.

'I'm good at classic cars, Miss Ferne. I don't know your married name, I'm afraid.'

'My dear, which name would I choose? I've forgotten the name of my first husband and there's no way Rex would permit me to use his. He was my second choice. I have no wish to use Charlie's name, and as for Harry's . . . that would be politically awkward at the moment.' Those green eyes twinkled again.

I couldn't resist the temptation to take this further – especially as she was clearly provoking it – so I fed her the question she was waiting for. 'Why?' I asked.

'He's eager to try a second round.'

'And you don't want to remarry him?'

'I haven't decided, Jack. May I call you Jack?'

'It would be an honour.' This was one game at least that I could play with caution.

'My name derives from the Latin, of course. It means I'm adored and so to you I must be Adora.'

From anyone else this would have sounded impossibly smug, but somehow it seemed quite natural coming from her – especially as it was probably true.

'And to show you how adored and adorable I am, or alas, in many cases was, I will show you my darling Jaguars, Jack. My zoo of panting lovers, my stable of husbands, my Lair. Come.' She took my arm as though we had been intimate friends for many years and out we went across the courtyard. Enthusiastic though I was to see the Jaguars, something felt wrong about this set-up. I decided to prod a little.

'Lair?' I asked. 'Isn't that a strange name for the collection given that Jaguars don't have lairs?'

'Mine do,' she retorted. 'Aren't they lucky? They all live together.'

She wasn't going to get away with that so easily. 'Apart from the thirteenth,' I said. 'I'm sorry I could not buy you the SS 100.'

Her arm jerked in mine as she stopped still. 'Dear Gabriel,' she whispered. 'So sad, so sad. But I shall get it, you know. I have to. It's the thirteenth car.'

TWO

What was so special about the thirteenth car? Now that Adora had repeated Danny's remark I realized its significance must be greater than I had guessed. Thirteen is deemed to be lucky or unlucky according to which faith, country or folklore you follow, but I decided to go with the positive approach – the thirteen of the baker's dozen rather than of the witches' coven. I hadn't had much luck so far, but with this particular commission I might be able to take it a stage further if I was to understand more of the background to the story – and if I were given the opportunity.

As we crossed the courtyard towards the collection, Adora walked amazingly quickly for someone in their eighties – I guessed she was eighty-four or eighty-five. I was in for my next surprise, however. I had been right in thinking that the modern building I had seen on my arrival did not house the Jaguar collection because we branched off from the courtyard and walked along an untarmacked track that had no apparent end for a while. It was no more than a wide footpath and took us first through a bluebell wood which, as with those I had seen on the way to Crockendene Farm, was about to burst into its mysterious best.

Through the shrubbery I at last glimpsed what must be the Lair, but it was a disappointing sight. From the bleak-looking black exterior it looked an uninspiring building, offering no more to the imagination than a home for farm machinery. There must be another entrance, I realized, as cars could not drive along this track, although there was no sign yet of another road.

Oddly, I could see no door in the black wall facing us. We had almost reached it when Danny Carter caught us up from behind, panting and reproachful at not being asked earlier to join the party. Adora made no comment, and indeed it seemed he was expected because when we were about twenty yards from the building she stopped, giggled and beckoned to him.

'Time to do your stuff, Danny.'

Whatever stuff this might be, it must be routine, as Danny was clutching a gadget in his hand. I presumed he was going to call someone, but I was wrong. This was a twenty-first-century version of abracadabra. Almost soundlessly the whole black wall slid upwards and Aladdin's cave was revealed, separated from us only by huge glass panels ten or twelve feet wide. Aladdin would have been disappointed, however. There were no jewels in this cave nor genies in bottles. Nevertheless, I'd not swap this treasure house for all the robbers' booty in the world!

'The Lair,' Adora chuckled. 'My little zoo. You might be right, Jack. These animals walk alone but for me they adore being together.'

Before us gleamed twelve shiny, gorgeous, leaping Jaguars. I goggled. Even from our position outside the glass I could see a blue E-type sports car and two saloons, a Mark II and a magnificent XJ 6 – and, yes, not only an XK 120, the two-seater car that had so wowed the Earl's Court Motor Show in 1948, but a red D-type racing car. Twelve Jaguars all at their stately, comfortable, glamorous best.

'Aren't they marvellous?' Adora commented. 'You can see why the thirteenth is so important to me.'

I could. No one looking at this splendid display could fail to do so, even if the word 'thirteenth' was beginning to have a distinctly ominous ring about it, set in context. In the centre of the twelve cars spaced along the length of the building was a raised platform, occupying a whole glass pane width and swathed in silk hangings as though an Eastern potentate were expected with entourage. This, I realized, must be the space for the SS 100 currently residing in Sussex (and, if the owner kept to his decision, for ever) with the Earl of Storrington. The missing thirteenth car.

It seemed to me as though the platform was making a statement on behalf of Adora and Gabriel Allyn. What it was I couldn't even begin to guess, save that there was more to this story than the whim of an elderly lady and an obstinate owner.

Without a word, Danny stomped ahead of us along the narrow path bordering the building to its far end, then stopped in disgust as he saw what awaited us around the corner.

'*He's* here,' he growled.

'Excellent.' Adora quickened her step. Taking my hand, she almost dragged me past Danny to the paved area in front of the building, on which sat a dilapidated Land Rover. Beyond it was a single-track road leading to the side of the building and in the other direction to what was probably a rear entrance to the farm. Adora took one look not at the Land Rover but at the man lounging by the front door to the Lair. Dropping my hand, she rushed towards him.

'It's my darling Harry,' she shouted back at me.

'Harry Gale,' Danny muttered gloomily. 'He's bad news.'

'Darling Harry' was a tall, burly man, about sixty, with a complacent grin, far too much carefully groomed hair and designer beard for a man of his age, and two eyes concentrating on Adora with what he probably fancied was his magnetic charm.

Bad news? I wondered. Coming from Danny this might be a touch of pots calling kettles black, although I had to admit I didn't take to Harry at first glance.

'Soaked her dry,' Danny continued, 'and now he's aiming for a comeback.'

I remembered now. This was ex-husband number three, or was it four? Danny was marching up to them, exuding disapproval at every step. Adora was clasped in Harry's loving arms so Danny was forced to tap her on the shoulder. 'Which car today, madam?'

Foolish of him to take on the enemy face-to-face, I thought. Adora didn't seem to mind, however, and her muffled voice replied, 'With four of us, I think the XJ saloon, don't you, darling? The one dear Charlie gave me, Jack. He won't mind.'

'Hey, babe,' quoth cheesy Harry. 'Let's not take a Jag. We'll take the Land Rover. Just the two of us.'

I could see why Harry figured that would suit him better. To get a Jaguar out, whichever it was, would take time, and he was after a quick getaway before she changed her mind.

Adora simpered. Or was that just a show for my benefit? 'Let's do that, Harry, darling. We have a lot to talk about, haven't we, sweetie pie? You can show Jack the cars, Danny.'

She followed this with a distinctly sexual giggle as Harry preened himself, detached himself from Adora with a loving kiss, offered his arm to her and led her to the Land Rover. She looked over at me as he helped her up into the passenger seat. 'Dear Jack, Danny will tell you all about the job you're going to do for me.'

I opened my mouth to protest at this switch of the situation, but I was too late. Danny got in first. 'What job?' he snarled.

Perhaps I'd been wrong; perhaps these were simply dotty elderly people having fun. Then I saw Danny's face and realized it wasn't fun at all. Whatever was going on here, it was deadly serious despite the frothy appearance of the situation. Harry already had the engine running but I wasn't going to let Adora get away with it that easily. I went firmly up to the Land Rover and opened the passenger door again.

'Would you tell me about this as yet non-existent job, Adora?'

'Just a few threatening letters,' she said airily, pulling the door shut again. 'Nothing much,' she shouted through the window.

I pulled the door open once more, to Harry's annoyance. 'I'm sure Harry won't agree they're nothing much if they're threatening you.'

Harry, thus trapped, glared at me. 'Better talk to him, babe.'

Adora stared straight ahead of herself then turned to me. 'If I really must, Jack.' She sighed. 'What do you need to know?'

'What are these letters threatening?' I asked.

'To burn down the Lair with the cars in it.'

I gaped at her. 'And you call that nothing much?'

'It's a joke,' she said lightly. 'No one would really do that, would they, Danny?'

Danny looked at me defiantly. 'Someone's just trying to upset madam.'

'That's what I said. A joke,' Adora said impatiently.

I was getting impatient too. 'If you thought they were a joke you wouldn't be asking me to investigate.'

A pause. 'Perhaps the last one was just a little scary. It did threaten to kill me, but that is just silly. Who would want to do that?'

'*Kill* you?' I said, stupefied. 'That doesn't sound silly to me.'

Adora waved an airy hand. 'Of course it is. Danny, be a dear and answer Jack's other questions. Show him the letters if he wants to see them. But I really must have a little talk with darling Harry.'

Harry's face lit up and he rushed round to slam the passenger door shut then back to the driver's seat before I could tell her there was no job yet. I was being manipulated and apparently Danny was too. Adora was pulling all the strings. Much as I was intrigued by Adora, this was not a good situation and my antennae were quivering like crazy. Don't take the job, whatever it is, half of me was instructing myself; the other half was already shooting up questions in my mind.

Still stupefied and more than a little annoyed, I watched them go then turned to Danny. 'OK. Let's go over to your office and you can show me the letters.'

'Thought you wanted to see the Jags.'

'Work before pleasure.'

He capitulated and back we went in silence to that spic-and-span office. 'Has Miss Ferne taken the letters to the police?' I asked when he indicated he was prepared to talk.

'No. Says someone's just trying to annoy her.'

'And if they're not?'

'Forget it. They're not serious and if they were there's a fat lot you could do about it. Her talk of another job is just to wind you up.'

'If the death threat *is* serious, there's a lot that can be done about it. Do you have these letters, especially that one?'

'No.'

'She said you had.'

'Madam told me to destroy them, so I did. Anyway, I told you they're not serious.'

'Then what is the reason for sending them?' I was beginning to think the whole thing was a fantasy.

Danny waved a hand in the rough direction of the Lair treasure trove. 'Check out those cars. There's the answer to your damn-fool question.'

This was not going well and there had to be a reason for that too. 'Look,' I said patiently, 'you love those cars and if there's a genuine threat to them *and* to kill Miss Ferne *and* if I take the job, I need guidelines. *Now.* How many letters has she had?'

He shrugged. 'Half a dozen or so over the last six months. I had one or two myself. Nothing to get worked up over. Nothing's happened yet.'

'But it might. Was your life threatened too?'

'No. I only had the ones saying the Lair would get torched.'

'Do you have one of those?'

'No. I torched the lot.' He appeared to find this funny but I was far from being amused. There was something odd about this. I had another shot at it.

'If you're both convinced they mean nothing, why should Miss Ferne hire me?'

'Just what I told her,' he replied smugly as I played into his hands.

I ignored this. 'What was her answer?'

'Madam doesn't always answer.'

That at least was believable. 'OK. Then why would anyone want to send the letters?'

A sideways look at me. 'Madam's had a long life. Upset people.'

'You as well?'

This time I had the advantage. I'd caught him and received a growl in reply. 'Plenty of folk know what the Lair means to me.'

Right. There was at least a crack in the deadlock. 'What does Miss Ferne imagine I can do?'

'She says you work for the police.'

'I do carry out freelance work for the Kent Police Car Crime Unit, but not this kind. These letters – do they come by post or email or hand?'

'Post.'

'The nice old-fashioned way,' I commented. Danny Carter was getting on my wick but he wasn't going to get the satisfaction of my letting him see that. 'Are you sure you don't have even one letter sent to you or Miss Ferne?' Once upon a time postmarks, fingerprints, handwriting, typewriting and words cut out of newspapers all provided *clues.* Nowadays the knowledgeable public could avoid all these traps, although it was true that computers open up different risks.

'No, I don't.'

'Then tell me what they were like.' I wasn't going to give up yet. 'What kind of paper? Typed or written? Or letters cut out of newspapers – you know the sort of thing.'

'Typed.'

'Computer or old manual typewriter?'

'Don't know.'

'You must have some ideas on who sent them, especially as it must be someone who is not only known to Miss Ferne but interested in the Jaguars. Suppose you tell me about them.'

'And you a so-called classic car expert,' he sneered.

I amended my somewhat ambiguous words. 'How did they come to be in the Lair?'

Anybody making this kind of threat by anonymous letter, real or not, firstly had to know that the Lair was here, secondly how much it meant to Adora and Danny, and thirdly have a personal reason for wanting to get back at Adora – and probably Danny too. With that in mind, I was fairly sure I didn't want this job but I wasn't going to give Danny the satisfaction of telling him that.

'Madam will explain,' Danny answered.

'She asked you to tell me.' I was getting bored as well as irritated by this man. Time to lock horns. 'I want to know the donor or seller and when Miss Ferne acquired each car.'

'Nothing much to it.'

I'd had enough. 'How long have you worked for Miss Ferne?'

This caught Danny off guard for some reason, although the question seemed straightforward enough to me. 'Over twenty years.'

'You look after the Lair and the cars; you take Miss Ferne for drives each day in one or other of them. You know these cars. *Show* them to me.'

He must have taken in the expression on my face and the fact that I was a foot taller than him and a lot younger. Another shrug and we set off back to those twelve lovely beasts awaiting us. He unlocked the door to Aladdin's cave and in we went. Once again, he hadn't spoken one word on the way.

Purpose-built premises for a collection should consist not only of their architecture but of the marriage between that and the contents. Never could a marriage be happier than the one that lay before me. The Lair had a high, rounded roof – something that I hadn't appreciated from the outside – painted light cream. This, with the glass panels on one side, and another cream-coloured wall with windows and the double doors facing it, was a perfect setting for the two lines of cars, which so far I had only admired from the outside.

Jaguar UK has its own heritage museum but for me this hall was almost as good. My initial impression was that Jaguar's whole history was encapsulated in this collection from the thirties to the eighties, with the latter heralding the glories still to come. Then I realized that of course I was wrong. What was missing was the SS 100, which in the thirties had signalled the way to all the magnificent beasts before me. The car belonging to Gabriel Allyn, now the Earl of Storrington.

I forgot about Danny as I marvelled at what was here. Both to my left and right cars were parked with their bonnets facing the outside world as though these splendid animals were all about to roar off on a path to glory. Twelve classic Jaguars and the space for the Galahad to arrive, the thirteenth car. Opposite the platform left vacant for it were the double doors for entry. On either side as I walked down the central aisle was – well, a hall of fame. I could think of no other name for it. It wasn't just the cars that seized my attention, from the XKs to the E-types and then the XJs. Displayed on the walls by each car were twelve enormous photographs in elegant oval golden frames; they were presumably of the men who had donated the cars, as also in each photo was Adora Ferne herself, arms entwined with her beloved, a hand on a shoulder or hand in hand. Were these merely loving mementoes of past loves or could it be a veiled threat that she still had a stake in these men's lives?

Erected on the platform on my left was a cream-painted board with another oval golden frame, but this one was empty. No prizes for guessing whose photo should be there, I thought. It was waiting for the donor of the thirteenth car, Gabriel Allyn. For the twelve cars in this collection more than photographs were on display. As I walked along the rows I saw a few mementoes arranged in the space allotted to each car. Photographs, a picnic basket, a theatre programme, a beach umbrella, a guitar – things that meant nothing to the casual observer but I guessed they were Adora's memorabilia of each former owner; memorabilia that might be dynamite now for the person with whom she had shared these loving moments.

At the far end of the hall was a raised recess, concave in shape. On this platform was a grand piano, a piano stool, a small table and, as far as I could see from where I was standing, a cupboard and – of course – a microphone. It didn't take a lot of imagination to realize what this was meant to represent. Here Adora Ferne still sang, at least in memory.

Danny was watching me suspiciously. Nevertheless, I needed to set a dialogue in motion. 'What's this for?' I asked, indicating the alcove.

'Obvious, isn't it? Know about the Three Parrots, don't you?'

'Only by reputation when Miss Ferne sang there. That's fifty years ago, though.'

Danny took this dismissive statement amiss. 'A high-class club, it was. Madam's second home. She made it famous.'

'Do any of the cars here stem from those days?' I guessed that several did.

'If you're thinking that their owners are planning to pop over here and torch the place, most of them are over eighty now. Not likely, is it?' he said in tones that indicated the matter was closed.

I decided to wind him up again. 'There were such things as gangs around then that took on commissions like that.'

'You telling me there aren't no gangs now?'

'No.' I thought of Doubler, the car crime king around these parts with whom I'd clashed on one occasion. Still, I saw Danny's point, although the idea of the Earl of Storrington or any other fifties' revellers contacting Doubler or any other villain to burn down the Lair was farfetched, as was their taking a spin over to Kent to murder a former sweetheart. Nevertheless, someone had it in for both Adora and the Lair, so I wasn't going to dismiss the notion out of hand.

'Which of the Jags are from Miss Ferne's former husbands?' I asked him.

He didn't have a chance to answer even if he'd been willing to, because to my surprise I heard the Land Rover drawing up outside and shortly after Adora appeared through the doorway, her flamboyant dancing skirt twirling with each step. Harry was hot on her heels.

'I changed my mind,' she said happily. 'I decided I wanted to talk to you again, dear Jack. Have you finished the tour? I do hope not.'

Harry lumbered menacingly up to us, as though I were going to whisper sweet nothings in her ear.

'No, madam. Just about to begin,' Danny told her.

'Excellent. So I'll take over. Look, Jack, at this XK 150. Darling Rex gave me this. Sweet of him. A divorce present in 1969.'

The silver two-seater sports coupé was a 1957 model and I could see the red badge commemorating Jaguar's success at Le Mans. I could also see the photo of a lean-faced, watchful Rex holding on possessively to a younger Adora at what looked like a theatre premiere. This car was a favourite of Humphrey Bogart and Clark Gable, so maybe he was hoping he could work the same magic.

'Rex was my first real husband,' she continued.

'Real?' I queried, hooked by this notion that husbands could also be unreal.

'I told you the first passed out of my life so speedily he didn't count.'

Count for what? I wondered. Even Danny looked disapproving at this rapid disposal of spouses.

'He's *Sir* Rex Hargreaves now, of course,' Adora continued. 'We were married for five years. What a time we had of it in this entrancing little car. Only a two-seater so it wasn't good for everything, of course. When Rex lets his hair down he's quite a lad. We had all sorts of capers in this sweet little Jaguar. That's why I wanted it – to remind me of a picnic at Broadstairs. Such fun with the wind in our hair.'

'A rotter,' Harry muttered savagely to me.

Rotter enough to threaten to kill her? I wondered. I looked at the photo of Rex's patrician face and a young and sexy Adora.

'Such fun,' Adora repeated. 'I was so wretched when he divorced me, all because of a stupid misunderstanding over my feelings for Patrick. I would never have left dear Rex. He is the father of my son, after all. At least I think he was, although Patrick always maintained . . .' Her brow wrinkled in thought. 'But there, that's past now. Poor Patrick, long departed from us. That's him over there.'

'Him?' I thought we had a ghost with us until I realized it was his car to which she was referring – a magnificent Mark II saloon. 1959, I thought.

She laughed merrily at my mistake. 'That's the car he so sweetly gave me when we parted. Dear Patrick. He was Irish. We had a wonderful time in the Mark II. So *comfortable*.' She gave me a meaningful look. 'He took me to Valentia Island once.'

'He was your second husband then?' I was getting confused.

'Good gracious me, no. I would never have *married* Patrick. He was far too happy-go-lucky. Wonderful lover, though.' She caught sight of my mesmerized face. 'You do know that these cars were gifts from my husbands or lovers, usually on parting?'

'I'd heard that rumoured, but—'

'You didn't believe it? Why not? It seems perfectly sensible to me.'

'It seems unusual to receive such gifts from someone from whom one has parted with some rancour.'

Adora looked shocked. 'No, Jack. Never with me. They all love me, you see.'

I glanced at Danny's wooden face and Harry's blank stare and wondered if they could tell a different story.

'Does Sir Rex still live in Kent?' I asked.

'Of course. Nothing would make Rex move far from me. Or indeed any of my husbands. Would it, Harry, dear?'

I turned to 'Harry, dear'. 'You married Miss Ferne after her divorce from Sir Rex?'

'No such luck.' Harry oozed what he thought was charm. 'That was Charlie.'

'My dear Charlie,' Adora explained. 'He kindly gave me the XJ 6 saloon. I did so love that walnut woodwork on it. Charlie followed Rex as my husband three years after the divorce.'

He must have been a generous man to give a car like that away, I thought. The last word in luxury, it handled beautifully and had won the Car of the Year Award for 1969. 'Does he live near here too?' My head was spinning already and I had only accounted for three of these cars.

'Oh, yes,' Adora replied. 'I was married to Charlie for ten whole years. I married him in 1972. He'd always loved me, of course, right from the Three Parrots days, and he was most annoyed when I married Rex instead. He even objected to Blake, although we were married by then.'

'Married to Blake?' I asked weakly.

'Goodness, no. He's far too boring. We had a brief affair but Charlie still can't stand him. Blake and I had the most marvellous trip to the Lake District and made love on the shores of Lake Windermere. His car is that 1970s' E-type.' She pointed to a gleaming silver sports car.

So much for Blake then. 'Was Charlie a member of the Three Parrots?' I asked.

'Oh, no. Charlie's father ran it and Charlie worked there too.' Adora looked at me anxiously. 'I suppose this does sound a trifle strange, doesn't it? But it was all such fun at the time.'

'What was Charlie's line of business?'

'He's some sort of car dealer, I think. Officially retired but he never does really.'

'Not Charlie Dane?' I exclaimed. Not the biggest magnate in

Kent to whom even Harry Prince kowtows – Harry's my bête noire who owns a string of garages and aims to add Frogs Hill to it.

'Yes,' Adora beamed. 'Charlie and I are great friends now. He was my husband when we first moved to Crockendene. He didn't begrudge giving me the farm and the car. After all, he is the father of my darling daughter. You met Melinda, Jack, didn't you? She loves Crockendene as much as I do. She was brought up here so it's a family home.'

Met was hardly the word, and nor from what I saw of Melinda was 'darling' a fitting description of their relationship, although one meeting wasn't much to judge by.

I couldn't imagine Charlie Dane being happy about handing over the farm and his daughter to Adora, particularly if there had been a gentleman called Blake in the picture. From what I'd heard in the trade, Charlie was tough but straight, and a good businessman for all his outward show, perhaps taking after his father, Tony – although the closing of the Three Parrots didn't sound as though it had been a profitable business even if straight.

I looked round this exotic parlour of cars. 'What about Blake?' I asked. 'Didn't you want to marry him after Charlie?'

'Oh, no. He'd gone long ago. Alan Reeve fitted in sometime around then. Such a dear man. We had a romantic parting, though, and Charlie still can't stand the sight of him any more than he can Blake. Alan insisted on giving me the other E-type sports car. 1975. Nice, isn't it?'

'Nice' seemed an inadequate word for this glorious maroon-painted gift. Henry Moore once described Jaguars as 'sculpture in motion', and here it was before me. Twelve of them, all belonging to Adora Ferne. What a lady! Two lovers at least still alive, plus at least three husbands and perhaps another lover or two. Plenty of room, I thought, for harbouring malicious thoughts towards Adora. I wasn't going to forget that death threat to her.

Adora looked pensive. 'Let me see, Harry, dear,' she continued. 'I had quite a period of being single – single in a way, at least, until you swept me off my feet. I can't quite recall when we married, though.'

'In 2003,' he grunted.

'Oh, yes. Four years, I believe, before you spotted that pretty little girl who worked at the pub.'

So the pussy cat had claws. Harry flushed. 'Didn't know what I was doing, babe. Come to my senses now. Only you – wonderful you.'

Adora just smiled. 'Such fun we shall have,' she said vaguely, 'in your XJ 8, darling.'

Of course. As an ex-husband he would probably have a car here. 'Is this yours?' I asked. There was little doubt as he was defending it aggressively from my inspection.

It was Adora who replied. 'Yes, it is. We had some splendid times in it, didn't we, dear? I was so pleased I bought it for you and you so kindly gave it back.'

He was, unsurprisingly, looking uncomfortable, and I decided to help him out by distracting Adora. 'Do you drive all these cars in turn?' I asked her.

'Of course not. I take whichever gentleman I feel like remembering on that day. Much more fun.'

It was clear that I needed a list from Danny of all the owners who had crossed Adora's golden path. That's *if* I took this job, I reminded myself, aware that everything was crying out that I should avoid it like the plague.

For once I listened to my own misgivings and when the opportunity arose acted on them. 'Any of these owners could have sent you those letters, Adora, and it's too wide a canvas for me to take the job on. You need the police to sort out the threat to your life. The letters could just be a matter of spite.'

A shadow crossed Adora's face which I couldn't interpret. 'But I will sniff around,' I added on impulse, 'free of charge. That would be a pleasure.'

Would it? Seeing the Lair again, yes, but stepping into the unknown? Usually this was a challenge I welcomed, but there was something about this case that smelled of more than petrol.

THREE

I left the Lair feeling as though I were on the losing side of an unwinnable duel – at least until I had worked out what was going on in this place. The name Crockendene Farm suggested a buzzing agricultural business but so far its activities seemed to be rooted in the past rather than looking forward to future growth. Certainly there was no sign of any farming going on. Fair enough, as the farm's owner was in her eighties, but the situation seemed more complicated than that. For a start, Danny, not Adora Ferne, considered himself in control of this kingdom, even if he did superficially show due deference to his employer.

It was blatantly obvious that Danny did not want anyone muscling in on his patch. He wanted no interference from me, the police or quite possibly Adora and her family too. If that was indeed the case, it could well mean that Adora was more worried than she appeared to be about the threat to herself, and that her calling me in was a gesture of independence, maybe even a declaration of war on Danny.

Walking through the silent woodland on my way back to the courtyard where I had left my car, however, it was easy to believe that there was more at stake than Adora trying to get one over Danny. From the death threat she received she could be genuinely worried that she was the ultimate target if the burning down of the Lair was merely a preliminary. Neither she nor Danny had so far been prepared to admit that this might be the case or to voice suspicion of anyone. Making a half-hearted offer to me to hunt down the culprit was as far as it had gone. The donors of the Jaguars remained for the most part just names; her family were shadowy figures merging into the general landscape. Not one letter was available, not one name stood out and Danny had been unenthusiastic about letting me have the list I asked for – until Adora insisted. I could swear there was something sinister going on here in which the letters had a role. Death threats on social media are common in our anonymous society but letters sent by post are a different matter.

It was strange that Danny's devotion to the Jaguars went no further than the Lair itself. Did he never speculate on why Adora Ferne had apparently attracted gentleman friends of varying degrees of affluence in her long life and why they were all so willing to bestow such gifts on her? And as they were mementoes of her past life with the said gentlemen, why were they all Jaguars and not some other classic car? Did none of them prefer Bentleys or Rolls-Royces or Austin-Healeys? To me it was interesting that although she was offering to pay handsomely for the thirteenth car, all the others had apparently been gifts, save perhaps for darling Harry's. Had she in fact bought some of the others? And if so, why? Happy memories of one's past tend to go only so far when it comes to forking out hard cash. Adora had not struck me as a fervent car lover and so why had she wanted them? Trophies? But if so, what had been the game behind them?

Unwillingly I came back to the unwelcome theory that gentle blackmail might have played a part. Husbands with new families to consider and past lovers with their pasts to conceal might prefer not to be reminded of follies long since committed. There was a hitch in this theory, however. If the threatening letters were from one of the donors, such follies could well go back as far as fifty years or more. Was it likely that past loves would still be burning as brightly? Then I thought of Gabriel Allyn, Earl of Storrington. Perhaps some flames among those twelve – thirteen – names had never died.

I wasn't happy about my impulsive offer to sniff around. I could be walking into a situation that not only needed disentangling in itself but which could have numerous tentacles reaching out in unforeseeable directions. It might not take much to extend one of them to carrying out that death threat that Adora seemed to regard so lightly.

This decided me. Sniff around I would, but I had been right to turn down a paid job. This was one for, first, Dave Jennings, and through him DCI Brandon. DCI Dave Jennings is the head of the Kent Car Crime Unit and the man who hires me for freelance jobs when he has a mind and the cash to do so. Brandon, who works in the same police HQ at Charing, is in the Serious Crime Directorate, and after a chequered beginning our relationship was rather more formal than with Dave. On the other hand, Brandon, like Dave, has been known to sign me up for jobs where my expertise might help. Whether Adora Ferne reported that death threat to her or not, I decided I should check in with Dave at least. There was, to my mind, a situation brewing and it wasn't looking good.

And then it became a whole lot worse.

I'd been walking along a footpath that I assumed would be a shortcut back to the farm courtyard. Instead it led me straight to the rear garden gate of a sizeable old house. Fortunately as I drew nearer I spotted a branch path which would take me round the house to what looked like a tarmacked drive beyond. Reaching the house, which bore the name Crockendene Cottage, I could see a Ford Focus ST parked in front of it. I registered where I had seen it before – and to whom it belonged. Just then its owner emerged from the house.

I was locked into a face-to-face situation with Rob Lane, Zoe's partner, and waving him farewell was the prettiest young woman I had seen in a long while. Although this incident could be entirely innocent, I guessed it wasn't. When he saw me, Rob looked as guilty as though I'd caught him climbing out of a bedroom window.

'Jack. Good to see you,' he cried out unconvincingly. 'What brings you here?'

He hastily exited through the gate, caught me up and encouraged me into a brisk march away from the house. Without waiting for my reply, he burbled on, 'Just dropped in here to leave a message for Simon Hargreaves. Know him, do you?'

'Afraid not, but Zoe told me he's Adora Ferne's son.'

'Did she?' Rob squealed at this unfair shot of mine.

'She did,' I said. Rob was so intent on removing me from the vicinity of Crockendene Cottage that I thought a gentle reminder was in order. 'Haven't you forgotten something?' I added.

'What's that?' He was completely thrown now.

'Your car.'

He went an even more interesting shade of brick red. 'Oh, yes, good Lord, so I have.' Light laugh. 'Actually, I'm only walking over to the farmhouse for a moment then going back to pick it up.'

'Of course. I'll come with you to pay my respects to Adora,' I told him cheerily.

He capitulated. 'Look here, Jack, fancy a pint in the King's Arms? Know it? On the A20. I take it you've a car here. I'll get mine and see you there.'

'Sure,' I agreed. 'Zoe's not expecting me back for a while.'

This unsubtle hint of mine was meant to convince him that it would be wise to turn up at our rendezvous. It worked, because fifteen minutes later we were both in the pub. He joined me at a window table, clutching a half of bitter as though it were a life-line. Rob's a chameleon – he changes colour depending on who he's with, where and why. I noted that his face was still red. The chameleon aspect is helped by his being neither fat nor thin, neither good looking nor unattractive and neither tall nor short. He nearly always wears designer clothes which match his usual self-confident bearings but make him an ill-assorted partner for Zoe when they are together. She specializes in old jeans and tank tops.

I let Rob down gently by chatting about Jaguars until he redis-covered what was left of his nerve. 'Look here, Jack,' he broke into my chat, 'I'd rather you didn't mention this meeting to Zoe.'

'Which meeting would that be?'

'With Alice.' He spelled it out through gritted teeth. 'Simon's daughter. Friend of mine.'

'Ah. The dancer. Is it serious with her?'

An ambiguous question in the circumstances, but Rob didn't have dancing on his mind, only his relationship with Alice.

'You know how tricky these things are, old chap,' he replied.

This old chap did, so I helped him out again. 'If this is going to hurt Zoe, Rob, I want to know. I'd like to be around when you deign to tell her. You've a week to make up your mind whether you tell her or not. But if Alice is just another of your fancies, I *don't* want to know.'

He considered this. 'Fact is, I'm not sure, but I appreciate that, Jack. Do the same for you one day, old sport.'

I suppressed my fury. Louise? Did he really think I'd play fast and loose with her? Being in my forties I know when I'm blessed. Rob really was a first-class idiot and Zoe would be well out of it. Should I chuck the rest of my beer in his face? No. Non-alcoholic or not, it would be a waste of good beer.

Instead I seized the moment to advance my own interests. 'What you can do for me, *old sport*, is fill me in on Adora Ferne, her family and this whole set-up.'

'Alice—' he began uneasily.

'Leave her out of it if you like,' I said obligingly. 'We'll take it that she's the most beautiful, innocent, sweet girl you've ever met.'

He cast me a look which made me regret this gibe, but luckily he still stuck to the bargain. 'What do you want to know?'

'I've met Adora and Harry Gale and had a session with Danny Carter. Start with Adora.'

'Not sure I can tell you much.' Predictable answer. 'She keeps her cards close to her skinny chest.'

Charming. *My translation:* Adora won't lend him any money for his daft schemes.

'Is she well off?' I asked him.

'House is falling down but only because she's tight-fisted. She's enough stacked away to repair the Coliseum.'

'Sure of that?'

'No, but coming from Simon it's a fairly sure bet.'

'What's he like?'

Rob considered this. 'A decent bloke. Under his father's thumb – that's old Sir Rex, Adora's ex – or one of them. Simon worked for his father. I wouldn't like to be in his shadow and nor did Simon. Took early retirement a few months back.'

'Rex Hargreaves is in insurance, isn't he?' I'd done my homework. Rob seemed to know Alice's family quite well, I noted. Not looking good for Zoe, I thought – from her viewpoint, that is. From my own and that of any other sane person, a bust-up would be only too welcome.

'That's what Alice told me.'

'Does she think the stories about the Jaguars and Adora are true?'

'Wouldn't know. But that's what she says her granny trots out and I've never heard differently from Simon or Melinda. I asked to borrow one of the Jags once to take Al— *someone,*' he corrected himself with a big wink, 'to a big do. Adora wouldn't even lend one to me.'

My translation: especially not to Rob.

Rob, I'm forced to admit, is likeable in some ways, they're just not *my* ways. There's a lot of talk about big deals and big dos and Zoe believes in them all, or so she tells me. How big they are and whether they exist is never clear, although I think he's basically honest enough. No scams for him. Far too dangerous. He's been on the Zoe scene for some years now so he must have some other good qualities, even if they escape me.

'Has Adora told you about these letters threatening to burn the Lair?' I'd hold back on the death threat. 'And if so, does the family think that any of the car donors could be involved?'

'Yes. Bit of a laugh, isn't it? Can't see Grandpa Rex Hargreaves creeping round with a can of petrol and a match. He handed over the XK 150 like a lamb, according to Adora.'

It was a handsome gift, even as part of a divorce settlement. 'Did he really hand it over willingly?'

'I wouldn't know. He may have had his reasons. He's a canny old bird and he and Adora go right back to the club days.'

Despite Adora's instructions, Danny had only very reluctantly returned to his office to pick up a copy of the list of cars and donors for me. I'd gone with him, fearing he might 'forget' to return, and on the way back to the Lair I had scrutinized the list, asking if he knew more about the men on it. Four of the men on the list were marked as deceased – Lance Benny, Travers Winton, Ivan Cole and Patrick O'Hara – but of the other eight I knew little save of Harry Gale, Rex Hargreaves and Charlie Dane, all three of whom had been married to Adora. Danny's answer about the other five was that they were still alive. Of course, I had met Gabriel Allyn, who had no wish to join the Lair. Like a true jaguar, he walked alone.

'The Three Parrots?' I asked Rob.

'That's the one. Rex married Adora after it closed and she waved goodbye to clubland.'

'She gave up singing too?'

'No idea, but this was the mid-sixties and she was a throaty crooner, not a Rolling Stone.'

'Do you know Rex Hargreaves?'

'Met him once or twice. My ma and pa know him. Lives in Kent near Sevenoaks but owns a chunk of Berkshire – unlike Charlie, the next husband down the line. He's from the London suburbs and not the fashionable side. As unlike old Rex as you can imagine.'

'Not the right schools?'

'Right for Charlie, maybe.' Rob sniggered.

My translation: Charlie didn't go to Eton.

'What was his attraction for Adora?' My curiosity was fully awakened.

'My guess is filthy lucre. He'd been after her for years but Rex nobbled her, so Charlie stepped in after the divorce.'

'Was he the reason for it?'

'No. That was some other chap.'

I remembered then. 'Patrick O'Hara?'

'That's him. Cheesy-looking fellow if his photo's anything to go by. Seen it in the Lair?'

I nodded. I wondered whether the donors knew about their celebrity status photos in the hall, and if any of them had taken objection to this in view of the fact that Adora featured in all of them and hardly in a supporting role.

'I gather Charlie was the son of the owner of the Three Parrots,' I said. 'That would put a distance between him and the club members, especially in the sixties.'

Rob snorted. 'Yes, and Charlie reaped the benefits. Both got out quick when it was closed down.'

'For drugs?'

'Probably. I wasn't around at the time.'

I tried another tack. 'Simon is Rex's son and Melinda is Charlie's daughter. Right?'

'Yes. She and Simon don't always see eye to eye, though they glue themselves together over their mother's affairs and Crockendene. Simon reckons Melinda moved in on his territory as a kid and is still doing it. He behaves like a kid himself over it sometimes. Simon has lived in Crockendene Cottage for yonks and didn't like it when Melinda came marching back.'

'When was that?'

'Some years ago. Five, maybe. She married a farmer who decided to plough more fertile grounds and Melinda couldn't wait to move back to the beloved home of her youth. Melinda's devoted to her mother – she's appointed herself Adora's guardian. Adora, however, sees her as the little baby daughter who needs the caring mother – the same one who pushed dear little Melinda off to live with her father when they were divorced in the early eighties.'

A touch of bias towards Simon's viewpoint there, I thought. 'What about Harry Gale, the next husband?'

'Also divorced from Adora but coming back for another go if he has anything to do with it. Luckily that isn't much. He took a dim view of being divorced eight years ago. The family view him as the black sheep, one of the few things that Simon and Melinda agree on. Rex and Charlie shared the same opinion.'

'And Adora too?'

He shrugged. 'Who knows? With Adora, anything goes.'

'Does Alice take after her?' I asked innocently.

'Good grief, no. She's a sweetie.' Rob looked very smug.

Time to take him down a peg. 'Adora might have been a sweetie, too, at her age.'

Rob looked totally thrown at this notion. 'Alice is off limits,' he snarled.

'Not mine. Does she have a mother around?'

'Divorced. Mother off the scene. There's a brother – Michael. Not the most popular lad in town. At present in disgrace but usually the rotten apple of Adora's eye. My opinion, not Alice's.' Rob was getting edgy.

Tough. 'What's the reason for the disgrace?'

'First he announced his intention of moving in with Charlie Dane's daughter – by his second wife, not Adora. Then he dropped that idea and said he'd take over the Lair. That upset Adora *and* father Simon, who'd been longing to do that for years.' Rob hesitated. 'The general opinion is,' he said awkwardly, 'that Michael's the most likely author of those letters. He can't stand Danny Carter for a start. Mind you, none of them can, except Adora. Michael's the most outspoken.'

'Any particular reason for that?'

'He's a layabout.' Coming from Rob, this was rich. 'He has his own ideas for the Lair but so does his father. Danny has his too, and usually gets his way.'

'And thus he's unpopular all round. Even with Melinda?'

'You bet. Neither she nor Simon can stand the guy. But he's just an employee, so they reckon he's no real threat to their lifestyle.'

'Is Adora herself a threat to that?' I slipped in as Rob sat back, clearly signalling that he'd finished cooperating.

Rob was caught off balance by this one and didn't have enough time to compose his reply. 'Big time – what do you think? Adora only has to marry again and everything goes up for grabs. And guess who'll grab it? Mr Harry Gale. She's walking on thin ice is Adora. And she knows it.'

This is none of my business, I told myself as I headed back through Charing. I didn't convince myself, however. This is *partly* my

business, I decided. Why, though? What was it that made me think
it was? The cars? The letters? A situation I couldn't understand? A
bit of all three? The letters were the lesser constituent, though, and
that at least I could offload on to Dave. I was heading straight for
Kent Police Charing.

Dave Jennings isn't keen on my just dropping by to see him, but
I was on my way. He's apt to be 'busy' if I call him on my mobile,
so I just breezed in. It must have been my lucky day. His eyes
actually brightened when he saw me.

'Drink?' he threw at me before I could get a word out. It was
late afternoon by this time so his usual getaway ploy of lunch wasn't
available, but drinks would fit in nicely.

'Suits me,' I agreed and we returned to my Polo. It's not a longing
to escape the office that lures him from his desk; it's the thinking
and discussion time he values. I drove him to our favourite pub on
the Canterbury Road and Dave sat down with a sigh of happiness.
He's a family man with young children, and to him a pub seems a
peaceful paradise, noisy or not. To look at he's the dreamy academic
type, but this is an illusion. He has a razor-sharp mind for every
tiny detail both on the crime side and the car side.

'Fill me in,' he said at last when we'd caught the measure of
each other's moods and were working our way through non-alcoholic
beers. He listened patiently to my tale of the Lair and Crockendene.

'What have you done so far about it?' he asked me.

'Nothing. I told Adora Ferne I'd sniff around but I'm turning
down the paid job she offered. It's the death threat to her that I
don't like.'

'Could be sheer fantasy on the writer's part or on hers.' Then he
pinpointed my concern right away. 'Using the post is odd, I grant you.'

'Elderly people involved?'

'Ageist,' Dave remarked dismissively.

'That's not the only point. Even though emails and tweets can
be traced if it's a serious threat, they're the easiest method so why
use post?'

'Because this is the work of a joker,' Dave replied. 'Trust me,
I'm a cop.'

'Not so sure, Dave.'

'You could be right,' he admitted grudgingly. 'This Adora Ferne
sounds a cute cookie. She probably knows more than she's let on.'

'So why drag me into it and not you lot?'

'Probably fell for your charms,' he remarked. 'Watch it. You'll be asked to give her a Jag soon.'

I ignored this dig. 'What's your conclusion?'

'Without the evidence, helpfully destroyed, we can't do a thing. But I'll put Brandon in the picture.'

At least he was taking the threat to Adora seriously, I thought as I drove back to Frogs Hill. I'd contact Adora tomorrow and tell her that I'd informed the police that I was sniffing around. On the whole, I reflected, cars were simpler than humans. True, they have complicated machinery and technology, but once one has sorted them out one can reckon with them. They don't have unexplained mysteries in the past or emotional lives that have to be taken into account. I never feel myself reluctant to tackle a car because I don't want to upset it. Human beings are different. Even though it appeared I would be holding my tongue over Alice for the next week, I was aware that I might have to look out for Zoe's well-being in the near future. I'd detected no major signs of turmoil in her recently (except when an ill-treated Austin-Healey came in). Nevertheless, I did what any normal man might do in the circumstances – I tried to avoid her.

I should have realized that this was not possible with Zoe. She cornered me on the farmhouse doorstep when I returned from Charing. I suspected she had been working this late on purpose, as it was seven thirty.

'You're not going into the farmhouse yet,' she informed me. 'Len and I want to know about those Jags.'

I obediently surrendered and went back with her to the Pits. On the way Zoe immediately displayed signs of true womanhood.

'Any sign of Miss Goody Two Shoes?' she threw at me.

'Adora?' I played simpleton.

'Alice,' she demanded.

'I glimpsed her at the door of her home but didn't speak to her.' She eyed me suspiciously. 'Did she speak to you?'

'No.' True enough, but I was glad when we reached the Pits and found Len there, which meant this inquisition would stop. He too was eager to hear from me, only not about Alice. He immediately lay down his tools to hear about the cars.

Relieved, I gave them a rundown on the Lair and the threatening letters, plus a detailed account of the cars themselves, which was really all Len wanted to know about.

'Are you taking the job this woman offered you?' Zoe asked as I'd mentioned the anonymous letters.

'No. Told her I'd sniff around, though.'

'Any nasty smells so far?' she asked crossly. 'Crossly' because she suspected I wasn't playing ball over Alice but couldn't identify what the ball was.

'Yes, but I can't be sure what they are.' Except for Rob, I thought.

'Drains,' Zoe observed.

'What's that mean?'

'Drains take nasties underground.'

'Could be a few,' I said cautiously, aware that Zoe was and would be examining my every word. I made a mental note not to chat too much to Louise about Rob when she returned. Louise and Zoe get on well, and if the sisterhood kicked in Louise might well drop a hint to Zoe that there was something nasty in the woodshed, i.e. Rob.

I wasn't sure when Louise was returning and when the phone rang just after midnight I was hopeful that she was on her way. She wasn't.

It was Dave bearing bad news. 'Thought you should know, Jack. There's been an incident at Crockendene Farm.'

I was instantly awake. 'The Lair? The cars?'

'No. But Brandon's on his way.'

'What for?' Then it hit me. Brandon – homicide. Death. 'Is it Adora?' I asked fearfully. Had the death threat been serious?

'No. But a corpse *has* been found in that Lair of yours. Identified as that of Danny Carter.'

FOUR

anny? That didn't make sense. At least, not to me. Accident? Suicide? Murder? A random killing? I mentally kicked myself. An image of a solo maniac tramp creeping through the woods and coming across Danny might be a convenient answer but was so unlikely it had to be discounted. Coincidences happen, but it would take a lot to convince me this was one of them.

I joined Brandon at the crime scene the next morning, and it made a grim start to Wednesday. I hadn't taken to Danny Carter, but the thought of the man with whom I had so recently been dealing now lying dead – and presumably murdered if Brandon was on the case – was chilling. Had Danny disturbed the arsonist of the threatening letters? Was Adora Ferne the intended target? Had Danny found out who was sending those letters and tackled him? This would get me nowhere because I had no facts to go on, and so I stopped speculating. The evidence would soon be all too obvious. As I turned into the driveway to the farm I could already glimpse the familiar vans and police cars ahead, so I parked the Polo behind them and walked the rest of the way to Danny's office, which was cordoned off.

At the Lair the crime-scene tape covered a large area round the building, reaching back as far as the woodland. As I drew nearer I couldn't see any sign of Dave but spotted Brandon on the forecourt. If this was indeed a murder case, I wondered whether Brandon would see the Lair merely as its location or linked more closely. As I said earlier, Brandon and I have had an up-and-down relationship but thankfully he has come to accept me as an annoying nuisance who buzzes around but whose help can be harnessed if needed on the classic cars front.

I made my way to the cordon entrance but Brandon had seen me and come out to meet me.

'Dave tells me you knew the victim, Jack,' he began without preamble.

'Not well. Met him twice. He came to Frogs Hill to commission me to buy a car for his boss and I came over yesterday to report on it. I expect Dave filled you in on Adora Ferne?'

'Yes, but tell me again.' His gimlet eyes were upon me.

I gave him a rundown on everything that had taken place, including the hate mail saga. I wondered how he would take the thirteen Jaguar lovers' angle, but as usual his non-committal expression failed to provide a clue.

'This death threat was sent to Miss Ferne, right?' he eventually said. 'Not Danny Carter?'

'To her. Have you met her yet?'

'Yes, and before you ask, her daughter's with her and one of my team.'

'Just as well. She's an unusual lady.'

'So I discovered,' he said drily. 'The daughter told me Danny Carter worked for her for over twenty years, but Miss Ferne seems to be taking it on the chin. She said something about a dog dying. Not hers, I gathered. Some other dog. I'd have put her down for dementia if it hadn't been for the rest of what she had to say.'

A dog? I too was thrown but then a bell rang. 'Did she say "The dog it was that died"?' I asked.

'Might have been that. What dog, though? It's a tough way to speak of someone who's worked for you for twenty years.'

'Not so much in context. "The man recovered of the bite, the dog it was that died", meaning that those who lash out suffer most in the end. "Elegy on the Death of a Mad Dog" by Oliver Goldsmith. It was one of my father's more mournful utterings when things went wrong.'

Brandon stared at me. 'Does that help us?'

'It could suggest the threat to kill her was serious but it hit the wrong target.' I hesitated. 'How did Danny Carter die?'

'First estimate, shot between eight and ten last night. No weapon found. Not suicide.'

'He wasn't the type—'

'What is the type?' Brandon said dismissively, silencing me. 'Chap who found him was called Fred Fox. He lives nearby, often takes an evening stroll through the grounds – knows the owner, he says – thought he saw movement around the Lair and went over to have a look. Door unlocked. The only sign of a break-in was a smashed window.'

Fred Fox. I knew that name. I grappled for it and succeeded. It was on Danny Carter's list. 'There must be an alarm system,' I said. 'Didn't anyone hear it?'

'Apparently not. The system shows it rang last night and that's what probably brought Carter over here. The alarm's set only to ring in his office and home.'

Typical, I thought. Very possessive over his job.

'Fox roused the son, Simon Hargreaves, who rang us. The body was sprawled beneath that empty platform.'

The thirteenth car's place. Was that significant? I wondered.

'Want to have a look?' Brandon continued.

I nodded. There's nothing I like less than seeing dead bodies, but I reasoned that this one would be gone by now so, duly kitted out, I followed him in. The forensic team was still working its way along the aisle, but I could see the pencilled shape on the floor by the platform and it didn't take much imagination to transfer a mental image of Danny's body to it. The blood alone was a guide and there were plenty of signs of that left, even on the board above him and on the empty photo frame.

'Did you find the keys on him?' I asked.

He glanced at me with a slight look of amusement. 'Yes.'

We both realized what followed from that. If Danny were the first to go in or went alone, he would have unlocked the door. His murderer would have no need to lock it after him. But how did the murderer get in? Answer: he set off the alarm by some means, probably that smashed window, knowing it would bring Danny over here, waited for him, followed him in and shot him. But that suggested either that the killer was acquainted with the alarm procedure, or that the killer didn't care whom it brought over provided it meant he could get inside the Lair. I'd go with the first option. It takes a very short time to shoot someone if you have come prepared.

'Fred Fox was one of the twelve Jaguar donors,' I told Brandon.

'Do you know him?' When I shook my head, he added, 'Odd fellow. And this is a weird place.' He looked round at the twelve Jaguars patiently waiting for the thirteenth. Or perhaps they weren't, I thought fancifully; perhaps they hated the idea of that supercar SS 100 joining them. 'These cars,' he continued. 'Is the story that Miss Ferne spun you about their being gifts true?'

'I believe there's at least some basis to it.' I told him a little more about such stories as I knew and even my brief descriptions made Brandon's eyebrows shoot up. His own home life from what I knew of it bore little resemblance to Adora Ferne's.

'Any relevance to this murder, though?'

'There could be.'

'Ten to one it'll come down to family in the end.'

'Danny's or Adora Ferne's?'

'Good point,' Brandon said. 'His. There's an ex-wife in south London who's already been notified. There's a son too, but she was vague over contact details. The team are working on Carter's computer and that should winkle it out. Will all these car donors be on it?'

'Yes. He printed a list off for me if there's a problem.'

Brandon pounced on this. 'Why?'

I mentally groaned. Dave hadn't filled him in on this angle. 'Adora Ferne asked me to do some work on tracking down the author of those anonymous letters,' I told him. 'I turned it down because the single death threat seemed your pigeon, not mine. I did say I'd sniff around in case I turned up anything. On the threats to the Lair, that is. Not the potential danger to her. That's your field.'

Brandon didn't exactly pat me on the back for conscientiousness. 'Why didn't she report it to us?'

'She didn't take it seriously.'

'But you did.'

Brandon can put one on the defensive quicker than a Ferrari off the grid. 'Yes, but that was only yesterday,' I said.

'That could be why she's asked to see you,' Brandon said reflectively.

'Has she?' I was wary about this. 'Any objection if I go?'

'I can't stop you, but you know the rules.'

I walked back to Crockendene through the woods, debating my next move. I'd have to give a formal statement but I couldn't just walk away from the case after that. It was possible Dave and Brandon might offer me some role if the cars came into it, but the threat to Adora would now be part of the police investigation. Colby's help not needed. Or was it less clear-cut than that?

The fresh smell of the trees combined with the scent of the mass of bluebells was a heady mix. Perhaps, I thought, I wasn't seeing the wood for the trees. Danny had been the victim but was the reason for his death to clear a path to Adora herself? If so, the story of those thirteen Jaguars could be relevant if they stemmed from a shady and mysterious past.

The farmhouse door was opened as before by Melinda, but this time her eyes were red with weeping. With her defences down, she seemed far more vulnerable. By all accounts Danny had not been close to the family, save for Adora, but the effects of the shock were no doubt kicking in with everyone.

'I told the police it's lonely over there,' Melinda blurted out. 'You never know who's prowling in those woods. We try to keep prowlers out but it's hard.'

I didn't comment. A prowler or poacher to my mind would run away, not come armed with a gun to draw attention to himself. But if the prowling maniac theory helped Melinda and Adora, I'd let it do so.

Melinda led me to a different room than the one I'd seen the day before. This one looked as if it might be a communal parlour with its log burner, several armchairs, a sofa and TV. Adora was sitting in an upright wing armchair opposite a middle-aged man with greying hair who I guessed must be her son, Simon Hargreaves. I recognized his daughter, Alice, who was keeping a low profile in a chair behind her father, but there was no sign of her brother, Michael. Simon looked a mild-tempered man by nature but his expression did not suggest I was any more popular with him than with Melinda. Even Adora looked a shadow of yesterday's dancing lady, but she was the central figure of the four. Very still, very poised, very strong. Both her children were perched sitting sideways, turned towards Adora, eager to please. No one asked me to sit down.

'This must be a huge shock for you all,' I said. It was an understatement, but useful as an opener.

Only Simon and Melinda acknowledged my gesture. Alice just stared at me and Adora merely accepted my presence.

'Danny was a valued employee,' Simon managed to say, sticking to the rules.

'Poor Danny,' Melinda moaned. 'Why would anyone want to kill him?'

Adora eyed them acidly. 'None of you liked him. You didn't even try.'

No one replied at first. Slightly odd, I thought. Why should they *try*? Because Adora was close to him?

Simon folded his arms defensively. 'He *worked* for you, darling. There was no need for us to *like* him. He was efficient.'

'*I* liked him,' Melinda said self-righteously. 'You just wanted to take over his job, Simon.'

'Not his job. I'd have been working *with* him. Taking the Lair in a new direction,' Simon said somewhat unconvincingly. 'He wasn't an easy man to work with, I admit.'

'Dad's right,' Alice joined in. 'I'm sorry he's dead but he was a horrid man.'

Melinda leapt on this bandwagon eagerly, changing her position as the voice of tolerance. 'He took advantage of you, Mother.'

Adora ignored her. 'Sit down, Jack,' she commanded me. 'You took on a job for me yesterday. Now it's changed.' She was still in fighting mode, although I could see it was a struggle.

I didn't correct her on facts. 'I can't take any job on with the police involved, Adora.'

'Of course you can.' She was quivering with what I identified as rage, though why I couldn't tell. 'I understand you can't get in the way of the police, but I want *you* to find out who killed Danny.'

I tried again. 'Even if the police agreed, I couldn't do it. I'm a car detective, not a murder specialist.'

'You are when you wish to be,' she snapped. 'I have made enquiries. However, if you prefer I merely ask that you continue to investigate who sent those letters to me. There we have Danny's killer.'

'The police will be following that line up.' I was still weighing up what I might be able to do, if anything. 'Can you be sure that the letters are linked to his death?'

'Yes.' She twisted irritably in her armchair, one hand fiddling with the long blue scarf wound round her neck.

I braced myself to ask the obvious question: 'Do you still think there is a threat to you personally, Adora?'

She looked astounded. 'He would never hurt me. That's why he killed Danny.'

He? Someone gasped, but it wasn't me. All shocked attention was on Adora. 'So you do know who killed him?' I asked.

Adora smiled – somewhat complacently. 'Naturally not,' she said, 'or I wouldn't wish to employ you, Jack. I knew the letters were never serious as regards myself, but they must have been sent by one of the twelve generous donors – it should be thirteen. Some to my great sadness are no longer alive, but most certainly are. Terrible though it is, one of them killed dear Danny.'

'Why would any of them threaten to burn the Lair down if their real motive was to kill Danny? Was a threat to you a step too far?' I asked, reasonably enough.

Adora drew herself up in the armchair, her graceful hands on the arms to indicate she was fully in control; there was the woman who fifty years ago had only to lift one of those slender fingers to have any man she chose at her command, who had captivated all who watched and listened to her magnetic performance and who, I reminded myself, was still the same woman exercising those same powers.

'Because,' she answered with dignity, 'I am Adora Ferne.'

That silenced us all. I could hear in my mind the sound of her voice in song, and for the moment could think of no logical reply.

'Mother . . .' Simon began, but his voice trailed off. Alice looked stunned and Melinda distinctly displeased. The floor was mine.

'I'll put that explanation to the police,' I said gently. 'And I'll do what I can. *If* I can.'

She inclined her head graciously. 'Thank you, Jack.'

It wasn't a surrender, I tried to convince myself. I was just buying time. After all, those Jaguars could still be under threat – as could Adora herself, for all her belief in her protected status.

There was also the matter of the thirteenth car. Was the arson threat the reason that the Earl of Storrington had refused to sell his classic, because he knew it might be in danger? Could it even be that he was the writer of the letters? I couldn't believe that, even if Adora was right about one of the donors being involved.

As I left the house, I saw the police were still active in Danny Carter's office and headed towards them. Alice, however, had come racing after me and caught me up halfway across the yard.

'Rob's told me about you, Jack,' she panted. 'You're good.'

'At what?' I asked cautiously, amazed at this accolade from Rob. Currying favour, no doubt, in the hope that his romantic dilemma would vanish.

'Sorting out this kind of business – it's awful really. Poor Granny. She doesn't show it but she's very upset.'

'At Danny's death or the letters?'

'Both. It isn't fair. She's being very brave, so we do want you
to find out what's happening. And please don't just say you'll
have to work along with the police. I know that. We all know that.
We just want you to help us. Be on our side.'

Looking at her, in her Alice-in-Wonderland full-skirted dress and
long hair, and with a face of misery that couldn't possibly be faked,
it was hard to think of her as a vamp who had stolen Rob away
from Zoe. I wondered if she even knew about Zoe's role in Rob's
life. But that was outside my remit.

'I want to be on your side but how can I be sure none of you
are involved? It's theoretically possible,' I replied. It sounded harsh
but it was true.

She took the point. 'You can be sure,' she said. 'We've nothing
to hide – none of us. It's those awful cars that are causing all this
trouble.'

I couldn't agree with the wording, but was inclined to agree with
Adora that the Lair and the car donors were top of the list as the
motive for Danny's death. My telling Alice this sent her off somewhat reassured, and I continued on to Danny's office. Dave Jennings
was there but not Brandon, which was frustrating but useful, as I
could sketch out the problem to him first.

'Do you want this job?' Dave asked me when I'd finished.
'Looking into the car angle?'

'Yes and no. It intrigues me but I don't see Brandon cheering
about any involvement from me if it merges with his case.'

'Could be good.'

'For whom?' I asked suspiciously.

Dave afforded me a grin. 'Me, the Crime Unit. Brandon's inclined
to the family path. Adora Ferne's *and* Danny's. He's chasing both
up. So if you're on a different tack, playing Jaguars, that could suit
us all.'

Brandon didn't look as if he wanted to suit anyone when he
unexpectedly appeared in the office. The non-committal expression
had given way to a rare fury. And it was directed at me.

'What the hell do you think you're doing, Jack?'

I was taken aback to say the least. 'Here to see you.'

He dismissed this impatiently. 'That batty old woman has just
rung across from the farm to tell me you're investigating this case
for me and I should consult you on anything I wish to know.'

A worst-case scenario. 'Wrong on all counts. I said I'd do what
I could on the Jaguars if I had your blessing.' Plus, though I didn't
add this, Adora was not a batty old woman. If she were, she might
be a whole lot easier to handle.

He calmed down then. 'Assuming that's true,' he began, then took
one look at my expression and nodded. 'OK. I'd already agreed to
that before Carter's death, but now the situation has changed. What
do you propose to do about the job she claims she's given you?'

'Sleep on it for the rest of the day and then convey my decision
to her.'

'I need your answer now. And you wouldn't be working for her,
but me. Agreed?'

My mind spun round like a dodgem car. I thought of those Jags.
I thought of Adora Ferne in the fifties and sixties belting out songs
such as 'Milord' and I thought of Danny Carter, probably killed in
the line of duty to those Jags. If those cars might lead to discovering
Danny's murderer, I couldn't leave it there. I had to know.

'Agreed,' I told Brandon.

'Keep to the cars, because I reckon you're on the wrong track.'

'It's happened,' I meekly conceded.

Brandon unbent a little. 'It's those letters. Death threats following
threats to property stinks of a smokescreen.'

'Screening what?'

'His family, Jack. Or maybe hers but *not* long-lost lovers from
the past.'

We parted on reasonably good terms and I went straight over to
report to Adora. She and her family were still huddled in that room.
As I went in they were talking about Danny's funeral and the need
to ask the former Mrs Carter or her untraceable son what their
intentions were. Blank faces therefore greeted my statement on what
I'd agreed with Brandon.

The only person who queried it was Simon. 'Does this mean
you're limited as to what you can reveal to us?'

'It does.'

Adora broke the silence that followed. 'Make the thirteenth car
an exception, Jack. I need to know everything.'

I was by no means sure I'd done the right thing but was relieved
that I was working for Brandon rather than Adora's family. I left

the forensic team still working in the office and made for my Polo. The press had already gathered and I decided to give them a wide berth. The last thing Brandon would want would be my shooting my mouth off to the newspapers. He's on the economical side when it comes to press releases.

I managed to avoid the press but had another visitor I couldn't escape. Lounging against my Polo was a youth in his early twenties clad in designer jeans and jacket and with a gleam in his eye. He unrolled himself meaningfully from my car.

'I wanted a word with you,' he informed me grandly. 'I've heard about you from Alice. You're Jack Colby and you're cosying up to Adora.'

'I've met her twice. Neither occasion was particularly cosy, especially today. I take it you're Michael Hargreaves, Simon's son?'

'You've sweet-talked her into paying you for sticking your nose into those letters and checking out the Jaguars.'

'Is that any business of yours?'

'Yes. I'm in charge of the Lair now.'

Was he, indeed. That seemed debatable. 'Good,' I replied cordially. 'When I have written authority from Miss Ferne that this is the case, I'll be contacting you *if* I need help. And incidentally, you're misinformed. I'm not working for Miss Ferne; I'm working for the police.'

'So you say.'

I sighed. 'Just believe me, Mr Hargreaves. It's easier that way.'

I unlocked the Polo, got inside and started the engine. I thought at first he was going to throw himself in front of the car, but he didn't. He stood aside and watched with a look on his face that suggested I'd have no friends in the Hargreaves household if he had anything to do with it. Luckily, I didn't think that amounted to very much. Nevertheless, cocksure and aggressive young men can never be discounted in sizing up a case.

When I reached Frogs Hill again I deliberately avoided the Pits, though I guessed that Len and Zoe, particularly Zoe, would be agog to hear what was happening at Crockendene Farm. It was unfair of me but I needed downtime by myself. Instead I took myself off to our local pub, which has a garden overlooking the weald of Kent – a good spot to brood by oneself with work and a pint. I took Danny's list with me to re-read, trying not to think of his horrible death.

Rex Hargreaves topped the list: in 1969 he had donated (or otherwise) the splendid XK 150 sports coupé 1957 model; Charlie Dane had handed over the 1969 XJ 6 in 1972; the lovely Harry an XJ 8 saloon from 1994 donated in 2007; Patrick O'Hara (deceased) a 1959 Mark II saloon donated in 1968; Lance Benny (deceased) had been the proud owner of a 1956 Jaguar D-type racing sports car bought from his estate in 1965; Noel Brandon-Wright had donated a 1962 E-type roadster in 1969; Blake Bishop a later E-type sports car from 1971 donated in 1980; Valentine Paston, fortunate owner of a 1949 XK 120 sports car donated in 1964; Travers Winton (deceased) donated his 1958 XK 150 in 1963; Alan Reeve donated a 1975 E-type sports car in 1984; Ivan Cole (deceased) a 1975 XJ 6 donated in 1977; and Fred Fox – he who had discovered Danny's body – donated a 1975 XJ 12 in 1994. Add to that Gabriel Allyn, now elevated to the peerage, a 1937 SS 100 *not* donated, and it was an interesting list.

I was just revving myself up to face Zoe's and Len's reproachful expressions the following morning when DCI Brandon called me.

'I've got something for you, Jack. Can you drop by? It changes things.'

I could indeed drop by. Only too pleased, as I could see Rob outside chatting to Zoe. Craven of me, but I couldn't face a cheery conversation with him today. Anyway, his week's grace for making his decision between Zoe and Alice still had four days to run, and so after a quick word with Len I shot off to Charing.

Brandon actually looked pleased to see me as well as rather pleased with himself.

'We've got some interesting data from Carter's computer,' he told me, leading me up to his office where one of his team was bent over a laptop. The constable straightened up and ceded his seat to me. He looked excited, as well he might, because I found myself staring at something familiar in subject matter in a Word file. For a moment I couldn't grasp the significance.

'Danny wrote the letters himself?' I asked incredulously.

'Either that or he carefully typed them all on to his computer when Miss Ferne received them. We've checked with her that she handed them all over to him, except for the one with the death threat. Thought it might upset him! But it's on the computer along with the rest. Funny sort of chap, eh?'

There I agreed with him. I also remembered that he'd shown no sign of surprise when Adora had mentioned the death threat. I could see why. I could also see the point of the letters by post now. Email would be too revealing if he used his own address.

'Did anyone else have access to this computer or share it?' I asked.

'Not that we've found out so far. Not likely either. He worked alone, no assistant, so anyone popping in on the off-chance to type and print them all out isn't a viable possibility.'

'What time of day were they typed?'

'Working hours. He doesn't seem to have bothered much about security, though. Not even a password.'

I couldn't get my head round this. Why would a man devoted to a collection like the Lair and with a secure and presumably good job write letters like this to his employer? It couldn't surely be a serious threat, but what advantage would there be in threatening her at all, much less threatening her life?

'What the hell did he do it for? He was wedded to the place,' I said.

'You tell me, Jack,' Brandon replied. 'You think the cars are behind the murder. How would this fit into that theory?'

'I haven't a clue but I'll do my damnedest to find out,' I said slowly.

'It means we can rule out Adora Ferne being the intended victim.'

'Does it? Not so sure there.'

'Why?' he threw at me.

I tried to fix on what was worrying me. 'Danny could have hounded those donors as well as thinking that one of them might have had Adora Ferne in his sights. She could still be someone's ultimate target. As she said, "the dog it was that died".'

As I drove into the forecourt at Frogs Hill I saw to my pleasure that there were lights on in the house. Len and Zoe have keys to the farmhouse but it was after their working hours so the betting was that Louise was home early, as sometimes happened when she was filming. I couldn't see her car but she had probably garaged it for once. All was right with the world. She had only been away a few days but it's amazing how quickly a house can empty itself of one's beloved's atmosphere and then quickly spring back to life again on their return. Today was no exception. Louise was home again, and it took a while before I had the time or desire to fill her in on the Adora Ferne situation.

It wasn't until the next morning that I was back on course. Even then I had to drag my attention back to Danny Carter rather than just appreciating how lucky I was to be starting the day with Louise. Her calm Madonna-like face framed with her dark hair was the satnav I needed (even if the calm couldn't *always* be guaranteed).

Back to Danny Carter. 'My fault,' I said. 'You warned me not to go to Sussex.'

'From what you've told me, Sussex sounds the least dangerous part of it.'

'True. I liked the earl and I liked his car.'

'You might even like his poetry.'

'Have you read any?'

'Yes. Dated, but good. It's not Adrian Henri style but it's a long way from Betjeman. Romantic in flavour.'

'Unusual by the sixties.'

'Yes, that's what makes it interesting. Have a look at some. Try "Café in Boulogne".'

'*Why* did you warn me not to go to Sussex then?'

'Because the commission was mixed up with Adora Ferne and there always seems to have been an aura of trouble around that lady.'

'She's had a lot of husbands and many more lovers, but what's the root trouble? Drugs or drink or scandal or what?'

Louise wrinkled her delightful nose as she thought. I love watching this process, as it indicates she is on the verge of a breakthrough. And so it was in this case.

'I think – *think*, mark you – that it was murder.'

I don't think I actually fell off my chair physically but I certainly did mentally.

'*Whose* murder? What murder?' I demanded.

'That's what I can't remember. I *think* it was all mixed up with that club she sang in.'

'The Three Parrots? Was that why the club closed down?'

'Perhaps. I wasn't alive at the time,' she said pointedly.

'Nor was I. Who got murdered? Who did it?'

'A blank, my lord.'

'Stop quoting the Bard of Avon and think, my lady. Who died?'

'Some racing driver? And I've no idea who killed him, even if the case was ever solved. But my father used to talk about it sometimes. Lance something.'

'Benny?' I asked, with a quickening sense of progress at last.

'Possibly.'

'Correct that to probably,' I said. 'Lance Benny was one of Adora Ferne's lovers.'

FIVE

Montague Greene – a name so familiar, and no doubt a familiar face as well, but I couldn't put the two together. I would know him, Louise assured me, from his TV appearances alone. She had told me that it was he who had been her informant on the Three Parrots and on Lance Benny, and that being gossip-minded he would be only too happy to expand on the story.

Whether it was useful or not, it was good to be travelling to London with Louise and in the springtime residential areas such as Kensington would be looking their best. Montague Greene lived in just such a street, lined with trees and graceful white-painted terraced houses three or four storeys high. Montague came to the front door himself when we buzzed the entry phone, and I did indeed immediately recognize him. In the old theatrical stock companies he would have been classified as 'character actor', the quintessential eccentric English gentleman whether he be detective, villain, lord of the manor or itinerant beggar. Now he was before us, Montague Greene himself: short, plump, alert and definitely eccentric. He was wearing a large checked green jacket and a bright green cravat, a scarlet handkerchief peeping out from the top pocket, slippers and bright blue trousers.

'Come in.' He beamed at us both. 'Louise, my *dear.*'

The extensive kissing that ensued – which I feared might extend to me – suggested his first sexual choice would not be female.

'Jack. So you're Jack.' His eye ran over me. 'Follow me, my dears, and you shall hear all.'

We obeyed and he led us to what appeared to be a ground-floor flat, although it also included the basement and, judging by a small inside staircase, perhaps part of an upper floor too. 'Down below is my stage, my books, my den,' he informed us, waving a hand in the direction of a staircase. 'But here I reflect on life.' The room we were in was a spacious and splendid living room that ran the length of the building.

'The view from the front windows, as you see,' he continued, 'is a perpetual reminder of the mundane world of today with which we must all contend. But here' – he trotted to the far end of the room overlooking a garden – 'is Jumbly land. "Far and few, far and few are the lands where the Jumblies live", according to our friend the late Mr Edward Lear. Such a dear man. Over my garden, beyond the rows of dreary houses and one simply terrible modern road, is their home. It lies over the hills and far away in Kensington Gardens, the trees of which can be glimpsed in the distance. Such an inspiration, gazing at Jumbly land. I can gallop away to Bohemia, to Verona, to Agincourt.'

'"Once more unto the breach" . . .' I murmured knowledgeably.

'Indeed, indeed. I have never yet played dear Henry Five. Falstaff, yes. Such is life. Now, Louise dear, you and this young man wish to consult me.'

It was a long time since I'd been so termed. 'Adora Ferne and the Three Parrots club,' I said.

'Ah, yes. The adored one.'

'But was she?' I asked. 'Are the legends true?'

'All legends are true but they rarely tell the whole truth. She was indeed adored. I even adored her myself. In a platonic way, of course. Even in those days one had preferences. You must try some of my chocolate crumblies. I made them myself.' He promptly disappeared through a door and I tried to curb my impatience as coffee cups then arrived together with delicate plates and paper napkins portraying the kings and queens of England. Trust an actor to walk off stage at crunch point. At last the coffee and the promised crumblies made their appearance – and they were indeed delicious.

'You're remarkable, Monty,' Louise said, amused.

'I know, my sweet. Now to our muttons. I gather from Louise and our splendid national press that foul murder has been committed on Adora's farm. One of her employees.'

'A key member of staff. Did you know Danny Carter?' I asked.

'Good gracious, no. I have had little to do with Adora for very many years. I see her at events, we pass civil words but all true communication ended after *it* happened.'

My opportunity at last. 'The death of Lance Benny?'

'Precisely. My parting with Adora was not linked to that, but these things happen.'

Mysterious. And interesting that he even thought I might be linking it.

'Forgive me,' Monty said, 'but why should my humble memories be of interest to you when this poor Danny only entered Adora's life at a far later date?'

'You've heard the rumours about how Adora acquired her twelve Jaguars?' I asked.

'Who has not? In suitably hushed tones, of course,' he replied.

I explained Danny's role in looking after the Lair but held back about the letters. 'Six of the cars in the Lair stem back to the Three Parrots days, although two of their donors are no longer alive.'

'Of whom one was Lance Benny,' he murmured. 'But, dear Jack, can you really believe that four gentlemen of advanced years are going to travel to Kent to murder an employee of a former singer? To my knowledge two of those four reside in residential care homes and would most certainly be missed should they embark on such an escapade.'

His eyes were very sharp and I was temporarily checkmated. Then I answered mildly, 'I make a point of not believing or disbelieving anything about a case I'm involved in until proven otherwise. The roots of a case are very often hidden in the past no matter what branches might be waving around above.'

I was pleased with this flowery explanation but I don't think Montague Greene was. He finished his chocolate crumbly very deliberately and I could see this interview was in the balance. I took a risk.

'And there is Gabriel Allyn,' I continued. 'He was a member of the club. That makes five members in Adora Ferne's circle. Excluding yourself.'

That did it. A brief flash of venom.

'I was a member, but not for obvious reasons in Adora's close circle. I admired her singing voice – who could not? – but an admirer in any other way, certainly not. Indeed, the opposite. One of the gentlemen on your list, by name of Valentine, was a particular friend of mine. He betrayed me, naughty boy, and fell for the charms of Adora. Tell me, Jack dear, this Danny Carter – was he too one of Adora's playmates?'

'I doubt that very much. He was about twenty years younger than her.'

'Not that that would stand in her way.'

'Nevertheless,' I said patiently, 'not a chance.'

A sigh from Montague. 'And you assume this murder is to do with Adora rather than this Danny's other interests in life? No doubt he had some.'

'He had very few, so I do assume it.'

'Then why, if I might ask, did Danny die and not Adora herself? It does sound the wrong way round. Like the dog, you know. The one—'

My patience was wearing thin. 'That died,' I finished for him. 'Danny was found among the Jaguars. It's a link.'

Montague seemed satisfied with needling me. 'Dear boy,' he said, 'then let us proceed.'

'Rex Hargreaves, Charlie Dane, Noel Brandon-Wright, Valentine Paston, Gabriel Allyn. Lance Benny and Travers Winton are no longer alive, but what part did the other members play in her life?' I asked.

'Charlie was *not* a member,' he said indignantly, 'although he was always *there*, behaving as though he were. As the manager's son he gave himself airs, pretending he was one of us: a role he found hard to sustain. Rex, however, was the opposite. How very superior he was to everyone, including poor me. He was merely a business magnate, however, whereas I have commanded air, sea, land and all manners of peoples in my career on stage and screen. That is where my heart and mind lie. It's only this wretched body of mine prevents my being offered leading roles. Inside, I am Hamlet, I am Lear, I am Othello. Like the poor Dan Leno. You know of him, of course?'

Louise looked as defeated as I did on this one, so I shook my head on her behalf as well as mine.

'The greatest clown of all time, excelling even Grimaldi. A masterly comedian and yet he died broken-hearted because he could not play Lear.'

'The Three Parrots?' I reminded him gently.

'Ah, yes. Noel Brandon-Wright, a leader of men, a classicist, a scholar, a pilot, but now bound by the four walls of a residential home. Travers Winton has long left the world's stage. And then there is naughty Valentine Paston, an artist of great talent – until he met dear Adora. He chose her over me and our ways parted. He took over his father's grocery business after that – just fancy – which was duly eaten alive by a supermarket, after which ordeal my poor Jonah emerged from the belly of this whale straight to a care home. And then there is the Mighty Gabriel, Earl of Storrington. Then he was but a thin and scrawny youth scribbling his verses for his adorable Adora, after which his poems vanished into anonymity.'

'Did she return his passion?'

'Adora returned everyone's passion, dear boy. Have you not grasped that? Gabriel was her devotee, her constant squire – for a while. Alas, poor Gabriel.'

'What about Lance Benny? Was he a constant squire too?'

Montague threw up his hands in ecstasy. 'What a fairy tale, what a romance,' he exclaimed. 'Rumours abounded. Whom would Adora honour with her hand in marriage? Whom was she honouring with an entirely different part of her body? Whom was anybody going to marry? In those days you understand there was little *public* talk of illicit relationships, though in darkened corners old friends might well fill a passing hour on the subject. I've no doubt the same applied to Valentine's relationship with me, which of course was still *very* illicit.'

'The night that Lance Benny was murdered?' I reminded him gently when he paused for breath. I could see Louise was trying not to giggle.

'Quite.' Montague beamed as he prepared to launch himself on this topic. 'You should understand, my dear Jack, that whether his death had anything to do with the club was never proven.' He helped himself to another crumbly. 'These were the glory days, the days of Noël Coward, of Larry Olivier and Vivien Leigh, of Louis Armstrong. Days of glamour, but also the days of whispers and intrigue—'

'Stop playing, Monty,' Louise cut in. 'Jack needs to know about that murder.'

A sigh. 'If you wish, Louise. But it's not nearly as much fun.' Monty looked appealingly at us – all part of the game.

'Lance Benny, please,' I said firmly.

Another sigh. 'Your wish is my command. It was Thursday the twenty-fifth of June, 1964. It was a dark and stormy night—'

'Monty!' Louise warned him.

His turn to giggle. 'A gala night at the club. We were all there.

By "all" I mean both Adora's close coterie and many others not so close to her. I was among the latter but because of my agony over Valentine's betrayal I was sharply aware of what was going on. Adora was magnificent as always in her performance, but to those who knew her well there was something special about that evening. At first her power and zest predominated. She performed in half-hour sessions from nine thirty p.m. with half-hour breaks in between. She took her bow at midnight for her break that evening but by her last session at twelve thirty her mood had changed. She was captivating but sad, bitter, enchanting – all those things. That mood spread over her audience. It thinned out but those remaining were restless, febrile, uneasy. Newcomers arrived but that did nothing to lighten the heavy atmosphere. Of course, I might be biased. It seemed Valentine had deserted me. When I finally saw him again he said he was not feeling at all well and would leave immediately.

'But to return to Adora, *if* I must,' he continued. 'Valentine had done me the honour of confiding in me that there was a shock in store for us that evening and that Adora and Lance were involved. I hoped – how I hoped – that the shock was that they were to be married.'

'They were that close?' If this was the case then I could be on the right track. There was much more to this Three Parrots line than I had dared to hope. But was it true? 'Wasn't Rex Hargreaves her great love by that time?' I added. 'She married him later that year.'

Montague was pleased with the effect his story was obviously having on me and proceeded to elaborate. 'Adora shimmered in a glorious golden dress that evening, and her evident excitement suggested I was right in expecting an announcement. But nothing happened, save this odd atmosphere. I could not help but notice that few of her coterie were around in the later part of the evening, and I assumed that there had been some quarrel either between Adora and Lance or between Lance and one of his rivals – perhaps even my dear Valentine. I returned home most dejectedly, especially as Valentine and I were no longer living together thanks to his betrayal.

'The next day I heard that Lance's body had been found in a doorway in Soho Square, about a hundred yards from the club. He had been stabbed. His death had no apparent connection with the club but his movements during the evening were closely examined by the police and we were all questioned. There is, as you know, a small garden in the centre of the square, and Lance seemed to have been walking around it. His body was covered with a coat and could easily have been mistaken for a tramp by any passers-by in the night. Suspicion naturally fell on the club but nothing came of the investigation. Valentine, with whom I was later reconciled, would never speak of it to me.'

'The club closed down that year. Was that connected?' I asked.

'Rumours grow in fecund ground. There was gossip. The coat was a good one but a well-known make and so could well have been Lance's own if he was carrying it. Nevertheless, it did not escape notice that the people on whom the police concentrated their enquiries were all in Adora's circle. Rumours still circulated in the club and in society generally that Adora had at last decided which of her lovers to marry – Lance. I cannot,' Monty added, 'claim that her lovers were all active at the same time, but passions, as I know too well, can linger, as can hopes of happiness.'

'What was Lance Benny like?' Louise asked.

'A glamorous and highly successful racing driver. He was congenial, social, gregarious, charming – and as unlike Adora's devoted Gabriel as one could imagine.'

'Yet she married Rex Hargreaves later that year,' I pointed out. 'Not Gabriel Allyn.'

'Indeed. That too was remarked upon in those dark corners.'

'Was Lance Benny in the club the whole evening? What time was he last seen there?'

'My dear Jack, cooperative though I am, this was over fifty years ago.'

'It was a major event, though. Details linger in the mind.'

'Oddly enough it was not much discussed in Adora's close circle. A discreet silence was maintained. This, after all, was a gentlemen's club. I naturally badgered Valentine for every detail but, as I said earlier, he would say nothing. He was very shaken, poor lamb, and like a lamb he returned to me. Nor would the other members of Adora's fan club speak. One has to admire them: a code of loyalty that has faded from our national mores. Fortunately I am not bound by it, but there is little more I can tell you.'

I thanked him. 'Do you have any photos from those days?'

'Not many, but they might amuse you.'

I spent a fascinating half hour while Louise and Montague argued happily over current interpretations of Shakespeare's plays. Each photo had been meticulously captioned in the album he had presented to me so I rarely had to interrupt their discussion. Most were groups with a young Montague in them, naturally enough. There was a spectacular one of Lance, however, photographed with the Jaguar D-type and with his arm round Adora. They made a stunning pair, even making allowances for a fifty-year gap in style. Both tall and graceful, both supremely confident. It was dated May 1964 – not long before Benny's murder changed everything.

Did that story have any bearing on the murder of Danny Carter, however? With this new light on the relationship between Adora and Lance I had taken a great leap forward – but where it was taking me I could not yet even guess.

'Any help?' Louise asked. We had decided to treat ourselves to lunch in Kensington Gardens after a walk to the Round Pond and the Peter Pan statue. Although it was a working Tuesday, yesterday had been a bank holiday to greet the arrival of May. The Round Pond was still well patronized with toy boats and the statue with tourists. Nevertheless, Peter Pan always fascinated Louise, so we spent some time admiring him.

'I played him once,' she said reflectively.

'Did you fly through the air on wires?'

'Yes, a highlight of my career. I felt above it all, above the cares of this world,' she joked. 'There's a bit of me still flies through the air in bad times.'

'We could fix you some wires in the Pits. Len wouldn't mind you whizzing overhead.'

'No,' she said seriously. 'The Frogs Hill part of me is grown up. And I love it.'

Her question about the meeting with Montague was not easy to answer but I tried my best. 'It's thrown me up in the air but I don't know where I've landed,' I confessed. 'Nor have I a clue where to wobble next. The case seems split in three: Adora, a fifty-year-old murder and a twenty-first-century one.'

'Adora at the top and the other two leading up to her in a triangle?' she interpreted.

'They must surely be linked at the bottom then. Taking Brandon's preferred route of family, there would be no link at all.'

'If you forget Lance Benny, that Lair must be worth quite a bit to the family.'

'How is killing Danny going to advance that?'

She grimaced. 'True, but since they want to take it over it would bring them a step nearer.'

'Weak, but a pat on the head for pointing it out.'

'I do my humble best.' She hesitated, then added, 'There's one angle I didn't mention. Montague is a gossip; it's his daily treacle, it's how he gets invited to places.'

'And so he might have spruced up the story?'

'Or glossed over some of it. Just bear that in mind.'

I would. Especially when, two days later, I went to see Sir Rex Hargreaves, former husband to Adora, father of Simon and prominent in the Three Parrots. I'd have to steer carefully. I would be walking on dangerous ground if Adora had only married him on the rebound after Lance's death. Gaining access to Sir Rex had certainly been tricky. I thought my police credentials would give me an easy passage, but his crisp reply to my request for an interview had ruled that out: 'For what reason?'

When I explained my role in the investigation of Danny's death, he had replied: 'I had no connection with Mr Carter and my past relationship with Miss Ferne has no bearing on his murder. Nor does the Three Parrots club. Nevertheless, I shall drive over to see you, Mr Colby, if you give me your address.'

No room for discussion on the venue. As he lived in the Sevenoaks area it wasn't that far for him to come, if that's the way he wanted it. Anyway, I was curious to see what this great man of insurance would be driving. I was not disappointed. It was a Bentley Mulsanne Turbo that drove gingerly into Frogs Hill forecourt (the lane to it is very narrow and scratches are most unwelcome for Bentley owners). Its driver could hardly be Sir Rex himself as I could see that the man leaping out of the car was only his forties. He held the door open for his employer and Sir Rex emerged. Tall, slender, elegantly and formally dressed, his keen eyes summed me up from my best casual shoes to my short haircut then swivelled round to look briefly at the Pits.

'Our restoration and repair garage, Sir Rex. Would you like to visit it?'

'Thank you. Later perhaps. Business first.' We left the chauffeur with Zoe and Len – I was aware of Len's reproachful eyes at this distraction from the day's work – and as it was a warm day we settled on the garden for our discussion. He appraised it, studied the view and remarked, 'Kent at its best.' The first sign of informality. We chatted on this subject for a few moments until he bore down on the issue of Danny Carter. 'You may begin, Mr Colby. You mentioned the Three Parrots.'

'Which may link up with the murder of Danny Carter and involve Miss Ferne,' I said. If he was laying down boundaries, I needed to stake out my claim.

'Mr Carter was merely a familiar figure when I visited my son, who as you know lives on the same estate as my former wife for some reason I have been unable to determine. I visit him rarely there, as he, Alice and Michael prefer to come to stay with me.'

'But you are still in touch with Miss Ferne?'

'Our life together finished in 1969. Now there is neither animosity nor a close relationship.'

'I understand the Jaguar XK 150 was part of the settlement.'

'I gave it to Miss Ferne as a gesture of goodwill when we parted.'

'Did you meet her at the Three Parrots?'

'Again, if relevant, I did. I answer these questions, Mr Colby, because of your role with the police. Otherwise I would regard them as impertinent.'

'There was a murder of a club member, Lance Benny, near the club, the same year that the club closed down.'

His face became a mask, as if he had been expecting – fearing? – this subject. 'There is no link between the two,' he said coolly.

'Were you there that night?'

'I was present every time my future wife was singing. I can assure you that Lance Benny's death had nothing to do with the club or with me personally, although the police interviewed us all at the time. The body was not found until the next morning and the death could well have taken place after the club closed at two a.m. I left well before that time.'

'With Miss Ferne?'

A pause. 'I cannot recall. I presume I escorted her home.'

Which meant he probably hadn't, I thought. It was time to stick my neck out. 'I'm told that Miss Ferne had been planning to marry Lance Benny.'

The mask came down again. 'Rumours multiply into fantasy. My former wife has a habit of reinventing the past. Take care, Mr Colby. Take great care.'

Interesting that he had assumed Adora had told me about her planned marriage. She hadn't.

Charlie Dane was, as Montague had intimated, poles apart from Sir Rex. For a start, he was only too happy to welcome me the following Monday morning. I could discuss anything I liked, he told me cheerfully. No problem, no holds barred. We were, he pointed out, in the same trade, just different branches. I could see his point, except that the Pits and Frogs Hill bore no resemblance to Charlie's classy modern building next to his car dealership near Canterbury. He reminded me of someone, but it certainly wasn't Sir Rex. Charlie was much shorter, much plumper and seemed much more content with life.

'You turn out good stuff at Frogs Hill, so I've heard,' he complimented me.

'Come along one day and see what's going on.'

'Thanks, I'll do that.'

Charlie also looked twenty years younger than his late seventies, the age he probably was given that he had worked in the Three Parrots. He was affable and jolly too, unlike Sir Rex, although on the whole people don't get to Charlie's position in life by being jolly; they tend to become jolly once they're there and can leave the serious stuff to others.

'This is about Adora, eh?' he said. 'You mentioned Danny Carter on the phone, but Adora's the key, as usual. That right?'

'Yes. I'm looking at the car angle while the regular police team are concentrating on other lines.'

'Too right. Heard all about that from Melinda. She's my kid, you know. When Adora and I split I wanted to take Melinda but she wanted to stay. So she did for a month or two until Adora got tired of her and passed her over to me. Melinda married a bloke I didn't care for. Told her it wouldn't work and now she's back at Crockendene. It suits Adora and Melinda couldn't wait to get back home. Why not? She and Simon Hargreaves – devoted to the place, they are. Home, they say. Know where my home was? East End in the Blitz. Bombed to blazes. That's why I like knowing my kid's in the home she loves.'

'You still own Crockendene Farm?'

'Think Adora would have let me get away with that? No way. Stung me for the whole estate. What a gal, eh? I love her to bits. Women, eh?'

I grinned even though my view on women in general was rather different to his.

'You must have known Danny Carter pretty well,' I said.

'That creep. Sorry and all. Don't speak ill and all that, but not much else to say about him. He arrived at Crockendene long after my time there but to visit the place after that was to know Danny Carter. Ask to see my old XJ 6 and Danny was right there in case I ran off with it. Melinda couldn't stand the creep either.'

'He seemed devoted to Adora.'

'Sure, for what he could get out of her.'

'When did you first come to Crockendene?'

'A couple of years after we married. Around 1974. Melinda was born the following year. I had eight years of living at Crockendene with Adora in wedded disharmony. I only gave way in the end to Adora over the estate because of Melinda. Funny little thing, she was. All big eyes and scared of her own shadow. And there's me and Adora the opposite.'

'Do you have other children now?'

'Yeah. Married again in 'eighty-five. My son Tom runs the business now. I cast the kindly eye, a genial godfather.' He laughed and I remembered of whom he reminded me: Harry Prince, the car dealer who has his eyes constantly on Frogs Hill hoping I'll default on the mortgage.

'Do you know Harry Prince?' I asked him. 'Neighbour of mine.'

''Course I do. Me and Harry go way back but I go wider than Harry, except in the midriff department.' He patted his belly but I thought Harry's was bigger. This man would be nippier on his feet, both metaphorically and physically. 'Good chap, Harry,' Charlie added.

'Sometimes,' I agreed, but kept my thoughts on the other times to myself.

'The Three Parrots,' I said. 'Your father owned it, didn't he? And you worked there.'

'He did. I did. Don't go there, Jack.'

'If I don't the police will. Danny Carter was linked to those twelve Jaguars, half of which go back to Adora's relationships at the club.'

He looked at me meditatively. 'You know what happens in those big museums? If the security alarm goes off the whole place closes down instantly. You're locked in, sealed, watertight. Nothing gets through and there are ways of seeing it doesn't. See what I'm getting at?'

'I take it that applies to the subject of the Three Parrots.'

'You're on the right track.' The bonhomie was gone.

'Lance Benny, for example?'

'Them and us, Jack. Talk to Rex Hargreaves and get one idea of the club. Talk to Adora and get another. My dad – he's gone now – had another. I was working there. I saw it happening. As manager you get to see a different side to things. Soho was beginning to get going in the late fifties and early sixties – if you see what I mean. The American Mafia didn't move into London for some years but there were plenty of gangs with drugs as their stock in trade.'

'Did your father have a policy?'

'Blind eye, Jack. Forget it. What happened to Lance Benny and the rest of them didn't have anything to do with that side of things.'

'What can you tell me about Lance Benny then?'

A long silence. 'You know what they say. Elephants and old men never forget. But you should, Jack. Believe me.'

There are ways of seeing it doesn't, Charlie had said. What did that remind me of? I had no problem remembering. It was Doubler, king of the car underworld in Kent. Our paths had crossed once and he had been silent since, but I had no doubt that he was still around. He had his own moral code, chilling though it was. If – and it was a big if – Danny Carter with his links to the threats to the collection had been a part of the Doubler underworld and betrayed it then that could well have brought about his death. Similarly, Charlie's father was manager of the Three Parrots, a job that could have brushed up against violence and gang warfare in the early sixties. Protection rackets were not unknown then, and Charlie would have grown up in that environment. It gave me food for thought.

SIX

'Your name's Jack Colby.'

I agreed it was. It hadn't been posed as a question, however, and it took me aback for a moment. I was still digesting the food for thought that Adora's choice of husbands had provided, the last one only yesterday, and couldn't get my head round what this extraordinary woman might be doing at Frogs Hill. The beat-up Honda she was driving did not suggest she was seeking our classic car restoration services, and nor did her truculent stance. It's not that I expect our customers to turn up on bended knee pleading for their jalopy's life, but the grim look on this woman's face defied any such categorization. She was around sixty, stocky, clad in a purple jacket over red trousers and was definitely not going to win any awards for charisma.

'Police sent me along,' she added. 'A chap called Brandon. I'm Di Carter.'

I was still blank, having first interpreted this as 'dicarta', not a word I knew. Then light dawned. 'Danny's ex-wife?'

'What are you going to do about it?' she demanded, brushing aside my condolences.

'About what?' I stalled.

'About those cars for a start. His Jags.'

His Jags? I sized up the situation and surrendered. 'Come inside,' I suggested.

Without a word, she stomped after me as I led the way to our living room and did my best to be an affable host with mugs of coffee. The latter seemed more acceptable than I was as she drained the mug and continued staring at me without a word – until I returned to the subject of cars.

I began on a cautious note. 'Danny was devoted to that Jaguar collection. Did you live at Crockendene with him?'

This at least brought a response. 'Went my own way, me and Sam. My son,' she added. 'What are you doing about it? That's what I want to know. The police aren't doing nothing.'

'They're a good team,' I began, assuming that by 'it' she must mean the murder of her husband.

'Arrest the lot of them,' she interrupted me. 'Them car owners.'

'Miss Ferne owns the cars.'

Another stare, indicating I was a prize idiot. 'Killed my Danny.'

'Adora Ferne killed him?' I was doing my best to keep up but it wasn't easy.

She let out a howl of disgust then calmed down. 'Look here, Mr Colby. I ain't got time to mess around.' Only mess wasn't her choice of word. 'Why should she kill him? She'd left the lot to him. That's what Danny told me a week or so before they killed him.'

'Who's they?' I was lost again.

'Family, that's who.'

If I interpreted this correctly, this was revving up the engine with a vengeance. 'Adora was bequeathing all the cars to Danny in her will? That was a generous gesture.' I'd already done a quick calculation and it came out at £400,000 at least. Of course, if the thirteenth car had joined it one could add another quarter of a million or so.

'I said the lot,' Di Carter informed me. 'You daft or something? House, grounds, the lot.'

To *Danny*? I couldn't get my mind round this. Surely it couldn't be right? 'What about her son's family and her own daughter?' I asked.

'Dunno. You ask the old witch yourself but that's what my Danny told me. Reward for faithful service, he said. So that's why I say they did it. That family of hers didn't like it and that's that.'

I could see why they didn't like it – and I could also see a few good reasons for their wanting Danny's removal from the scene. 'Did the family know about this will?'

'Must have done, otherwise why would they have bumped him off?' she shot back at me with impeccable logic (from her point of view). I noted the suspected guilty parties had now switched from the car owners to the family. Brandon was going to love that twist.

'My Danny didn't deserve that,' she continued. 'So now what are you going to do? I'll be done out of my rights if she goes and changes that will.'

The picture was now complete. Di Carter had been expecting to enjoy the fruits of Danny's will in her old age, ex-wife or not. Already she had seemed an alien presence in our living room, which normally has a pleasant, relaxing atmosphere. Now it was turning hostile. It was time to disillusion her.

'You have no rights,' I pointed out. 'You're no longer married to him.'

'That's what you think. Danny and I never bothered to get divorced, see? I'm Di Carter, married my Danny in 1971.'

The atmosphere grew even more hostile. I tried to imagine this sturdy, obstinate woman as a lively teenager being wooed by a young Danny Carter. I couldn't do it.

'So when the old bird drops her feathers, I get the lot,' Di continued gleefully. 'Me and Sam.'

I braced myself. 'Miss Ferne will probably rewrite her will.' No probably about it, I thought. Simon and Melinda – if they knew about this situation – would already have been on the case.

'If she doesn't pop off before she's done it,' Mrs Danny said smugly.

I was left dazed by the time this alien presence had been prised off my sofa and sent on her way. I had at last convinced her that my only role in this affair was to follow up the owners of the cars, and that nearly all of them had to do with times long before Danny had come to Crockendene. This was true. Not only did this apply to the six former members of the Three Parrots (seven if you counted Gabriel Allyn), but also to Patrick O'Hara, the gentleman who had interrupted the smooth flow of Adora's marriage to Rex, Blake Bishop who played the same role in her marriage to Charlie Dane, Alan Reeve and Ivan Cole. That left Fred Fox who found Danny's body and whom I had yet to meet, and the great Harry Gale who was very much on the scene. I hadn't mentioned him to Di Carter but he was another contender for inclusion in Adora's will.

I was still chilled by Di Carter's comments about Adora, remembering that threat to her life all too vividly. Another visit to her would be in order *and* I could pop into the Lair. The crime scene had been formally lifted now, but I still thought it good policy to clear a visit with Brandon's team before setting off.

I usually enjoy the drive along the Greensand Ridge to the Pluckley–Egerton road and then on towards Charing and the Downs, but today it held fewer charms. I had already turned on to the road to Pluckley when I realized that I was being tailed by a familiar car: Di Carter's. I had a sinking feeling she was heading where I was. Luckily I was driving my Polo and not a classic and managed to throw her off my tail at the Charing roundabout. Or so I had hoped. When I parked at Crockendene Farm, however, there she was. She must have taken a different route because she was already harassing the police constable whom Brandon had posted outside Reception.

I contemplated my next move but apparently this had been decided for me. She was insisting on seeing the Lair.

I braced myself and helped the PC out. 'Shall I escort Mrs Carter there?' I asked him.

'I don't need no escort,' she said. 'Where is this place?'

I ignored her – a ploy that seemed to work as she ceased to argue and followed me in relative silence to the Lair. The outer blinds were down and I didn't have Danny's magic instrument for opening them, but I didn't care. She would neutralize any magic left. She stomped along the path behind me to the door to which the sergeant had given me the key, pushed herself in front of me and stared at the cars.

'Did you come here when Danny was alive?' I asked.

'No. Where is it?' she demanded.

'Where's what?' I asked patiently.

'The thirteenth car. Danny was on about it. Pinched it already, has she? Danny said she'd get it sooner or later. It's valuable, that is. Where is it? It's mine.'

Ignorance was the best policy. 'All these cars belong to Miss Ferne, and so would any others that she acquired.'

'They all belonged to Danny,' she said matter-of-factly. 'He told me. He polished them, repaired them, drove them, knew them like his own kid – better,' she amended. 'Didn't take much notice of Sam did Danny. Sam was five or so when I walked out so not much time to bond, eh?'

'Is your son living with you?'

'He's around somewhere. Got out six months ago. Third time,' she added proudly.

So that answered that. Sam was an ex-con.

Her next gambit was: 'What about the old cove who used to do her gardens here before Danny came? Danny said the old bird hopped into one of the beds. His. We had a good laugh over that.'

'Would that have been Fred Fox?'

'Dunno the name but he and Danny never did get on, so Danny saw him off soon as he could. That chap could have done him in. Or one of the others.' She paused. 'What about that Harry Gale? Danny couldn't stand him either. The old witch bought the car for him and took it back when she sacked him in the divorce courts. Good riddance, Danny said. He was no good.'

And Harry was now back on the scene whereas Danny was dead, I reflected.

I eventually managed to offload Di Carter on to the PC again and could at last pay my respects to Adora. A few things needed to be aired between us. This time it was she who opened the door but we were not to be alone. Melinda and Simon were guarding her as closely as the giant statues of Gog and Magog had once protected the City of London.

'That nice police sergeant tells me you came here with dear Danny's former wife,' Adora said brightly as she waved me to a chair. She had regained some of her verve judging by the bright blue outfit. 'I suppose she has been saying horrible things about me.'

'She's a grieving widow,' I said diplomatically. 'She tells me she and Danny never got divorced.'

Adora promptly turned to her offspring. 'Then how glad I am that I've just changed my will, my darlings. You were quite right to advise me to do so as soon as Danny died. He said you weren't too pleased that he was to inherit my estate. It was very naughty of him to have told you. When was that? Quite recently?' There was a sharpness in her voice.

'He was horrid. He wanted to annoy us,' Melinda whispered, looking close to tears with the shock of this attack. 'It was when you began talking about buying that thirteenth car back. Danny thought it was a wonderful idea and said it would all be his inheritance anyway, that and the whole estate, including this house.'

'Melinda and I were rather surprised.' Simon's voice was more a squeak than his usual tone. 'Crockendene Cottage is *my* home just as this farmhouse is hers. We'd always assumed . . .' His voice trailed off as he no doubt realized this was neither the time nor the place for delicate negotiation.

'Don't be upset. I've no immediate plans to die, darlings,' Adora reassured them. 'And I most certainly wouldn't want to find Mrs

Carter living here when I return as a ghost. Poor Danny. She made his life a misery and he only knew what true happiness was when he moved here alone and could be with my cars.'

'You were too good to him, Mother.' Melinda failed to keep a snarl out of her voice.

'He was a sponger,' Simon agreed. 'Like Harry Gale – as you yourself used to say.'

'Did I? I don't recall that,' Adora said reprovingly. 'I *paid* Danny. He did an excellent job and the poor man has been murdered for it. And as for Harry—'

'That's nonsense, Mother,' Simon said bravely. 'He sent you those threatening letters, according to the police.'

'That was to protect me,' Adora replied.

I blinked at that. 'How does that work?' It was an interesting take on the situation.

'Danny wanted to draw attention to my vulnerability.'

That silenced us all. I fast-tracked it through my mind but it still didn't work for me.

'I think,' she continued, 'I'll take a little walk with you, Jack. It doesn't seem right to take one of the Jaguars for a drive.' Pity about that, but I understood. There was still a lost and lonely feel to the Lair.

There was an immediate offer to join us from Simon and Melinda, instantly rejected by their mother, and I was aware of their eyes following us as we left. I'd nothing against either of them in the circumstances. In their shoes I'm not sure I would have felt very warm towards Danny either. I doubt if it would have led to murder, though.

'Do you think there's a danger to me as the police believe?' Adora asked at last as we reached the woodland. This time she took a different path, not the one to the Lair or the Cottage but to the right, a track I didn't know.

'There could be,' I answered her.

'And does that stem from the former owners of my Jaguars?'

I chose my words carefully. 'It seems unlikely, but as half of the Jaguars belonged to former members of the Three Parrots the possibility has to be eliminated.'

'My life, my youth, when all was sunny and so easy.'

'Not always, Adora. One of those members was Lance Benny, the racing driver.'

I felt a jerk on my arm. 'Yes, Jack.'

'He was found murdered near the club and his killer never found.'

A pause, then she asked: 'How does that affect my Jaguars, even though one of them was his?'

'I've been told – but not from you – that you were planning to marry him.'

Adora was staring straight ahead of her. 'What a splendid detective you are, Jack,' she eventually replied. 'Your information is correct. It was one of the great tragedies of my life. Lance and I were very much in love. To be with him was very heaven. We were going to marry, but then – as you say – he was taken from me in the cruellest way.'

From the tone of her voice I thought she was crying as she walked ahead, still with such determination it seemed she thought that was the way to overcome her grief. The path we had taken had led us through the woods to open grounds at the rear of the farmhouse, skirting a small formal rose garden.

'I married Rex somewhat on the rebound, I fear,' she continued eventually, 'but I did have genuine affection for him.'

'Did you ever consider that Lance's killer might have been someone from the Three Parrots, one of the rivals for your affection?'

She answered that immediately – almost too quickly. 'So long ago, Jack. Everyone at the time was suspected. None of us could believe what had happened or that one of us might be involved. All we were told was that his body had been found the next day in the square, nowhere near the club. It was thought to be a gang of drunken youths.'

'Did you see him leave the club?'

'No. If I had I might have prevented it. I thought he had merely gone home. I think he was found at about six thirty in the morning. We had been planning to leave on the Saturday for a trip to Paris to celebrate our engagement. I wondered why I did not hear from him. Our plan had been to announce our engagement at twelve o'clock that night after my session ended, but I could not find him. I was told he had gone home. He lived close to the club. I'm afraid I was not pleased with him but assumed he had misunderstood the arrangement and would come round in the morning, but he didn't. The shock, oh, the shock. Some maniac killed him and my life changed for ever.'

'Why didn't you tell me, Adora? You made me think that Gabriel was your great love.'

'Oh, Jack. He was. You don't understand – how could you? It was so long ago. Lance was the burning ray, Gabriel the glorious sun and Rex the sheltering shield. But what,' she asked, 'can this have to do with Danny? Danny always had my interests at heart, you know.'

'Despite those letters?'

'Perhaps they were a warning, not a protection. A warning that not everyone feels towards me as warmly as he did.'

'It's an odd way of showing it – unless, of course, he *had* warned you. Had he?'

She bypassed this question. 'Danny was strange. But he understood me and I him.' A sideways look as we turned back towards the house. 'He meant a lot to me, Jack. That's why he was to inherit my estate.'

I didn't comment. 'Did you ever meet his wife?'

'Only once. We didn't take to each other. Danny might even have grandchildren for all I know. That would have been nice for him. I get so much pleasure from mine.'

'From Michael?' I wondered at this adroit switch away from wills. I could understand her pleasure in Alice, but my brief association with Michael did not suggest a warm relationship between him and his grandmother.

'A scamp,' she continued. 'But he is good at heart.'

So were a lot of the worst villains in history, no doubt. However, I wouldn't class Michael in that category – not yet, anyway.

Adora paused as we parted at the door to her home. 'We're having a little family gathering before lunch tomorrow. Would you care to join us? I think you'll enjoy it.'

'In remembrance of Danny?' There had been no mention of a funeral yet, either from Di Carter or Adora.

'Not quite, but I'm sure he would approve.'

I'd no great desire to carouse with Simon and Melinda but duty called, and besides, I was curious to find out why I had been invited if it had little or nothing to do with Danny or the cars. Adora was not the sort of person to issue invitations without a purpose. I might be overstepping the boundary into Brandon's territory but at least it was a passport to Adora's good books. I wondered whether any of the later lovers in her life would be there: Blake Bishop for example or Alan Reeve. So far these were just names to me but that had to be rectified.

At first I thought I was wasting my time. On the Thursday morning Melinda opened the door and ushered me in without a word. There was no sign of Adora or thankfully Harry or any other stray former lovers. Only Simon, Michael and Alice – and another familiar face to my horror: Rob was there. He looked as horrified as I felt.

'Morning, Jack,' he said uneasily.

'Good to see you, Rob.'

'It's lovely to see you, Jack.' Alice's voice bore an artificial jollity. 'Rob and I are off for a couple of days – we're leaving right after this party.'

If Rob's face could fall any further it would hit his boots as he took in my expression. It was over two weeks since our little chat. Had Zoe thrown him out or not? I pulled my attention back to Adora.

'What's this party in aid of?' I asked Melinda when she handed me a glass of champagne.

'I don't know,' she said crossly. 'Mother is odd sometimes.'

'This champagne isn't. It's OK by me,' I joked.

Melinda didn't do jokes. 'We're to be ready to greet her with it,' she told me sternly before I took my first sip.

And then the door opened. In floated Adora clad in a bright red lace dress that even someone of Alice's age would have difficulty in carrying off. Adora almost succeeded. But my eyes were on her companion.

It was Harry Gale, smartly clad with a carnation in his buttonhole. A terrible suspicion came to me.

'Darlings,' Adora beamed, clinging to his arm. 'I want you all to know as soon as possible. Harry and I have just got married.'

For once work at the Pits was at a standstill after I returned that afternoon. Zoe and Len both abandoned their posts but I was so shell-shocked at Adora's announcement that I didn't even mind facing Zoe.

'Harry Gale,' Len repeated slowly when I reported the news of the wedding. 'Met him once. Didn't take to him.'

Zoe wasn't interested in Adora's marital affairs. 'Was the ador-able Alice there?' she demanded.

I nodded cautiously.

'Looking her sweet lovely self?'

'Yes.'

'And Rob?' she shot in like a dagger.

This was the junction at which I had to take the road of truthful-ness (with some satisfaction, I have to confess). Rob had had his chance and blown it. 'Yes.'

She slammed down the front boot lid of the Renault 4CV she'd been working on. 'That does it,' she yelled, and she wasn't talking about the Renault. 'He told me it was over with that cow!'

I offered feeble hope. 'Alice has her eyes on the bright lights of London. I don't see her dragging Rob along when she has the world at her feet. He'll be back.'

She gave me a sweet smile. 'Not to me, he won't.'

Louise did not return until late that evening and it was only after she had eaten my carefully prepared pasta carbonara that she told me she had had a call from Montague Greene that day. 'He thought you might like to go to a care home,' she said, straight-faced.

'Love to. When do I move in?'

'Not till we're old and grey. He's going to a gathering on May the sixteenth. This Saturday. Thought you might like to go with him.'

'Gathering of what?'

'Veterans of the Three Parrots.'

'Yes,' I said promptly. 'Why the care home?'

'Noel Brandon-Wright now lives there. He can't travel and so he's invited them all there.'

'This,' I pronounced, 'sounds interesting.'

I rang Monty back early the next morning and received a full dose of his cordiality. 'Come as my guest, dear Jack. Valentine will be jealous, I fear, if he remembers who I am. Alas, unlikely. I must warn you, it is a reunion for *all* members. What you might not be admitted to is the inner circle, those particular chums of Adora's who were present the night that Lance died. There's never been a reunion of any sort before, so this is somewhat of a surprise. Hence I deduce it's a cover for the inner circle to get together without drawing attention to themselves. I'll email you a list of the attendees.

Poor Travers is dead, but the other fans will be there, including my sweet Valentine – and Gabriel, of course. Also, I fear, Charlie Dane.'

'Gabriel's coming?' I repeated in astonishment.

'Rather surprisingly, yes.'

What, I wondered, did they intend to discuss?

SEVEN

Gatsford House on the outskirts of Tunbridge Wells looked a pleasant stone mansion, no doubt once the pride and joy of some Victorian business magnate and now a residential and nursing home for the sick and aged. From the outside it seemed a gentle retreat from the hurly-burly of life, but I had no doubt that it brought its own trials and tribulations for its residents. Its grounds were spacious and as I parked in the gravelled area in front of the house with my passenger I could see a few residents soaking up their daily dose of vitamin D on the seating provided in the gardens. Judging by the assembled cars, Gatsford House was at the luxury end of care homes. An Aston Martin and a Mercedes did not suggest impoverished families.

When I had picked him up from the railway station Monty Greene had been ecstatically enthusiastic about the event to come and chatted inconsequentially on the subject for the entire drive. Fortunately he was not as eccentrically clad as before but was still definitely making a statement with his golfing cap combined with a dress suit that would have graced Buckingham Palace – albeit the suit was some-what tight on his rounded figure. He bristled with excitement, either because he was shortly to see Valentine again or because of the first-class opportunity to collect and relate gossip.

I could see Rex Hargreaves' car – a Bentley, of course – and I mentally assigned a Chrysler 300 to Charlie Dane. I was glad that I had decided to give my stately British Gordon Keeble an outing today. I had thought Monty might enjoy my 1965 treasure. I don't think he had even noticed it in his pent-up anticipation of the pleasure to come.

'I've told them you're my carer, dear boy,' Monty told me grandly.

I was hardly flattered, for all sorts of reasons, but gritted my teeth in the cause of duty. I had feared I was going to stick out like an old-fashioned trafficator at this gathering, but I need not have worried. We were conducted to a light, airy room at the rear of the mansion which was already full of 'our' party. I could see

Rex there and Charlie – not hobnobbing together, I noted, but each with his own coterie. There was no one else I recognized as yet, which was hardly surprising. To my relief, there were other 'carers' in evidence, several women of an age to be wives of the Three Parroters and others of both sexes, perhaps family members or drivers. Tables were set for an interesting buffet lunch and glasses of wine, sherry and orange juice were doing the rounds. Nevertheless, there seemed little animation in the conversation I could overhear and the atmosphere was flat.

Until, that is, Monty took a hand by waving his sherry in the air and crying out mournfully to the room at large: 'My dears, how we have descended in this world. Where, one might ask, is the champagne?'

'In your dreams, Monty,' someone shouted back.

Nervous titters all round, which set the ball slowly rolling. Monty beckoned me to follow him to the bay window where a distinguished-looking grey-haired man was sitting in an armchair with an empty wheelchair at his side.

'Our host,' Monty declared, so I realized this was Noel Brandon-Wright, donor of the 1962 E-type. 'Dear Noel,' Monty continued, 'pray meet Jack Colby, my carer for today and a great friend of Adora's.'

Perhaps it was my imagination but was there a note of warning in his voice? Whether this was so or not, the welcome in Noel's face promptly disappeared. He was courteous enough but distinctly guarded. I decided not to mention the name of Danny Carter unless someone else did.

'I trust Adora is well?' Noel asked politely.

'She is,' I replied. 'In fact, she has just remarried.'

Noel looked astounded. He seemed to be a man whom life had treated well, save for the infirmity that had put him into a wheelchair; once he would have been chairman of the cricket club, the parish council and any other organizations he could collect. I wondered what had replaced them in his present mode of life. He still carried the air of leadership about him and his eyes were keen, so I guessed that if there was any rallying of the troops in this home for social events or complaints to management or whatever, he would be in the driving seat.

'Married whom?' he enquired.

'Another round with one of her previous husbands.'

'Brave chap.' A guffaw from Noel – almost one of relief, but that again could be sheer fancy on my part. 'Not Rex or Charlie, I take it? They're both here and both look to be in their right minds.'

'Is it charitable to point out, Jack, dear,' Monty observed thoughtfully, 'that a celebration of marriage hardly seems fitting at present in light of the murder that took place on her land so recently?'

Evidently Monty was ready to stir things up. Not necessarily a good thing, I thought, but I followed his lead. 'I gather Adora always had her own way of handling matters,' I answered.

'Indeed. A lady adept in many ways, whether it touches the heart or the purse,' Noel replied.

'It was her heart in Three Parrots days, so she told me,' I said. 'She was involved in another murder then, wasn't she?' I added innocently.

I expected Monty to leap on this with relish given the opportunity my remark gave him, but he did not. 'Dear Jack. Always so to the point. If you'll excuse me, I simply must chat to Valentine.' He swanned his way along to the next bay window where I could see another wheelchair, whose occupant had remained in it.

'Is that Valentine Paston?' I asked Noel, as no one else seemed eager to answer my question. Noel nodded. 'Does he live in this home?' I asked.

'If one calls it living,' he answered me ruefully. 'Poor chap.'

I could see the frail old man was taking no notice at all of Monty's chatter, just staring into the garden. 'Alzheimer's?' I asked.

'Yes. He's quite gentle with it fortunately.'

I watched as Monty sat down at Valentine's side, talking to him quietly without stopping. Occasionally Valentine's head turned towards him with a vacant smile, but from what I observed no word or look indicated that he knew who Monty was.

'Your mention of another murder,' Noel said to me abruptly. 'Did Adora tell you about that?'

'No. And incidentally I'm hardly a friend of hers. She asked Danny Carter to commission me to buy a car. I'm a classic car dealer.'

He shot me a caustic look. 'Rather more than that, I hear. Carer you might be today but I've been told you work for the police. I imagine you're involved in this Carter affair.'

Word had got round quickly. 'Only as far as the classic car angle is concerned.'

He grunted. 'Can't see what you hope to learn by coming here. We're hardly likely to have banded together at our age in order to rid our former friend of her pestilent knave.'

Former? That wouldn't please Adora, I thought. 'Before Carter's death,' I pointed out, 'Adora received threats to burn the Jaguar collection down – and a threat to herself. It's possible there's a link to Carter's murder.' Well, that was true enough, even though we knew Danny was the sender.

Another grunt from Noel. 'Seen my Jag in her collection?'

'Yes. The splendid E-type. And your photo, of course.'

He did a double-take. 'What photo?' he demanded.

Just as I thought. He, and perhaps the others too, probably never visited the Lair and had no idea of its contents. If the Hargreaves had their way their plans for it might include opening it to the public, in which case the donors might be far from delighted to see Adora's bright notion of including their photographs and other memorabilia. There was no point in my holding back, however. They had a right to know sometime, so I described the Lair's layout, including the display of photos of Adora with each of her lovers. As I suspected, Noel was horrified.

'Damned woman. What photo of me did she dare to put there?'

I racked my memory. 'I think it was a blow-up of a snapshot of you both and the car by a lake.'

'Lake Windermere,' Noel said grimly. 'No wonder someone threatened to burn the place down if that's the kind of game she's playing. Is the car safe if there have been threats?'

'The police think so and so do I. The letters were just a means of getting Adora rattled in all probability.'

'Hardly surprising. That woman's got the nerve of the Devil. We had our fling in the early sixties. It was seven years later when she demanded that car. She'd even checked that I still had it. Said it was a sad time for her as she'd just got divorced from Rex and she wanted to remember the happy times we had together. I most certainly did not. I was married by then with two-year-old twins.'

He paused, staring straight ahead of him but not at me. 'You know, Jack,' he continued, 'that lake. 1962. I'd just bought the E-type. I believed I was the only chap in her life but she gaily told me she'd just been to Monte Carlo with Rex. Driven down the N7 to the Riviera in the XK 150. Taught me something about women, I can tell you. If I didn't give her the car, she implied, she'd tell my wife about our jaunts. Not that Betty would have cared but I didn't want that woman hanging round my neck like an albatross, so I let her have it. Thanks, she said. It was only to remember the happy times we had in the past. Happy times, my foot.'

'Weren't some of them happy?'

He gave me a shamefaced grin. 'Maybe. Enough said.'

'Have I put my foot in it?'

'It's your job to put your foot in it,' he said drily. 'It's mine to decide whether to keep it there.'

'Then I'll go right on. The Three Parrots?'

'Fair enough. Closed at the end of 1964. I married two years later and put those years behind me.' A pause. 'When we had our fling she had her eyes on bigger status and money than I was likely to earn or inherit. Only when she was divorced by Rex for adultery did she start cashing in on the past.'

'Why cars not cash, then?' I asked.

He stared at me. 'Cash. Now that's interesting. Why not then? I've no idea but my guess is this: Adora means the adored one, but there's a difference between being adored and being loved. There are some women, as you must know, Mr Colby, who have a power over men that has little to do with lasting love. Adora was, and no doubt still is, one of them. Ever read that poem by Gabriel Allyn, "Café in Boulogne"? Still sets me going, if you know what I mean.'

I had read it after Louise had recommended it and knew exactly what he meant.

'It's my guess,' Noel continued, 'that Rex's settlement left her financially secure but to have the cars from those earlier days gave her enduring power over us – in her mind alone, I hasten to add.'

'You could be right,' I agreed. Indeed, he might be, but I couldn't believe this was the whole truth behind the Lair. Then I dropped my next penny in the slot. 'Lance Benny.'

He was clearly ready for that and clicked into action.

'Ah. The old club scandal. Don't harbour any suspicions on that score, Mr Colby. There is no deep, dark secret. From the evidence, all that happened is that a gang of youths who were high on LSD or some such drug were lurching towards Soho Square. Lance had left the Three Parrots on his own at the wrong moment; they picked a fight with him and he ended up dead. That was the police's conclusion and that is why no killer was ever found; there were many such gangs around in those days and no DNA profiling to help track them down.'

I had been watching Noel's hands. He appeared so relaxed and yet those hands were gripping the arms of the chair so tightly the veins stood out.

'Adora told me that she and Lance were very much in love. She made it sound as though he were the great love of her life.'

He laughed. 'Mr Colby, we *all* were.'

'She claims she was going to marry him.'

'Alas, false memory syndrome. Lance had other plans. I do recall he was *one* of her admirers, although the full extent of the admiration was then unknown to myself, who after that disastrous Lake District revelation had fondly imagined that Rex was my only rival. Lance was of no more consequence than the rest of us. Except, of course, in the romantic hindsight on which Adora always tends to rely.'

'And was she of no more consequence to all of you?'

His face darkened. 'Mr Colby, if I am correct, five of us from the Three Parrots donated cars to her, and she later *bought* Lance's car. The rest of the collection was donated by later gentleman friends in Adora's long romantic career.'

'You're right,' I agreed. 'And there was a sixth among your number who did not donate his car.'

An elegant eyebrow was raised. 'How fortunate,' Noel murmured, 'that Gabriel Allyn has just joined our number here today. You may question him yourself. However, do believe me, Jack, when I tell you that Lance Benny is irrelevant. His sad death was over five decades ago.' He was trembling now, but with rage rather than infirmity. Somewhere I had hit a nerve.

The Earl of Storrington had entered the room without my noticing, but I could now see him quietly sipping a glass of wine, talking to Monty. I realized that for some reason Monty was not part of this inner circle. Was the earl? I guessed that he was. Monty had no car in the Lair and nor had the earl, but for far different reasons. I wondered how Gabriel Allyn – as he was known to his friends here – had arrived. Had he driven and if so . . . I looked through the window and could scarcely believe what I was seeing.

It was the SS 100!

I could see no sign of a low-loader and so amazingly he must have driven it here himself. There it was in all its gleaming green glory, currently surrounded by a crowd of admirers. Gabriel Allyn did not strike me as someone who followed a mere whim or acted without thought, and so I speculated on why he had made this gesture. I was about to join him when I was forestalled. Rex Hargreaves was walking purposefully towards me.

'Ah, Mr Colby,' he greeted me. 'You are indefatigable in your pursuit of Danny Carter's murderer. I take it that is why you are here?'

'Sheer pleasure,' I assured him. 'Look at that SS 100 outside.'

'Not solely pleasure,' he replied. 'I hear you arrived with Monty Greene. A good fellow but don't take too much notice of anything he tells you.'

'About what?' I enquired. 'Lance Benny's death?'

'I've already told you that had nothing to do with the Three Parrots.'

'Save that Lance was there that evening.'

'I also told you he left early – about eleven thirty at a guess. Adora had just begun the next session of her performance. Lance was attacked some way from the club.'

'Adora must have been very upset. She told me they had wedding plans.'

He stiffened. 'I would be most surprised if that were the case. Lance had many girlfriends, of whom Adora was one. Adora had many admirers of whom *I* was one.'

'Who were Lance's other girlfriends? Were they there that night?'

My persistence paid off as his patience ran out. 'I have no idea about either question.'

He was rescued by Charlie who thumped him on the back, to Rex's evident distaste.

'How are you, Rex? Need a word with you later on.'

'That would be good,' Rex said unconvincingly, taking his chance to depart and thus handing the baton to Charlie.

'Didn't interrupt anything, did I, Jack?' Charlie said innocently.

'Not at all. He was telling me all about Lance Benny.'

'Sure he was. Monty Greene told me you were poking into that old story. Thought it was Danny Carter you were after and those poison pen letters. The things that happen in this day and age, eh? Thought poison pen letters went out with the ark. Tell you what, Jack. Seriously. Keep to Danny Carter. Unless you find out who did him in you'll have another corpse on your hands. Adora.'

That shook me. 'You know the death threat was for real?'

'Can't tell, but it's a warning, eh? Forget about Benny.'

Not yet I wouldn't. 'Was Adora the only woman in Benny's life?' I asked, interested to see what reply I would get this time.

'No way. He was smitten by someone else and made no secret of it. So that shows you. Adora's having you on if she says they were an item. In her dreams. Lance was just a passing fancy. Does she strike you as the type of woman who would let some other bird take the worm she wanted herself? Ripe old sparrowhawk, she is. I should know. I had ten years of it. Spots her prey, drops right down on it and gobbles it up. Rex was her real victim. She had her eyes for years on Allyn's title but he'd no cash. I tried my luck with her often enough, but old Rex was having none of that. I had to wait a few more years before it was my turn to be gobbled.'

He departed with a wink. I'd now had several versions of the relationship between Adora and Lance. I wondered which – if any – was true. I thought it was time to seek another.

After the crowd around the SS 100 had dispersed I strolled outside to admire it, and Gabriel must have sensed what was coming because he came out to join me. We stood in silence for a while, both ostensibly taking in the beauty of its graceful lines, its stylish headlights and its sheer breathtaking driver appeal.

'How did she run on the way here?' I asked him at last.

He smiled. 'William Lyons would have been proud of his creation. How are your enquiries going, Jack? I gather your remit has broadened since we last met. I believe Danny Carter's death is now your concern?'

I was cautious. 'Only to seek background information.'

'And you believe Miss Ferne's Jaguars have something to do with his death?'

'That's the line that I am following through, Your Lordship.'

'Come now, Jack. Here I am Gabriel. I am among friends. If we are to examine the past then I am Gabriel Allyn the poet, although that concept seems long past. Days when I was twenty-two years old, eager, impassioned, fresh down from Cambridge and very much in love with Adora Ferne, a passion that continued for five years until 1964, despite my absence for two of them while I did my National Service. Does that help your enquiries?'

'Perhaps,' I said gently. 'Thank you.'

'Not at all. We are all here, I imagine, to talk over that very matter and what she meant to us.'

'The adored one, and yet few, save you, have spoken of her with affection,' I observed.

'Perhaps that is understandable. Few people see the past with clarity. They mean no harm. They see only—' He broke off.

'Only?' I prompted him.

'The clouds of history. We were all young then, Adora too, although a few years older than many of us. She was a symbol of glamour. We were all in love with her. She may or may not have slept with at least some of us, but somehow when she glided out on the stage it was intoxicating, magical; she was leading us up a staircase to heaven. Did you ever see – no, you are too young. I was going to ask if you saw Josephine Baker perform. She had the same mesmerizing quality. Ella Fitzgerald, Edith Piaf . . . But at the Three Parrots we had Adora Ferne. There was no reason any of us would want to kill Lance. We all loved her, but we accepted that Lance was the one she favoured.'

'Not Rex?'

'No. Lance was the chosen one. He too had a special star quality so it seemed quite natural that she would choose him.'

Another slant then. 'She was going to marry him?'

'I believe so. But we will never know because Lance left early and it is believed that hooligans killed him.'

Believed? I wondered at his use of this word. Believed by whom? Just the police? 'Could Adora have changed her mind about marrying him?' I asked. 'Or did Lance do a runner? Could another jealous lover have killed him?'

'No to all three questions.' Gabriel stopped suddenly. He switched off and I had to restart the process by pressing on marshy ground.

'Can you be sure of that? Would her other admirers have felt the same way as you though? Forgive me, but your companions at the club may have had less charitable thoughts.'

'Charitable? I fear that there you are mistaken, Jack. I have no charitable thoughts towards Adora. Compassion, perhaps, and the tolerance that the years bring to most of us. But not charitable. This car that you so rightly admire – the car that I will not donate to her – has a story. A story of love and rejection. A common story but nevertheless one that still bites deep when I delve into it. I seldom do, save when this motor car is the issue.

'I have said I was in love with Adora,' he continued – to my amazement that he was speaking so freely and so calmly after his former reticence. 'She is older than I am and yet it seemed to me then that she was an innocent at heart and that I could give her the happiness she craved. Wrong. I had assumed the bliss of our relationship, both physical and emotional, meant as much to her as it did to me. It did not. The day that it happened we spent together. I drove this SS 100 – even then an eye-turner – to Richmond Park. We took a picnic, we laughed, we were happy. It was there that I asked her to marry me. I could not conceive that she would say no. She did. She looked amazed and said that surely I realized that Lance was the only man for her. He was all that I was not – handsome, carefree, exciting – and he adored her. They were going to announce their engagement on that fatal Thursday evening. I leave you to imagine how I felt.'

He paused, glanced at me and perhaps interpreted my stupefied reaction correctly, for he smiled. 'I have told you this, Jack, although to speak so openly is quite foreign to my usual practice – so that you may understand why the thirteenth car will never be Adora's. It is the symbol both of rejection and of rebirth; it had to be put aside and yet remembered if I was to surmount what had happened to me and enter the different life that awaited me. What had I to offer Adora? Only love and a title. She rejected both. As W.B. Yeats wrote of a similar situation, I had nothing more to bring to her. "Nothing but a book." My poems could be my only other gift; I had written most of them for her and I have written nothing since.

'Lastly, Jack, you asked me why I encouraged you to visit me in Sussex to plead for the sale of this car to Adora when I had no intention of selling it. I did not answer you then but I will now. Our past is never quite as buried as one thinks. My mind has never queried my attitude to Adora and never will, but sometimes it revisits those days against my wishes – perhaps to be sure I still feel as I did then. Seeing you, hearing of her, allowed me to know that I had taken the right path.'

All I could blurt out was: 'You won't sell it? Not to anyone?'

'No. The earl might sell it but the poet would stop him.'

Back inside the house, the buffet lunch was in full swing. It was a good one – too good as it took me some time to realize that although Monty was still here, none of the inner circle, including Gabriel and even Valentine Paston, was present. They had slipped away while I was engrossed in coronation chicken and salad. Their cars were here but they were not to be seen and my guess was that they would not reappear until they had finished discussing their own business. And what could that be but the death of Danny Carter and the threat of death to Adora? That told me instantly that there was more to this story than I'd yet been invited to share.

Monty summed it up as I drove him back to the station an hour later: 'Dear boy, they have kept their secrets for fifty years. Do you imagine they will part with them now?'

EIGHT

I t's rare to see Len emerge from the Pits at all on a working morning, let alone for him to stalk into my office in the farmhouse, arms belligerently folded across his chest. I'd watched him stomp across the forecourt on Monday morning with some trepidation and rightly so. Trouble was not only in the air but standing in front of me.

'We've got that Bugatti replica in.'

'A problem?' Perhaps it was just a technical hitch, I thought hopefully.

'Zoe. Not in today.'

My hopes vanished. This was trouble in a big way. I had received no phone call, text, email, nothing. 'Tried her mobile?' I asked. Len isn't mobile friendly so this would be a big step for him.

'Voicemail.'

He must really be worried to have gone so far. 'All quiet on the Rob front?' I asked. Zoe had been suspiciously quiet on the Friday after I'd had the honour of meeting Rob just about to set out with Alice for a day or two. Not that I breathed a word about it. I wouldn't have dared. In any case, I had presumed that all was over between Rob and Zoe. If so, where was she now?

'That young man's as reliable as a cardboard tyre,' Len snarled.

'I'll call him.'

It was a noble gesture on my part but it took us nowhere. Rob too was on voicemail. I tried his landline – based in his so-called office at his parents' amazingly well-run farm. 'So-called' because the word office usually implies active work participation, and in this case that element was missing. The farm is only well run because Rob seldom sticks his paw into it. Someone answered the phone but it wasn't Rob, who was apparently only just returning from that couple of days away with Alice.

This did not bode well. A week or so ago Zoe had mentioned that she and Rob had plans for yesterday, but had that happy event taken place she would most certainly have rung in to say she'd be late. Instead we seemed to be at crisis point. I wasn't sure whether Len's concern was for Zoe or the Bugatti or both, but I opted for the one I could do something about.

'If Zoe doesn't turn up I'll give you a hand later on today,' I told him, 'when I get back.' I like keeping my classic car restoration skills finely honed at the sharp end, but Len's continued silence confirmed that I was the last resort. Nevertheless, an eventual nod suggested he was taking my offer with good grace.

I had two meetings arranged for the day, the aim of which was to probe deeper into the jungle of the Jaguar donors. I'd covered the Three Parrots brigade but the later surviving donors remained mere names. My first expedition was to meet Blake Bishop, who lived in Tonbridge, a reasonable drive from Frogs Hill. When I arrived at his grand mansion, however, I found Alan Reeve with him. He had been scheduled for the next expedition as he lived in Lamberhurst, not too far from Tonbridge. They explained that they had decided to save me the trouble of the extra journey. This was very considerate of them but I didn't believe it. To me it indicated that they thought there might be safety in numbers, just as the Three Parrots' former members had flocked together at Gatsford House.

Alan was a small, lively man in his late sixties, a complete contrast to Blake Bishop who looked some years older and a solid citizen type. Blake seemed even more bluff and hearty than Noel Brandon-Wright, despite allowing for a few years' gap in ages. Alan, however, was sharp and quick-witted, and so it didn't strike me that these two were natural chums – save perhaps in the event of a threat to joint safety.

I wasn't offered coffee, which I took as a hint that my visit was intended to be a short one – a hint I might or might not take.

Blake opened proceedings, which didn't surprise me, as he seemed to be a man in retirement missing his former status. 'You told me you wish to talk about the cars we have donated to Miss Ferne,' he began ponderously.

'Yes,' I agreed. 'Was that at the time your friendships with her finished?'

Blake glanced at Alan. 'Speaking for myself,' he announced, 'I recall I presented my E-type to her about 1980.'

'Mid-eighties for me,' Alan chimed smoothly in. '1984, I think.

A splendid E-type, 1975 model. Both of us are still on good terms with Adora,' he added helpfully.

'Then you both know Crockendene and knew Danny Carter?'

Blake glared at me but it was Alan who rescued the situation. 'Good terms as on the principle that no news is good news. Neither of us knew Carter. And,' he added, 'we've already given statements to the police on our whereabouts on the night of Carter's death. Ridiculous farce, since we didn't know him, but we're both law-abiding citizens so we complied.'

Brandon's team had filled me in on this. Blake had been at a Rotary Club do and Alan at a concert. Probably neither alibi was cast iron but that was Brandon's province, not mine.

Blake waved a careless hand. 'The good terms merely refer to exchanging Christmas cards, that sort of thing. I haven't actually *seen* Adora for years. Have you, Alan?'

'Thank the Lord, no.' He grinned. 'Delightful though Adora was – and probably is – distance does indeed make the heart fonder.'

Blake didn't add to this tribute and indeed remained so stolidly disapproving of the whole subject that I wondered what Adora had seen in him in the first place.

'Even if you haven't met him, have you had dealings with Carter?' I asked. 'He began working for Adora in 1994.'

A united 'no' to this, so I pressed on. 'As you may have heard, Miss Ferne has been the target of a series of anonymous letter threats.'

'Threatening what?' Blake growled cautiously.

'To burn the Jaguar collection and one of them to kill her.'

Blake swelled with indignation. 'Are you implying *we* knew anything about this?'

'Did I suggest that? I don't believe so but you are two of the twelve Jaguar donors, which means you are involved in the investigation.'

'Remotely,' Blake snapped. 'Merely because we gave Adora those cars?'

'Yes, as memories of happy times in her life, she told me. That's evident from the photographs around the Lair.'

'What photos?' Alan asked sharply.

'One of each of you taken with Adora.'

Both gentlemen seemed somewhat upset by this, judging by their sudden pallor. Having caught them on the hop, I threw a punch at random.

'Did either of you know Lance Benny in years gone by?'

I hadn't expected much result from this, as Alan at least would still have been in his teens at the time and neither of them was a member of the Three Parrots. Blake, however, must still have been shaken by the news of the photograph for he replied all too casually, 'Racing driver of sorts, wasn't he? Carter said he knew him.'

The look Alan gave him for this faux pas was not a pleasant one.

'So you know that Danny, whom you *didn't* know, knew Lance Benny whom you also didn't know. Is that right?' I enquired politely.

'One meets people at car shows,' Alan snapped. 'That hardly constitutes knowing someone. We didn't *know* Lance Benny either but we heard rumours about some kind of charity or memorial fund in his name.'

'I'll check it out. What was it in aid of?' My simple statement was greeted with silence from both men. Why were they so defensive? I wondered. Lance had died fifty years ago so a memorial fund could hardly be very active now.

'Probably racing safety,' Blake replied at last.

'But Benny wasn't killed on the track.'

Alan took over. 'Perhaps he promoted safety. Does it matter? Jaguars, Mr Colby, that's what you're here for, not murder cases.'

'Lance Benny owned one of the Jaguars in the Lair,' I pointed out, 'and so it's highly relevant to Carter's death.' Silence from both of them. 'Did the rumours you've heard suggest the fund was set up when Lance Benny died or later?'

Blake shrugged. 'I've no idea. And it's still not relevant to us. We haven't all day to waste, Mr Colby, so please do keep to the point.'

'I shall,' I assured them. 'Was Adora Ferne still married to Charlie Dane at the time you knew her, Mr Bishop?'

At this Alan Reeve laughed, which annoyed Blake even more.

'Have you met Charlie Dane?' Blake threw at me.

'Once or twice.'

'Then you will appreciate that even after all this time I have no desire to remind him that I was seeing his wife while they were married. Pleasant and affable though Charlie was, and is, he had many contacts who weren't and even, I dare say, aren't.'

'Understood,' I said as gravely as I could. 'And you, Mr Reeve?'

'Rather the same motivation. Adora was already divorced from Charlie but he was still very much in evidence, as was another gentleman friend. I retreated and paid the price with my Jaguar, but I returned to the fray some years later. Unfortunately by then Adora was already friendly with yet another so-called gentleman who was bent on marrying the lady – despite the age difference. Cash talks and Adora was a wealthy lady by then, a fact he doubtless noticed.'

I could guess this one. 'Harry Gale?'

'Spot on. He too is pleasant and affable but he's no objection to getting his hands dirty if his interests are adversely affected. I didn't want him to know that my fun and games with Adora overlapped his own and Adora suggested that a second Jaguar from me might help her forget that fact. I refused and thankfully she did not persist.'

I remembered Monty Greene's words: the heart or the purse. Which of these, I wondered, drove the enigma that was Adora Ferne? And did this fund in remembrance of Lance Benny affect it? There was no evidence yet that either Blake Bishop or Alan Reeve was more closely connected with Danny Carter or the Lair or Lance Benny than they had told me, although they were certainly cagey where they were concerned. They might not have been members of the Three Parrots but it seemed to me they knew more about it than they were prepared to share with me.

When I reached Frogs Hill I hardly dared even glance into the Pits, even though I was looking forward to honouring my commitment to Len. Working with my hands on a classic car would be an excellent antidote to puzzling over Jaguars. I found Len still working there alone on the Bugatti in grim silence. No radio or headphones for him. The only music he likes is a well-tuned engine. When he noticed me, he glared, pointed to the Hillman Minx and told me I could 'get on with the oil change and chassis lub'.

I was happy to obey, if a trifle disappointed I wasn't to be allowed to tinker with the Bugatti and, after leaving a message for Brandon telling him about the memorial fund for Lance Benny which I would try to track down, I returned to the Pits to do my duty. Brandon would no doubt classify anything to do with Benny under mere trivia but at least it made me look conscientious.

Len and I worked in companionable silence for an hour, by which time it was mid-afternoon and Len decided to eat the sandwiches that Mrs Len always provided for him. He generously told me I could leave if I wished. I didn't wish, but I wasn't wanted, and so I decided first to have a go at checking out that fund and secondly to head for Crockendene to see if I could track down Fred Fox.

The first task took very little time because the name Lance Benny brought up little online, save for stray references to him in newspaper articles. The memorial fund in his name produced nothing at all, which suggested it had been wound up years ago. I wondered how old this rumour that had reached Blake and Alan was. I put this niggle on one side and set off to unearth Fred Fox from his den.

Apart from Harry Gale, with whom I'd at least rubbed shoulders, Fred was last on my list of surviving donors and the odd one out. The former gardener, once Adora's lover and still living at one corner of the Crockendene Farm estate, had been the person who found Danny Carter's body, yet he had not otherwise appeared so far over the horizon as a suspect. He had donated an XJ 12 saloon in 1994. Brandon's team had obviously interviewed him but I knew little of him, save that his fling with Adora must have ended in the mid-nineties and that according to Brandon's team he didn't like Danny Carter, which put him among the majority of Danny's acquaintances. Nevertheless, he had put up no objection when I rang to arrange a time for meeting.

The stone cottage was very close to the farm's rear gate but I decided to park by Danny's office so that I could walk through the grounds and – I must confess this – past the Lair, although I doubted whether it would be open. At least I could peer at those beauties through the small windows on the far side if the blinds were down on the other.

That accomplished, I could see Fred working in his garden when I approached the cottage, looking much older than the macho photo of him in the Lair. He looked a weather-beaten sixty or so, which meant at the time his fling with Adora ended he must have been about forty. And the mid-nineties was the time that Danny Carter had arrived at Crockendene. Could there be a connection? I wondered. All too possible.

Fred's garden was a splendid example of the old cottage system in which vegetables and herbs intermingled with flowers. It was mid-May now and every flower under the sun seemed about to burst into full bloom in this earthly Eden. I called over to him and he straightened up, took off his gloves and escorted me to a terrace table and chairs, moving easily with the assurance of a countryman who'd spent all his life on the land.

'Have a seat, Mr Colby. The wife's out so no need for hushed voices and all that. Fire away.'

'Thanks.' For all his bonhomie I noticed that his eyes were sharp and I was being rapidly assessed. This was a man I wouldn't want to cross, I thought.

'You said you wanted to talk about Miss Ferne and Danny Carter?' he rattled on. 'Doesn't everybody? Had the police round three times. The press are camping out in the lane and young Michael Hargreaves is pestering me all the time. Well, tough luck to the lot of them. And you,' he added cheerfully. 'I never heard a thing that night except a shot but that's nothing unusual round here. The alarm only goes off in Danny's place. Took my walk, glanced through the Lair's window at my old car, saw something lying there, tried the door, unlocked, went in, found Carter. That's it. Satisfied?'

'Thank you, yes.'

Fred seemed amused rather than aggressive. 'Police searched my place and all,' he went on. 'Wife didn't like that, I can tell you. Blamed me for shooting my mouth off about Danny Carter once too often.'

'Does your dislike of him have anything to do with Adora Ferne?'

''Course it does. Why else? She and I had had a nice little arrangement for years not doing no one any harm. I was single when Carter pushed his way in here, my first wife having taken off with the kids. Miss Ferne and me took a trip out in one of those Jags most days and had a little fun on the side – and a romp or two in the gardens. Ever tried it on newly mown grass clippings, Mr Colby? Messy, but who cares, eh?'

'Adora would have been about sixty then.' I was fascinated with the images of Adora this threw up.

'So what? Fine-looking woman. Still is.'

'Do you still get on well with her? That was twenty-odd years ago.'

'And getting on for forty since we had our first roll in the hay. 'Course I get on with her.'

'Most of the other men in her life have mixed feelings.'

'Well, I don't. Never went off her. Even when Danny ousted me.'

'Danny did?' I asked incredulously. 'But he wasn't her lover.'

'No. Leastways, I hope not. But Danny, he liked control, see. So once he realized the way things were between me and Adora he made sure he got me out of the way permanently. He got me sacked.'

'How did he manage that? Adora would have had some say in it.'

'Not much of a conscience, had Danny. Made out I was fiddling expenses and Adora believed it. So that was that. She treated me well, though. Didn't hold it against me. She did buy the old Jaguar from me, so there's me up with the great and the good in the Lair. Danny hated that. Gave the Jag a kick or scrape every now and then, but if Adora saw him then it was my car she chose for her daily jaunt next to punish him.'

'He got you sacked, yet you live here. How did that happen?'

'Danny couldn't do much about that. I bought it fair and square ten years earlier when it came on the market. Charlie had sold this place when he divorced Adora. Livid, he was, when he found out it was me who bought it. He knew I'd been having it off with Adora. Danny wasn't pleased about my getting the house either. Threatened to burn the place down, he did.'

That struck a familiar note. 'Did he ever try?'

'No. Too scared I'd tell Adora.'

'Did you ever rekindle the affair with her?'

'Head has to rule heart sometimes. Danny had some funny friends – and so does Charlie Dane, so I watched my step.'

'Any ideas on who killed Danny?'

He shrugged. 'Plenty of folk would like to have seen him vanish, me included, but not that way. There was no love lost between Adora's family and Danny. Nor that Harry Gale. The Hargreaves are mostly OK but I can't stand that bloke. Ugly tempered, he is, when she's not watching. I'm told she's married him again. Some folk never learn. Wouldn't have happened if Danny had been around.'

'Could he have stopped it?'

'You bet he could. Adora listened to Danny – she did over me. Only time she didn't was when Harry got his hooks into her and married her. Danny did everything he could to break it up and succeeded first time round, so our Danny boy was incandescent when she started talking about another round with him. Got her in such a state she said she wouldn't do it.'

Now this was interesting – if true. 'How do you know all this?'

'The wife. She cleans up the house for Adora and for Mr Hargreaves – and did Danny's office and all. So she knows what's going on. Take those letters Adora received threatening to burn down the Lair – the wife reckons Danny wrote them himself.'

'If you want information,' I observed, 'forget the police – ask the cleaner.'

Fred chuckled. 'So she got it right, did she?'

'Why would he do it, though?'

'You've stumped me, Mr Colby. He was a funny chap, was Danny, but he could never have burned the Lair down or hurt Adora. I reckon he was out to show how indispensable he was, saving her from all those wicked folk out there who wanted to hurt her. Power, that's what it boils down to. Power in his hands, not the family's.'

'Did he get on with Adora's family? They don't seem to have liked him much.'

'With reason. Mr Simon's got plans for the Lair and Danny would have none of it. He wanted to be number one with Adora and was a real thorn in the flesh for them and Mrs Melinda – even young Alice. They none of them had any time for him and nor did I.'

'But now he's gone.'

The jolliness had vanished now and I noticed how cold his eyes were. 'So he has, Mr Colby. And good riddance.'

I took the longer route back through the woods to reach my car again because I was considering the wisdom of calling on Adora. Halfway there I decided against it, partly because I wanted to weigh up all the varying comments I had heard about her and partly because when I reached the Hargreaves' home I was diverted.

Outside it stood Zoe's clapped-out Fiesta in which she still chugs around. There was no mistaking it and it did not bode well – especially as I saw that it wasn't just Zoe's car parked there. Rob's was there too. Whatever was going on inside could scarcely be a reconciliation meeting judging by the noise – among which Zoe's voice was prominent. That meant trouble and any trouble for Zoe rubs off on Frogs Hill, and so as her employer I considered I had every right to knock and enquire why she was not at work.

The situation grew more ominous as the level of noise increased.

My hand was poised to knock but the door opened and out marched
Zoe. She didn't seem surprised to see me, but the angry flush on
her face suggested that she had other matters on her mind. As indeed
she did.

'This time it's over,' she yelled back over her shoulder into the
house, and then in case I hadn't heard, turned to me. '*Over.*'

'Who won?' I asked, trying to look compassionate but actually
delighted at the disappearance of Rob from her life.

'I did,' she retorted, slamming the door behind her. 'I've turfed
him out for good. He had the nerve to say he was coming back to
me. Big deal. I told him not to bother. *Ever.*'

'Oh,' was all I could manage in return.

'Do you know,' she swept on, 'that man told me he and the lovely
Alice have been in Brighton for the whole weekend. Imagine. It's
insulting to choose Brighton and Alice instead of me and Pluckley.'

I tried to be rational as she wrenched open the door of the Fiesta.
'But is this what you want to happen, Zoe? You want to split up
for good?'

She calmed down. 'I don't know,' she muttered.

'The trouble is,' I pointed out, 'leopards and similar animals don't
change their spots.'

'And you think Rob is a similar animal?' she snarled.

Careful, I thought. I had only to say one adverse thing against
Rob and she would turn on me and rush back to him. 'You know
him better than I do.'

A scornful look. 'Coward.'

'Me or Rob?'

'You. I've finished here. There's a Hillman Minx to fix.'

'I know. I did the chassis lub earlier on.'

She uttered one unrepeatable word, muttered 'that means I'll have
to redo it', slammed her car door shut after her and drove off.

I watched her for a moment or two as I walked down the path,
genuinely worried. Then I heard running footsteps behind me – light,
dainty ones. They weren't Rob's. It was Alice who caught my arm
to stop. She was looking particularly fetching today in tight blue
jeans and a snazzy pink top.

'She's taken it hard. I'm sorry, Jack.'

This time I thought I could intervene. 'I take it it's serious between
you and Rob?'

She didn't answer that. What she did say was, 'Zoe seems rather nice, although it wasn't the best of times to meet her. Do you often see her in a rage?'

'Not over a man. Over a mistreated car, yes.' Try to keep light-hearted, I thought.

Luckily she giggled. 'She's misunderstood. Rob and I truly aren't an item yet. He came to Brighton only to see the ballet I'm in. I told him to help front of house and he could see it three or four times.'

'Are you planning to be an item?'

She flashed a smile. 'Not sure. If he can two-time Zoe he could two-time me as well.'

I was impressed. Such wisdom. 'It's possible.'

'I've got my career to think of and that's not in Kent.'

'Your career's more important than Rob?' This sounded hopeful.

'Than any man,' she replied. 'Than *anything*. I do like Rob, though.'

'And that,' I agreed crossly, 'is the trouble. There are occasions when I even like him myself. Today isn't one of them.'

A pause. 'Granny Adora is very unhappy too. Have you found out who killed Danny yet?'

'That's the police's job. I'm merely doing research for them.' That sounded grand but it didn't fool her.

'With those Jaguars? They have to have played a part in it, don't you think?'

'It's possible.'

'That seems to be a favourite phrase of yours,' she observed.

'It's a useful one.'

'People are odd, aren't they? You never really know them, do you? Only if they're family, and perhaps not even then.' A pause. 'You can tell Zoe what I've just told you – if it helps, that is.'

'Who knows whether it would or not? It might sentence her to life with Rob.'

Another giggle. 'It's possible,' she mocked me.

Before I left Crockendene I checked my messages, something I don't do often enough. It was lucky I did because there was one from Brandon asking me to drop by at Charing HQ. What was all this about? I wondered. I'd only left my voicemail for him a matter of hours ago so it was unlikely to be a response to that. Brandon had added a tempter too before he rang off: 'You'll like this one, Jack.'

Would I? I wondered. It depended on Brandon's mood when he said it. Still, it sounded hopeful. I set off post-haste as it was already past five o'clock, and was flattered to be met by Brandon himself and Dave too. This must be important.

'You'll like this one.' Dave repeated Brandon's assurance.

Brandon's outer office team looked up with interest as we swept through. In his partitioned office only one lone sergeant was present, with a laptop which I recognized as Danny's from the football team transfer stuck on the top.

'Coincidence, Jack,' Brandon said. 'You left a message about a Lance Benny Memorial Fund. Have a look at this.'

I peered over the sergeant's shoulders and before my incredulous eyes was a screen showing a bank account in the name of the Lance Benny Memorial Fund. The address was River Cottage, 2 Crockendene Lane.

'Carter's home address,' Brandon told me.

'A charity, yes?' I guessed, wondering what, if anything, Adora knew of this.

'Depends on how one interprets the word charity. Have a look at this.' Brandon put a printed-off bank statement into my hand and I whistled.

'Getting on for half a million. Good balance for a small charity. How much goes out?'

'Interest regularly, capital from time to time.'

'Who are the beneficiaries?'

'We're tracing that now. But I can tell you one thing: there's one sole signatory to the account and it's not a registered charity. The signatory is Danny Carter.'

'Adora must surely be involved then,' I commented. 'Or perhaps not. This could be a Danny Carter sole fundraising venture for himself or a mask for some plan of Adora's.'

'We've already tracked the regular contributors,' Brandon told me.

'Noel Brandon-Wright?' I guessed at random.

'Yes. The first one we traced was Rex Hargreaves. There seem to be four regular contributors over the years: those two, Charles Dane and the Earl of Storrington. Two regular contributors no longer subscribe.'

'Don't tell me,' I said. 'Valentine Paston and Travers Winton.'

'Been doing some homework?'

'Not much needed. They were the six Jaguar donors who were present at the Three Parrots club.'

'Present when?'

'The night Lance Benny was murdered.'

I stayed another hour or two at the station, and by the time I reached Frogs Hill again the house was in darkness. Louise wasn't yet home, and with low spirits I let myself in and went to the kitchen to see if there was a note from her or a missed landline call. Nothing. Then I heard a noise in the living room and there seemed to be a light on in there so, fool that I was, I rushed in.

'Louise?' I called out, puzzled.

It wasn't Louise. I was greeted by a hulking great man with a balaclava masking his face. The shape was somehow familiar but I didn't have time to contemplate where I had seen it before something hit me in the midriff. A large fist. As I was gasping for breath, another one caught me and I collapsed on the floor.

My attacker stood over me and I heard him growl in a somewhat familiar voice: 'Keep your nose out of it, Colby.'

NINE

I was lying on the floor semi-conscious when Louise arrived home half an hour later – fortunately after the departure of Mr Balaclava. She naturally assumed the worst, so I struggled to get up to show her I was as fit as a fiddle. I failed.

'Stay there,' she ordered as I painfully whispered what had happened. I was only too happy to obey her instruction and she held my hand until the paramedics arrived. They conferred so briefly about me I knew I wasn't going to get off lightly. I was in for a painful journey to the Accident and Emergency department of the nearest hospital, where in due course I was informed that I was lucky.

'Lucky?' I whispered.

'Only a cracked rib or two.'

I knew what that meant. There was nothing they could do to help except give me painkillers. I'm not fussy – I accept whatever's going where pain is concerned. It would take some weeks to get me back to normal with the first week or so off driving.

'Who was it?' Louise asked eventually as we drove back with the dawn. 'And why?'

'I haven't the faintest idea on either count. It can't be the Danny Carter case. I've only forced my unwanted attentions on some elderly gents who would hardly leave their Zimmer frames behind to rush into my home and deliver a punch worthy of Mohammed Ali. But I think I've met whoever it was before,' I added.

'Someone you've dealt with recently then.'

'Rob Lane,' I said, as if inspired. 'Zoe's chucked him out and he's blaming me.'

'Very funny,' she retorted. 'Take this seriously, Jack, or he'll be back again – and I don't mean Rob.'

'Yes, Louise,' I said meekly.

'There was someone you talked about who wasn't over eighty. Michael Hargreaves, was it? And Mrs Carter. Didn't you say—'

By golly, she was right. 'There was a son,' I broke in.

'Did he belong to anyone in particular?'

A terrible suspicion crept over me. I fought it but I lost the battle, scrabbling furiously through the records I haphazardly store in my mind. And I groaned. I knew now who Danny's son was.

'Yes,' I answered her. 'Mrs Danny Carter. A son called Sam.'

'And that means?'

'Slugger Sam.' I'd met him a few years ago on another case. Slugger Sam who packs a punch and is therefore the darling of anyone looking for a reverse bouncer for hire – reverse because Sam doesn't deter violence like most bouncers but deals it out on behalf of grateful clients. I now recognized that solid muscle shape. Of all things he was back in Kent. It had to be him. Mrs Danny talked about his being 'out' after all. Not out shopping – out of prison.

'What's this charmingly called Slugger warning you against?' Louise was anxious to know.

She had managed to doze while I'd been waiting for tests. I'd had no sleep and every time I breathed it hurt, so I didn't care why he'd done it at this precise moment. 'Not clear,' I mumbled, adding a few brief words of explanation about the gentleman.

'It's clear to me.'

I surrendered. 'Speak, O Delphic oracle.'

'His mother must have more to do with her husband's murder than you reckoned.'

'Danny was shot, not punched to death.'

Even so, I hadn't thought of that angle: Mrs D. Carter and Son. Out of the whole bunch of interested parties, they had the best motives for killing Danny – and here was I assuming the guilty party lay within that silent body of elderly gentleman who didn't want the past raked up.

Louise was on to that too. 'Do you think your Sam could have killed Danny on his mother's behalf and his own, lining their pockets from the inheritance they fondly imagine they're going to get? They could hurry that up by doing away with Adora as well. Stranger things have happened.'

'True.' I forced myself to concentrate. I hadn't yet told her about the memorial fund but that could be another source of expected income for Mrs D., the grieving widow. 'Although, even if Mrs Danny suggested to her baby boy that I needed to be warned off,' I continued, 'he of all people would know from past experience that was unlikely to work.'

Then I reconsidered. I wasn't going to be able to move far physically or drive for the next few days – did that leave them a clear killing field if they did indeed plan on ridding the stage of Adora? That was an uneasy thought. Or did they just want to throw the spotlight on the Jaguar donors so that Mrs Carter and Son could quietly disappear from Kent in the fond but surely misguided hope that they would inherit the estate as Danny's next of kin?

The former theory was a distinct possibility and one I should put to Brandon, but there was a snag to the second one which was wobbly anyway. Why bother to warn me off if they intended to disappear quietly into the blue? Answer: they weren't the brightest pair in town.

I crawled out of the car with Louise's help and headed hopefully for bed. I couldn't make it, however, and was ordered hot milk and pills by my beloved. I hadn't drunk hot milk since Hector was a pup, as an American friend of mine used to say. But it worked and I managed to climb the stairs. Louise threatened to have a stairlift installed if I was going to make a habit of courting the likes of Slugger Sam, so I quickened my step.

'Sometimes,' I said to her as I crawled into our bed, for which the only use for a while would be to sleep, 'I think I'm a better car restorer than detective.'

'Sometimes you might be right,' she blithely replied, making me feel less than a million dollars. Then she added, 'But *much* more often you're completely wrong.'

I cheered up. 'Len would be the first to agree with you.'

Brandon graciously came to see me later that day after Louise had reported in to him on my behalf.

'Thought I'd spare ribs – in this case yours,' he quipped to my amazement. Quips aren't in his usual repertoire so I concluded I was privileged to share a private side of Brandon that I usually never glimpsed. 'So old Slugger Sam is up his tricks. Why pick on you?'

'My guess is that his name is Carter, son to the late Danny and to the lovely Mrs Di Carter.'

He looked quite interested. 'We'll follow that up.'

'For the Carter murder or on behalf of my ribs?'

'Carter, but your ribs might come in useful.'

'I'm so glad,' I muttered.

'All in the line of duty. Put an extra hour or two on your invoice.'

'Thanks.' I was in fact genuinely grateful for small mercenary mercies. Mortgage lenders tend to expect incapacitated freelancers to ignore their injuries when it comes to monthly payments.

'This memorial fund for Lance Benny – it's getting even more interesting. Want to hear how?' Without waiting for my enthusiastic reply, he continued: 'Sir Rex Hargreaves, to the tune of seven thousand a year. He's the former husband, right?'

'Yes, and there's another one. Charlie Dane.'

'Ten thousand a year,' Brandon said.

'Are these regular or sporadic payments?'

'Regular. Same for Noel Brandon-Wright. Three thousand. Two lapsed contributors, Valentine Paston and Travers Winton – two thousand each. Blake Bishop, Alan Reeve, Patrick O'Hara, Fred Fox, Ivan Cole, Harry Gale – no payments.'

'As I thought,' I observed. 'Just the Three Parrots members. How about Gabriel Allyn, Earl of Storrington? He was one of them, even though he didn't donate a car.'

'Yes, he's there. Three thousand a year. Everyone's duly paid up for the most recent payment. Payment day was sixth of April. Neat touch – beginning of the tax year. Charlie Dane paid ten thousand, but hitherto he'd only stumped up eight thousand. Same pattern for Sir Rex – in his case six thousand had been upped to seven. Brandon-Wright and His Lordship got away with their former payments. So were the first two just generous or were they pushed?'

'Having met them,' I said, 'I'd go with their being pushed. Brandon-Wright and Lord Storrington either weren't approached or didn't pay up.'

'Or they, maybe all of them, took steps to ensure that this payment would be the last. Danny Carter conveniently died. But what strikes me as odd is that we're not talking vast sums, taking into account that the victims were wealthy men. That's unusual for a blackmailer.'

'Taking care that the income continued,' I agreed.

There aren't many times when I can report that Brandon and I were mentally sprinting along the same track but this was one of them. I agreed with his reasoning but I didn't like where we were heading one little bit. He was waiting for me to pose the inevitable question, so I did: 'You need to know whether Adora Ferne was involved with this racket or whether it was solely a Danny Carter venture – plus whether it was sheer generosity that made them contribute to this fund or blackmail?'

'Blackmail. No doubt about that. No cash paid out save to Carter and I doubt whether he shoved it in the nearest charity collection box. No transfers to other bank accounts.'

I had to force myself to be objective. 'He could have given the cash to Adora so that she could pretend ignorance.'

'So he could. We're going to find out. Crockendene, Jack. Now. Your adorable Adora wants you to be there when I talk to her. Normally I'd tell her to take a running jump but as this will be a so-called friendly chat I'm willing to let her have her way.'

He paused as though he wondered whether he was tarnishing his reputation as a tough guy, and then added somewhat awkwardly, 'The lady's getting on in years. I'm going to get more out of her in her own home than by frightening her at the station with a formal interview.'

I felt it only fair to comment. 'I can't see Adora being frightened.' I didn't add 'even by you', but those words lay between us.

'Perhaps not, but you'll make her at ease. She may speak more freely. Stick to the rules. OK?'

I promised. However friendly a lion, one has to remember he's a hunter and I had to be careful not to become his prey. After all, there was my mortgage to consider. Unfortunately I had to submit to the indignity of telling Brandon I couldn't drive. He smiled – loving this moment – and told me that police cars were very comfortable.

Adora seemed subdued, although from my reading of her character I would have expected her to come out all guns blazing faced with a police 'informal chat'. She was flanked by both her children, which suggested she needed more support than me. Simon was trying to look laid-back but officious, and Melinda was grim-faced and clearly ready to do battle. Adora sat at the head of the table around which we were apparently all to sit. That was a smart move on her part as it meant Brandon had either to be distanced from her at the far end or conduct his interview from the far side of where Simon or Melinda were sitting. He took the far end and I took the sandwich position between him and Simon. Thankfully there was no sign of husband Harry Gale.

'How good of you to come, Jack,' she greeted me mechanically as I sat down stiffly. She didn't seem to notice that. This was not the bouncy, resilient lady I had met hitherto. She was even wearing a rather drab beige skirt and top rather than her usual bright colours. Was this an act on her part for Brandon's benefit? I wondered.

'The Lance Benny Memorial Fund, Mrs Gale,' Brandon began.

'Ferne,' she corrected.

'If you prefer that, Miss Ferne.'

'In the interests of accuracy, I do,' she answered coolly. 'It's true I was once Mrs Gale but that marriage is over.'

I was stupefied. 'You were only married last week.'

I wasn't the only one to be puzzled. Melinda and Simon looked as confused as I felt. A small, self-satisfied smile crept across Adora's face. 'Now is not the time for long explanations, my dears, but it is true, however much Harry and I might have pretended the opposite.'

'You're *not* married?' Melinda squeaked.

'That's very wise, Mother,' Simon croaked, once he could take this in.

'I'm glad you're pleased.' Adora began to look even more cheerful. 'Do take our announcement in the spirit intended. It seemed such a funny thing to do at the time but I can see it was unfair on you.'

'Not just pleased, I'm delighted you're not married to that man,' Simon almost cried in relief.

'Ah,' Adora said, 'but I soon will be. With this sad business of Danny, Harry and I thought we would delay it and play a little joke on you.'

Melinda's and Simon's faces were a treat to behold. That was unfair of me as basically I was on their side, of course. Both of them would lose the stability of their homes and both of them would gain a fortune hunter in the inheritance stakes. Brandon was looking poker faced, as though regretting his impulse to give in to Adora's whim by meeting her here.

'I am sorry you so dislike my poor Harry,' Adora continued, 'but it can't be helped,' she added sweetly, patting their hands in turn as they lay clenched on the table – rather as though she was denying them sweets for the day.

While they were still assimilating the bad news, Brandon took control. 'The Lance Benny Memorial Fund which Danny Carter was running. Who set it up, Miss Ferne?'

'It seems that dear Danny did,' she replied. No hesitation there.

'At your request, since you knew Lance Benny?'

'Of course not. Danny must have done it to please me.'

'That man was a rogue through and through. Feathering his own nest,' Melinda said vehemently.

'He did have his faults, darling,' Adora murmured, 'but he was a good man at heart.'

Brandon had little time for hearts. 'It seems unlikely the contributors would have agreed to pay into a fund run by someone who was so close to you, Miss Ferne, without any of them mentioning the fund to you. Did Carter know Lance Benny?'

'It does seem odd,' she agreed, 'and it seems unlikely that Danny would have known dear Lance because he would only have been in his teens at the time Lance died. Perhaps he was a hero to Danny.'

'Then why ask only the members of the Three Parrots club for contributions and not the general public?'

'Because Danny knew Lance was a club member.'

Sometimes the simplest answers silence the best of interrogators.

Simon took advantage of the brief pause. 'It seems to me that this man set up this fund knowing that Lance Benny was a friend of my mother's and connected with that club; he used my mother's name to persuade them to contribute in order to further his own interests. Fraud, Mr Brandon, fraud.'

'Possibly,' Brandon said non-committally.

It occurred to me that increasing reluctance on the contributors' part to pay up – especially with the rate increase – might have led to those threatening letters being sent to Adora. Danny might have hoped the letters would drive Adora to contact the car donors – especially her former husbands – who would presume this was a 'polite' increase of pressure to pay up their dues to the fund. Danny might also have extended his range to ask for voluntary contributions from her later lovers, which would explain the reluctance of Bishop and Reeve to talk much about it. On the whole that was unlikely, I reasoned, although it was possible Danny went so far as to tell them about the fund. All these possibilities, however, depended on what I sensed was a lack of communication between all the parties. That was curious in itself.

Adora maintained her position. 'Of course that's possible, Mr Brandon. Danny adored me; there is nothing odd about that. All the people contributed to this fund for darling Lance because they loved me and knew how much he meant to me. Naturally they would give money if they thought I was backing this fund.'

'But you weren't?' Brandon asked again.

'I had no idea that Danny was doing this on my behalf. It was a sweet thought on his part.'

'Sweet?' gurgled Melinda. 'He was deceiving you.'

I thought Brandon might let this circular conversation flow on but he intervened. 'Did you receive any money from it?'

'No.' Adora looked puzzled, as if wondering why she was being asked all these questions.

'You're quite sure these men donated regular large sums because they loved you and you benefited in no way?'

'That is the case,' Adora said. 'Lance meant a lot to them and to me, and so they try to help.'

'Adora,' I asked gently, 'you must have talked to Danny about your love for Lance, otherwise he wouldn't have known about him. Are you sure the subject of the fund never came up?'

'Of course I told him about Lance, Jack. He couldn't very well call it the Danny Carter Memorial Fund, could he?'

We were still going round in circles. Brandon tried again. 'He set up the fund *without* telling you? Is that right or is it not?'

'I think so,' she said doubtfully, an indecision Melinda was quick to exploit.

'You're deliberately confusing my mother, Chief Inspector. She has already told you she knew nothing about the fund and that is final.'

'Nothing is final in a murder case until I say so,' Brandon whipped back with a voice of steel. 'I'm still not clear how much and why Carter knew about Benny, save that it was from you. Did you have a closer relationship with Carter in which your earlier life became a matter of discussion? He didn't come to work for you until thirty years after Benny's death.'

Adora rallied with some dignity. 'The reason I must have mentioned the name is because of the Lair. I'd been collecting

Jaguars for some time before Danny came here and I talked to him about all the donors, including Lance, of course.'

She had bought the Benny car, I recalled, which was reasonable enough after Lance's death. Had *any* of the other cars been freely donated, as she maintained, however, or was that too a kind of blackmail? It wasn't looking good for Adora, nor for all those gentlemen who paid up so obediently at Danny's orders.

'I must have told dear Danny how much Lance meant to me,' Adora continued brightly. 'Perhaps I even told him the sad story of Lance's murder by those thugs.'

I supposed her story hung together but it didn't convince me – nor, I observed, did it seem to convince Brandon. There had to be more to it. Then Adora floored us all.

'Of course,' she said reflectively, 'Danny spent a lot on the Lair, you know. It was his pride and joy. These cars take a lot of upkeep, even though I paid for insurance and road tax and so forth. I think, my dears' – her glance went round the table to include us all, even Brandon – 'that you will discover that's where the money went from this fund. It was for the upkeep of their cars.'

Simon's face darkened. 'There's no way of proving that the money was spent on the Lair, Mother, and even if it was, it's still fraud if Carter told them it was for Lance Benny. The fund was in his name.'

'We've checked,' Brandon said. 'The money never reached his estate. The family hadn't heard from you, Miss Ferne, or from Danny Carter. We'll need to speak to you further.'

That concluded the meeting, but Brandon told me he was meeting his young sergeant Judy at the Lair before he ran me back to Frogs Hill. No problem, so I gritted my teeth against the pain – the tablet I'd taken before leaving was wearing off – and looked forward to another peek at those Jaguars. Simon was keen to accompany us once he had opened it up for us, but was firmly told this was police business. There were a few mutterings about search warrants but as Brandon merely said he'd get one and return on the morrow with a full team, he shut up.

The Lair seemed to grow in magnificence every time I saw it. Even Judy, whose idea of a good car was the one quickest to hit the blues for an emergency – demanding sirens and lights – seemed impressed. Adora's face looked out so innocently and beguilingly from the twelve huge framed photographs that it was hard to associate her with blackmail.

I became so busy studying the cars that I didn't at first notice where Brandon was heading. He was less interested in the cars than in the alcove where the piano and other memories of Three Parrots days were stored. While Judy inspected the cupboard, Brandon studied the sheets at the piano and the photos pinned on the walls and eventually remarked: 'If these men were forking out good money for a non-existent memorial fund they must have assumed Adora Ferne was at least in the background, which would account for the relative hostility they've shown towards her. She may think they all adore her but that's not the impression either we or you have got from them.'

He was right, as far as that took us. 'The joker in that pack is the fact that Carter sent those letters to Adora,' I said. 'He might have sent them to all the fund contributors as well.'

'It's possible,' Judy contributed. 'We've only been able to trace the one on screen, though.'

'Why would he do that?' Brandon asked flatly, looking at me as though Slugger Sam had had a crack at my brain rather than my midriff.

I thought rapidly. 'In the expectation that they would all believe it was one of the others in the group who refused to pay higher rates.'

'That's a possibility,' he said grudgingly. I was still basking in glory when he damped it down. 'They'd hardly pay up if they thought the threat to burn the cars might be put into effect anyway. If it was Adora behind the fund they'd assume she was bluffing.'

I tried again. 'OK, let's go back to the first idea. Danny wanted to get Adora in on the blackmail through the back door. He thought she'd contact the donors to say their cars were at risk. Danny would then insist on the higher rates.'

A scathing look. 'But she didn't contact them.'

'We don't know that,' I pointed out, 'and we don't know Danny didn't.'

'Could be. Complicated, though. We're not there yet, Jack. Something's going on but the true story is probably much simpler.'

'The family or the great Harry Gale?'

'Never discount them.'

'Do I keep forging ahead on the club angle?' I tried to sound as nonchalant as I could. I needed this job.

'These are murky waters, Jack, but there's some rhyme or reason to it all somewhere. Keep going – temporarily. How about your ribs, though?'

'No problem,' I said airily. 'I'll get someone to drive me.'

There was a problem about that, in fact. Louise was leaving that evening to film at Pinewood and would be away until after the coming bank holiday weekend at worst or a day or so earlier at best. Sometimes solutions come out of nowhere, however – although they often come at a price. In my case, it was a heavy one.

I was sitting in the garden on Sunday morning trying to persuade myself that the ribs were improved enough to cut my week's denial short. They weren't ready, I realized as I swung round to see who it was – and nearly cracked another rib.

My visitor was Rob Lane. I was staggered at his cheek. For one thing, he'd come on a Sunday in order to avoid running into Zoe.

'Glad to see you, Jack. Heard you weren't too well.' He plonked himself down in a garden chair at my side and I was glad Louise wasn't here to see this. Her disapproval rating of Rob is even higher than mine.

'Brought some grapes for the patient?' I enquired.

'Bottle of Prosecco actually. Care for a glass?'

'No, thanks,' I said. I didn't mind putting my foot in it with Rob, though. Zoe's face was constantly grimly set and a beautiful reconciliation looked unlikely. 'Are you hoping to crawl back to Zoe through the back door?' I asked bluntly.

'Yes.'

That's the trouble with Rob. He really is likeable sometimes, and as he lounged there grinning at me this was one of those moments. Luckily it rapidly passed.

He removed the grin. 'Look, Jack. Zoe's serious about chucking me out and I know you don't give a damn about that, but . . .' His voice trailed off as he stared at me hopefully.

'But?' I was *very* wary now.

'I'd just like to hang around for a bit in case she changes her mind. She has before.'

Was this man mad? I wondered. 'What about Princess Alice?' I threw at him.

'Ah, well, that's the thing. She's off to London shortly so my hopes of bliss look doomed.'

'Hardly flattering for Zoe to be second best.'

That riled him. 'Zoe and I see eye to eye,' he said shortly.

'Do you? I've seen Zoe's starry eyes when they were nowhere near you. Remember that episode?' She had indeed fallen briefly hook, line and sinker for someone else.

He pounced on this. 'Exactly. Now it's the same for me. I just had a little stroll outside the compound. OK with you?'

'No. What role do you have in mind for me, not that it matters? Whatever it is, I'm turning it down flat.'

He looked hurt. 'It's not a role, Jack. I heard you were up the creek with those ribs and I know the Pits is busy at the moment. Thought you might need a driver for a few days.'

I gazed at him in dismay. What hellish plan was this? Not only was I not allowed to drive but I had to consider enduring Rob's company as driver?

'Drive me where?' I asked suspiciously. 'The supermarket?'

'Nowhere as exciting, old chap. Thought maybe Crockendene would suit us both. You've been invited to a tea party tomorrow afternoon.'

I blinked. 'I have? Where?'

'Crockendene Cottage. Simon Hargreaves' place. We can have a spot of lunch before we set off.'

TEN

Rob drew up with a flourish outside Crockendene Cottage. He's a good driver, which is surprising given his casual attitude to life, and he loves showing off his Porsche 911. We were in it today and as it isn't his daily driver, this must be to impress the Hargreaves. He's given up trying to impress me. Today's venture seemed to be a last throw of the dice on his part. That was closing the stable door, I thought, as the horse – Alice – had announced her firm intention of bolting up to London. Nevertheless, he was nattily dressed in a red jacket over smart-casual grey trousers and a pale pink shirt. Put together that made a statement: look at me before you leap into the unknown. It remained to be seen whether Alice was listening.

The drive over to Crockendene had been bearable because by silent assent we had kept off the subject of his love life and talked about cars. Car talk provides neutral ground and this being a bank holiday Monday a great many classics were on the road, either making their way to and from car shows or out for a holiday spin. There was therefore a lot to look at as a diversion from Rob.

I was wondering who would be at this tea party and whether it had been arranged solely for my benefit. The probability was yes and it would be interesting to see what lay behind it. I doubted whether Rob was a factor even if he was bent on showing Alice what she would be losing if she abandoned his advances. It was far more likely that Adora was about to pull more strings, and yet if so why pull them at Simon's home and not at the farmhouse?

The house was larger inside than it appeared from its facade, with high ceilings and a wide entrance hall; it extended further than I had realized. With three adults living here it needed to be a fair size but I wondered why Simon had chosen to remain here so close to Adora. Close to his inheritance? Or sheer concern for her welfare? Perhaps the divorced wife had taken the lion's share of his assets. I could see at least one reason that Alice needed to move on, however. Comfortable size though this house was, it was stuck in the middle of a wood miles from anywhere. I'm all for that, but it's not something the average twenty-year-old relishes.

Simon ushered us to a large conservatory overlooking their garden where the family was assembled – or rather, most of it. Alice and Michael were there and so was Melinda, but there was no sign of Adora. At one side of the room a table was loaded with cakes, dainty sandwiches and chocolate biscuits, and with Alice's help Melinda was busy distributing cups and saucers.

'Harry Gale decided to drop in to see her,' Melinda snapped when I enquired after Adora. 'She won't be coming.' 'Harry Gale' I noted, not 'Harry', which might have implied some kind of acceptance of his coming role in the family.

'Not setting a date for the wedding, I hope?' I jested. Nothing like throwing out a red rag for the bull.

'That won't happen,' Simon replied quietly. Was it he or one of the others who had thought it a good idea for me to be present? 'Our mother is much too sensible ever to marry him or anyone else,' he continued. 'As she said, it's just a joke.'

I hoped for his sake he was right, but I had my doubts. The word 'sensible' wouldn't be my first choice to describe Adora.

'She knows very well,' Melinda explained earnestly to me, 'that Gale only wants her for her money and that once his grubby hands are on it he would squander every last penny.'

'I fear you're right, Melinda,' Simon chimed in.

'But she'd never marry a murderer on the loose,' Michael drawled.

'Suspect for murder,' I corrected, wondering whether this sudden switch to murder was the result of a pre-arranged plan.

'How high up the list is he?' Michael shot at me.

Simon backed him up. 'Top, I hope.'

I was aware that all eyes were upon me, and not because I had just dropped a piece of cucumber from a sandwich I was daintily attacking. I was, they thought, the key to the police investigation, and that was why I had been invited. I was about to disillusion them.

'Outside my province. I'm restricted to Jaguars.'

'A subject that involves Harry Gale,' Simon immediately pointed out. 'My mother had to buy that car for him and then he made her pay for taking it back for the collection. The nerve of the man. He's just after her money.'

'I disagree,' Alice said brightly. She was looking even more Alice-in-Wonderlandy today in a full-skirted short dress that suggested she was about to pirouette onstage in *The Nutcracker.* She caught me staring at her and smiled. Just like Rob, I couldn't see this girl harbouring any wicked thoughts about anyone, but I forced myself back to neutral ground. 'Grandora – that's my name for her, Jack – is entitled to be happy.'

'What makes you think she'll be happy with that thug?' her brother promptly shot back. 'He'll bump her off the first opportunity he gets.'

'Nonsense. Harry tries to look after her,' Alice ploughed on.

'Only while we're watching,' Simon said. 'She divorced him once over that girl.'

Alice stuck to her guns. 'Grandora says he's learned his lesson.'

'Sure. He's disposed of the opposition by ridding the world of Danny,' Michael retorted.

Here we go again, I thought. Theme number one was to nail Harry for Danny's murder and who was I to say they were wrong? Brandon was keeping his cards very close to his chest over his line of thinking.

'Quiet, Michael!' cried Simon without much conviction.

'I'm not shouting. You are,' Michael pointed out. 'And I'm serious. Who else could have killed Danny, Jack?'

I stalled. 'There's a whole raft of lines the police are following up.'

'We never hear a word from them. They've given up on the case,' Melinda said aggressively. 'It's Gale they should be concentrating on.'

'The police are hunters,' I told her. 'It's when they're silent that they're at their most dangerous. That's when the hard work's in progress.' I had a pleasing image of Brandon prowling through the jungle at night with his tin hat and a big stick to attack his prey.

'You mean the forensic stuff?' Alice commented.

'They'll have to hurry up,' Michael said, 'or another one of us is for the chop if Gale gets a chance.'

Then Rob unwisely chimed in. 'If Gale has all of you on his hit list, even Adora might smell a rat.'

That went down like an ice cream in a snowstorm. Alice looked scared, Melinda aghast and Simon furious. Michael, however, laughed. Even so, Rob must have realized he'd put his foot in it.

I decided to help him out by taking him seriously – as indeed I did – and see what transpired. 'Could Harry Gale have been at Crockendene that night?'

'He lives in Ashford so he could have been,' Melinda said eagerly. 'The rear gate's shut at night but not locked, so he could easily have entered the grounds.'

'In fairness, so could all the world and his wife,' Simon pointed out.

Alice looked doubtful. 'How could Harry lure Danny to the Lair at night? Danny would have smelled a rat.'

'Carter *was* a rat,' Michael muttered.

'The answer's easy, Alice,' Melinda informed her. 'The Lair is alarmed to ring in Danny's house so the slightest noise would bring Danny rushing over.'

'Melinda's right, Jack,' Simon said. 'Danny would have unlocked the door and his killer followed him in.'

'He wouldn't willingly go in with *Harry* following him,' Alice pointed out. 'They loathed each other.'

Time to intervene. 'Anyone have any ideas as to why Harry Gale would want to kill Danny?'

Four eager voices (Rob wisely abstained) began to speak and Simon won. 'Danny was fiercely opposed to his marrying my mother.'

'So were you all,' I pointed out. 'You knew he was due to inherit the whole estate. Danny was no threat to Harry, however, because on marriage the will would be redone.'

This was hardly a comment they would appreciate from a guest at their table but I wasn't here to win a good conduct prize. There was a deadly silence. Only Rob looked as though he might burst forth into speech, but a look from me quelled him.

'Danny would have made quite sure that she did not marry him,' Simon answered nervously, beginning to lose whatever cool he had. 'That's motive enough for Gale to want him out of the way.'

There were so many flaws in this theory that I had no need to point them out. Simon was avoiding eye contact, Alice looked embarrassed, Melinda sat with pursed lips and Michael was almost purring with pleasure at this impasse. I was now in the driving seat – and this was a situation in which I *could* drive.

'I'm getting two pictures of Adora,' I told them. 'One that she is in complete charge of her own affairs, the other that she is at the mercy of any rogue who comes along. Which is right?'

I saw Rob looking round nervously. It seemed to be dawning on him that in his eagerness to have an excuse to come back here by driving me he had doomed any remaining slight chance he had of success in his own cause. The expressions on our hosts' faces implied they were regretting having wasted their cream cakes on either him or me.

It was Alice who picked up the baton. 'Grandora,' she said firmly, 'knows what she is doing. She always has and always will. Why else did all those men give her their cars?'

Why else indeed? The case swirled round the answers to that, just as it did around Adora's nearest and dearest. And at the centre of both circles the enigma of Adora still remained. Was she victim or manipulator?

Rob bashfully indicated that he wanted a one-to-one with Alice after the tea party came to a sluggish end. That suited me as I was hoping for a one-to-one with Adora, so I told him I would make my own way home.

The Hargreaves family must have been disappointed if they were expecting a shortcut to Brandon through me, but if they had wanted to highlight Harry Gale as a suspect they might be a little happier. I did indeed focus on Harry as I walked somewhat painfully to the farmhouse. If he married Adora her will would be revised with no need for him to kill Danny, but the future of Adora's son, daughter and grandchildren would be far from secure. That in theory gave the family a good reason to want Danny out of the way, although that didn't add up either. Both Hargreaves and Charlie Dane were wealthy enough to ensure their offspring didn't starve. It was true Simon's and Melinda's homes might be forfeit, but that again was a financial problem that could be sorted out with their respective fathers.

Adora was only too delighted to see me when I reached the farmhouse. I'd been relieved to see no sign of Harry Gale's car. Adora was in a bubbly mood, as was evident from her tight jeans, bright green top and Mexican shawl. 'Did you enjoy the family conference?' she asked brightly.

'The cakes were excellent,' I told her. 'Pity you weren't there.'

'My dear, I don't care whether I'm there or not. They can talk about me all they like but it makes no difference to me.' She led me to the room that I had mentally dubbed the dancing studio, although today there was no music playing. Perhaps that was why she seemed subdued. 'I heard you were housebound after an unfortunate episode, Jack.'

'With a masked opponent who might have been Danny's son.'

'Ah, yes. Dear Sam.'

'Not so very dear to me.' It was a hard adjective to connect with Slugger, though doubtless his mother would have approved. 'You've met him?'

Adora smiled but didn't reply to that. Instead she said, 'It's time we got to know each other better, Jack. Let's go out in the XJ 6, my Charlie's gift. I'm starved for jaunts out at present now that Danny has gone. Harry never seems keen on taking me and Freddie and I are no longer on those terms. I gather you have no car, so we can take a spin out and then I'll drive you home.'

I leapt at the chance. Away from here it would be easier to talk. It was easy to see why the XJ 6 had won Car of the Year in 1969; it was one of the best saloons ever made. It was luxury on wheels, handled like a dream from my experience of it and breathed power with every movement. Even being a passenger was quite an experience, especially driven by its remarkable owner. Adora brought the car to the farmhouse door and we drove out on the North Downs above the Pilgrims Way, a comparatively recent name for the track which is thousands of years old. Pilgrims would have turned towards Canterbury before this point while the drovers continued along the line of the Downs to the Channel ports of Folkestone and Dover.

We were parked high above the village of Wye, a favourite spot of mine as well as of hers, and sat in silence for a while. With such a view as the Downs falling away before us, it was possible to get life into perspective, and perhaps Adora felt the same. To our right was the so-called Devil's Kneading Trough, a smoothly rounded indentation in the folds of the hillside; in front of us were prehistoric settlement sites going back into far history; and in the distance was the well of St Eustace, the saint who had the power to heal all ills. I considered making the journey over there to cure my remaining bruises but decided it was too far to walk. The body could heal itself but the mind needed the help of this view.

Adora at last broke the silence. 'I must know who killed Danny,

Jack. You realize that. Sometimes I think you are the only one who does. My family only cares about Harry and my will. Danny's wife cares only about the money and not Danny's loss. My friends of long ago have turned into enemies because of Danny's peccadillos. And Sam – I don't know what Sam thinks. I haven't met him for many years and he wouldn't even remember me.'

'You were Danny's employer and you must have known him very well.'

Her reply was: 'Did one of my family kill him? I can't believe that, but if not then the truth lies in my past life with my past loves, all gone in the mists of time. We'll all join them, Jack. Join their ghosts like those who walked this track before us.'

'In time we will.' In time, I thought, when Louise and I were old and grey and full of loving sleep. Would we have children together? There was still time. Or would the ghosts just be Louise and me on our own rainbow path to the other side?

'My past life,' Adora repeated, more to herself than to me. 'Which of those ghosts hated Danny so much that they killed him?'

I tried to cheer her a little. 'The likelihood is that he was killed not for who he was but for the threat he posed.'

'The memorial fund money?'

'Blackmail, Adora,' I said gently. '*Why* did he do it and what did he do with the money if he didn't give it to you?' So far Brandon's team hadn't traced any savings accounts. All withdrawals had either been in cash or paid into his current account.

'He must have spent it on the Lair. Why would he do that, Jack? I have money but he seldom asked me for any.'

I thought this through. 'The amount he demanded from your friends was carefully thought out. It didn't go over the top. Also, I think it gave him a sort of indirect power over you.'

She took this in. 'I see that could be it. Perhaps we all have a need for power in some way. It's my fault, of course.'

'How could that be?' I asked. 'The need for power is inborn in some of us, it doesn't only stem from the people and situations we meet in life.'

She did not reply, so I risked switching back to the here and now. 'Of those from whom Danny received money, who would be the most likely to have retaliated with murder, either by himself or by a hired assassin?'

She sighed. 'It makes a nonsense of my life to look back and wonder who might have betrayed me. Who was true and who was false. Yet I must know who killed Danny.'

'Let's look at the possibilities.' Something, I hoped, might emerge from this. 'Valentine must be excluded because of his mental state.'

Adora brightened up immediately. 'Dear Valentine. I did so love him for a short while. I knew about his affair with Monty Greene so I didn't expect our own affair to be a permanent one. We had such fun in his XK 120, though. That name makes it seem so impersonal and yet it was a living part of our affair. We drove in it to Reculver Towers once, the ruined monastic church built on the site of the Roman fort on the cliffs. No one was around and so you can imagine how we spent the time.'

'And the other Three Parrots members? Noel Brandon-Wright?'

'Dear Noel. Such a *manful* man, he was. I had such happy times with them all. None of them would wish to hurt me in this horrible way. I send Christmas cards to them all but I'm afraid I receive only a few. I expect their wives tear them up. I used to visit all my loved ones from time to time but men are fickle, Jack.'

I wouldn't get sidetracked by this sad comment. 'I can't see what motive the later donors would have for Danny's murder. Blake Bishop and Alan Reeve, for example?'

Her face lit up. 'Darling Alan. He spent most of his time at parties. Once I told him someone I knew was throwing a party in a castle. Let's go, he said. It's in Dundee, hundreds of miles away, I told him. Then we should leave now, he replied. And we did. He presented me with a rose every time we made love. We laughed all the way through our love affair. Blake was the opposite – so serious, so much in love. Such a wonderful voice. We sang "Passing Strangers" in duet once. He was quite irresistible.'

'And neither of them would have had reason to engineer Danny's death?'

'Of course not. They love me. I *do* have Christmas cards from them.'

I'd left the delicate matter of her former husbands till last (plus one other, the thirteenth owner). 'And Rex Hargreaves and Charlie Dane?'

'The darlings. Chalk and cheese. They, at least, never desert me. They would not dare.' Adora laughed. 'After all, we share our children. Charlie adores Melinda and Rex is so proud of Simon and the grandchildren. You wouldn't believe how romantic Rex could be when he took off his stuffed shirt and Charlie is a hoot. Every casino in France knew us. But why would they kill Danny? If they had anything against him they would talk to me first.'

'Which brings me to Harry Gale and Fred Fox, neither of whom got on with Danny.'

'But why would they want to kill him?' she asked indignantly.

'I don't know, Adora,' I answered her. 'But then I don't know your new plans for inheritance. That might prove a factor.'

'That's my affair, Jack.'

Having gone too far, I decided to keep going. 'And the donor of the thirteenth car you long for?'

'He has nothing to do with what we're discussing.'

I thought that was that as a silence fell between us – hardly surprisingly. But then at last, she sighed.

'Gabriel. My poet Gabriel. I suppose you must put me through this, Jack?'

'I'm afraid so. Do you know why he won't sell you the car you want so badly?'

'No.'

She was a bad liar but I'd get nowhere by telling her so. I tried a different tack. 'It seems odd that he paid into the Lance Benny Memorial Fund, the money from which you think was spent on the Lair, and yet he wouldn't let you have the car.'

'He would not have known that the money went into the Lair – if it did.'

'Then why did he submit to what in effect was blackmail from Danny?'

She flinched. 'I don't know, Jack. I don't *know.*'

There was an air of finality about the way she said that. If she did know the answer she wasn't going to tell me. We sat a few moments longer and then she began to sing. Her voice was perhaps a little deeper but still had the same haunting quality that I had heard in recordings galore.

Who knows what love is,
Only we;
Who knows where love has gone,
Only me.
I've searched the skies, the moon, the sun, so tell me please

Where love has gone.

'Was that one of Gabriel's poems?'

'No. Just a lyric he dashed off for me one day.'

'When you ceased to be lovers?'

Her silence confirmed it. She drove me back to Frogs Hill, singing softly all the way. There were songs I'd heard from Edith Piaf, from Elvis, from Sarah Vaughan and Billy Eckstein, and finally one whose lyric I recognized, 'Café in Boulogne'. I wondered whom she was thinking of as she sang them. Was it all her former lovers or just the one? Gabriel Allyn.

I thought she would turn round and leave straightaway when we reached Frogs Hill but she didn't. Instead she drew up with a flourish on the forecourt in front of the Pits, which to my surprise, as it was a bank holiday evening, had first Zoe and then Len coming out to admire the cream-coloured Jaguar XJ 6. The earlier ones are relatively cheap to buy second-hand now but they still look a million dollars. Zoe glared at me but Adora proved such a hit with them both that Zoe was disarmed.

'Are you Zoe?' Adora asked, jumping out of the car like a twenty-year-old.

'Yes,' breathed my employee, with stars in her eyes.

'My dear, pray don't believe that gentleman friend of yours would be any more true to Alice than he has been to you.'

Usually Zoe would treat such a remark with frosty disdain but not now. Not coming from Adora.

'He's history,' she said. 'I've thrown him out.'

'Dear child, no lover is history. They live on for ever, though it seems to me Rob has been remarkably foolish. Shall we talk about it?' They walked off together towards my garden, leaving Len and me to do the things that men do in such circumstances: admire the car.

The first thing I found after Adora's departure was a message from the Earl of Storrington that, subject to my telephoning to cancel, he would be coming to see me at Frogs Hill on Tuesday morning – tomorrow. Coming hard on the heels of Adora's memories this seemed too good to be true. What had brought about this *volte face* on his part? I wondered. It had been nearly a fortnight since the Gatsford House meeting, so it couldn't be a follow up from that.

I'd put my money – what little I had – on its being the Lance Benny Memorial Fund. The truth behind that could hardly have pleased His Lordship. It was that, not fond memories of past love, that must be disturbing him.

He arrived promptly at ten o'clock and took his time to come to the point, admiring my garden with a knowledgeable eye. It takes a man of confidence to do that and age does not always bestow that gift. I wondered whether the young Gabriel Allyn had been so assured. I doubted it. In his poetry I had met a far different man, an eager, passionate youth, who now had perhaps vanished for ever either with age or the way life had treated him.

At last, Gabriel spoke out. 'The Three Parrots club, Jack. And Lance Benny. I'm concerned that you might still believe they affect the death of Danny Carter.'

'Very much so.'

'The motivation in your view being the payments to that fund or do you believe Lance's death to be the issue?'

'They could be linked.'

'I feared as much. Your theory is that we are all paying hush money into this fund because we know more about Lance's death than we revealed to the police at the time.'

'*Do* you know more?'

'Yes.'

I blinked at this straightforwardness. 'Are you officially telling me?'

'Unofficially in the interests of justice, if that is not a contradiction in terms. And on behalf of my fellow surviving members of the club who were involved.'

I could see the snag. 'Why not tell the police?'

'I realize you may feel bound to tell them yourself if circumstances demand it. If not, it will lie buried as it has done all these years. As to why we did not speak out, I hope what I have to say will answer that.'

I nodded. 'Go ahead.'

'As far as the police know, Lance Benny was found at six thirty in the morning in a doorway in Soho Square and their evidence pointed to a gang of drunken or drugged youths having set upon him late the previous evening. That was Thursday the twenty-fifth of June 1964. In those days and at such a place there were often scenes of rowdiness. That night, however, the gang was not particularly drunk or drugged and it was in fact composed of club members.'

I could scarcely believe what I was hearing. 'But—'

He held up his hand and I stopped mid-protest. 'We did not murder Lance there or anywhere. His body was found first not long after midnight by one of the club waiters in the passageway outside its side door. The passageway led then as it does now from the street to the rear of the building where the dustbins were kept. The waiter panicked and rushed straight inside to find the club owner, Tony Dane, who promptly rushed down to call Travers Winton, who was a doctor. I was sitting at the same table as he was, as were several others of us, and naturally we became involved. Lance had been knifed in the chest and was dead. No weapon was ever found.

'Tony was in a tough position,' the earl continued. 'Drugs certainly circulated in the club although they weren't controlled by any of the gangs. The scandal of a murder probably connected with the club would be bad news for us all and that was an understatement when one considers Lance's fame and the horror of his death. Someone suggested a group of us including Charlie Dane walked the body into Soho Square acting like a crowd of drunken young men. That was nothing unusual for Soho. The square was about fifty yards away and we agreed. The first plan was to conceal the body in the bushes of the garden in the middle of the square, but that, we discovered too late, was locked, so with great haste we found a doorway and laid him down with a coat covering him so that he would look like a vagrant sleeping for the night.

'The next morning we regretted our action,' he continued, 'but it was too late. The coat we had thrown over Lance was mine, and it was a good one, but it could have come from any one of the many clubs around. The police interviewed us but all traces of blood had been removed from us and from the passageway outside by the time they came. We suspected the police realized the body had been moved but there were many places from which it could have come around and near the square, so the task proved in vain, even though they paid particular attention to us as Lance was a club member. However, rumours spread, Adora stopped singing there, membership fell away and the club closed a few months later.'

I tried hard to absorb the enormity of what he was telling me. One obvious question came to mind: 'Didn't it occur to you that one of the people in the club, including those in your group, might have been his killer?'

'Perhaps each of us silently wondered whether that was the case but if so we had no proof of it and nor did the police. It could have been any one of the club members or the staff. No DNA profiling then, of course, and nor did we have any reason for killing Lance. The police interviewed all of us and were apparently satisfied that the killer was not among us.'

'And yet you pay hush money to Danny Carter,' I bluntly pointed out.

That riled him and he flushed. 'Hardly. Do you think we felt no guilt at treating Lance's body so disrespectfully?'

'And masking a murderer?'

'We did not see it that way. Guilt, yes, but not blame.'

I left that issue for the next obvious question. 'There's another factor,' I said. 'Adora Ferne. Did she know what you had done?'

'It's possible she might have suspected.'

'Was she involved with Carter's blackmailing memorial fund?'

'I dislike the word blackmail. It implies our guilt. However, I realize our payments could be looked at in that light. I hope Adora had no knowledge of that fund but Carter must have gathered his information from someone.'

'Is that the reason for your hostility to her or does that stem from your earlier relationship with her?' I asked bluntly. I was beginning to sound like Brandon, not through choice but through the very awfulness of the story I was hearing.

'Perhaps,' he replied evenly.

'Where was she while you were moving Lance's body?'

'She was in the middle of one of her singing sessions.'

'Did Adora know that he was dead? She was to marry him, after all.'

'Did she tell you that?'

'Let's say I was told that was the case. What happened when she found out he was missing?'

'As far as I recall, she assumed he had left early and was extremely upset. I do not know when she was told that Lance was dead.'

'Why did you do it? Despite her love for Lance you all loved her enough to do that and give her the cars.'

'Not all.' He smiled and I knew I would get no further. 'As you know, I have not. However, let me tell you about Adora Ferne. The one I knew.'

'I'd like that.'

'There was nothing mean or paltry about Adora and perhaps there still isn't,' he began matter-of-factly. 'There are four of us from that group who are still alive and reasonably active and others who have died or become incapacitated. Adora has no doubt told you that we all loved her and that is true. That is the reason that six of us agreed to Carter's outrageous demands at the time he first made them. Travers has since died and Valentine – well, Valentine is no longer able to contribute. We assumed Adora did know about the fund.

'We were all young in 1964,' he continued after a moment. 'My poems were influenced greatly by her. We all felt the hurt passions of youth, the pangs of rejection, the ecstasy of love, and Adora was the centre of our devotion. Even when she had passed her favours on to someone new she remained our goddess. She was magical, not just a symbol of sex, but of the anguish and joys of love. It might seem to you therefore that any of us in the group might want to kill Lance for stealing her from us if he intended to marry her, especially myself.

'You would be wrong, however,' he continued quietly. 'None of us had any reason to kill him. Adora had been full of joy earlier that evening, telling us that Lance would announce their engagement after her eleven-thirty session ended at midnight. Hot-headed as we were, that might have led to mild violence from one or other of us had it not been for the fact that Lance himself joined six of us at a table at about eleven fifteen as we waited for her to appear again on the stage. He told us that he intended to back out of his commitment by vanishing during Adora's next session. Adora would be furious but he had decided he wasn't going to marry her. So you see, Jack, none of us had any reason to kill Lance.'

Once upon a time I was lost in the snow in the Yorkshire Dales. I was so close to where I was staying but I couldn't find the path back to the village. Earlier it had seemed obvious but all directions look the same in the snow. No paths were visible, no signs pointed the way to go. I was in that position over this case. Louise was still away filming so I couldn't discuss it with her. Should I report what

I'd been told to Brandon or should I see where this new information led me? Lance Benny's death was not Brandon's pigeon, and the Three Parrots connection was supposed to be my concern. I decided to sleep on it.

Nevertheless, I was still grappling with it late that evening when I was taking the hose round the garden to water the tomato plants I'd promised Louise not to neglect. Then I heard a noise. The gate at the rear of the garden gives on to open farmland but once through it there is a path leading round to join Frogs Hill Lane much further along. It was from that path that I could hear someone whistling.

The sound sent shivers down my spine. The last time I had heard that sound it had meant big trouble was on the way.

And it had just entered my garden once more, in the form of a slightly built, middle-aged, middle-height man in a raincoat who came through the gate. A nondescript sort of fellow. Nothing to alarm you. That's if you don't know who he is. When, like me, you *do* know, you also know there's no escape. No point running, evading – he would catch you sooner or later.

It was Doubler.

The silent king of the Kent car underworld was back in my life. He gave me a friendly wave as he approached. I stood frozen to the spot, hosepipe in hand.

'Evening, Jack,' he said.

ELEVEN

'Good to see you again,' Doubler added to his greeting. He had all the appearance of sincerity and might have been any old acquaintance dropping by to see how I was doing. I had to remind myself that he wasn't. He was Doubler and every hair I had was standing up on end yelling for help.

I swallowed. 'Take a pew,' I said as airily as I could manage and waving at the garden chair I'd hoped to relax in later. I busied myself finding another one, which gave me time to assess the situation.

He hadn't changed much. He was the same non-charmer I remembered from the past. Some people, of whom he is a shining example, walk in a permanent envelope of chill; it encases them, it sends out warnings, it allows no one close to them.

He sat down, never taking his eyes off me as I hauled up another chair and positioned it as far away as I tactfully could.

'To what do I owe this honour?' I asked brightly, aware that this man could have a dozen assassins rushing to do his bidding at the merest nod of his head. Exaggeration? Perhaps, but I wouldn't want to put it to the test. After all, I'm in the car trade and cars are Doubler's sphere of operations. Within that sphere, if people get in the way of his wishes they pay for it, although for him the cars remain the central hub around which we merry-go-rounders merely spin. In this case, what was Doubler's hub? No prizes for guessing it was twelve Jaguars.

And at last, he spoke. 'I owe you, Jack.'

Those were the last words I would have expected from him. Nevertheless, caution was required. It was true that in a way I had done him a favour in the past, but only because there had been no chance of pushing him into the path of his just deserts.

'Good to see you too,' I lied.

'I'll take a cup of tea, if you please.' He eyed the glass of wine I'd poured for myself with great disapproval.

'I've a malt whisky I can offer you.' I was getting overanxious to please.

'I don't drink while I'm on a job.'

Bad news. 'What job's that?'

'Yours, Jack.' I stopped in my tracks at this sinister opening. I'd been about to move indoors to grant his wish for tea but this wouldn't wait.

'Danny Carter?' I blurted out. '*You* sent Slugger Sam after me?'

'*Slugger?* Jack, Jack, you underestimate me. You really do. Would I fall as low as that?' He looked genuinely insulted.

I bit back my instinctive 'yes' in my own interests. 'He's Danny Carter's son,' I pointed out.

'Is he?'

Again, I could have sworn his surprise was genuine but I don't bank on anything where Doubler's concerned.

'Well, well,' he continued, 'amazing the things you know, Jack – and the things you *don't.*' His voice had changed like a whiplash. 'Suppose you get me that tea, Jack.'

I was only too pleased. I was quivering like a leaf at that last exchange, but the brief respite inside the house helped restore me. I chose the very best biscuits for him, presented him with a porcelain teapot full of the very best tea and donned my very best smile. He looked pleased at the attention. It might have been any old visit, any old day, but it wasn't and I wasn't going to relax yet awhile.

'What things don't I know, Doubler?' I asked at last, as though I hadn't much interest in the subject.

'You be very careful, Jack. They're out for blood.'

Not good. 'Who's they?'

'That's the word going round.'

My mind was going round too – at top speed. The former Three Parrots clientele? Adora's other ex-lovers? Her ex-husbands?

Time to struggle for control. I'd have a go anyway. 'Doubler, I appreciate your coming here but you tell me there are things I don't know. I agree. As far as the Danny Carter case is concerned I seem to know less and less.' I was pleased with this frank admission.

Doubler dismissed it. 'You don't know what you know and what you don't.'

'Accepted. Where's this threat to me coming from and why and how did you hear of it?'

He took a sip of the tea. 'Most enjoyable.'

'Cars,' I pursued him, trying to keep my cool. 'It has to be the Jaguars. The Lair.'

'You're on the right track – roughly speaking.'

'The Jags go way back. Why now?'

'We all go way back, my friend.'

Me? A friend of Doubler's? Brandon would have a fit. What on earth was Doubler getting at? The story of the Lair – or more scarily, the death of Lance Benny? It seemed unlikely my connection with that story had reached Doubler already but it was possible.

'You mean through our fathers and grandfathers and all those that went before?' I tried experimentally, keeping to his elected method of veiled hints.

'I do. Indeed I do. But Danny Carter died in the here and now. Be careful you're not next. I wouldn't like that to happen. Very nice, this tea. Good to have seen you, Jack.'

And with that he rose to his feet, ambled back to the rear gate and disappeared into the green fields and the blue yonder.

Perhaps I'd dreamed it all. Perhaps I'd missed something. Doubler seemed to be implying he'd been hired for some job to do with the Three Parrots (possibly), Lance Benny (possibly) and Danny Carter (certainly) – and the unpleasant corollary was that Jack Colby was standing in the way. Had Rex hired him? Gabriel? Noel? Blake Bishop and Alan Reeve? Or – a sinking feeling now – Charlie Dane?

Charlie equalled cars. He was the likeliest of the bunch to have connections to Doubler, and yet I couldn't see Doubler working *for* him. They were both kings of the Kent car world but one ruled the underworld, the other above ground. They wouldn't work together unless their interests were the same. And even if Charlie Dane had an interest in Carter's removal from the car scene, I couldn't see how Doubler fitted in. Perhaps that was the point. He didn't. Could he have heard a rumour about Charlie and me and thought he would look me up as I appeared to be on Charlie's hit list? How, though? And why? *Things I don't know . . .* There were all too many of them.

Louise arrived home late that night, long after I had given up gazing with unseeing eyes at the garden and had retreated to the house, still hopelessly lost in my mental maze.

'Bed,' she said firmly, sizing up the situation.

Nothing I'd like better, but today I knew I'd be tossing and turning until I got my head round both what Gabriel had told me and Doubler's rearrival in my life, followed by what I hoped would be a permanent exit – for him but not me.

'I'll sit up for a while,' I told her.

'Forget Danny Carter's murder. I'm getting the six o'clock train to London. I told you,' she said patiently, obviously seeing the look of horror on my face.

She had misread it. The words 'train' in conjunction with 'murder' had grabbed me as memories of old detective stories flooded back, one of which had included the then brilliant and new idea of more than one suspect joining together for murder. Could that have happened in the case of Danny Carter? All the family, or all the surviving Three Parrots members joining together to fight against blackmail? It was at least a possibility.

As Samuel Pepys said, 'And so to bed.' We went.

When the clear light of morning dawned, I couldn't see Brandon entertaining this theory for a moment. He would fell me with two words: 'evidence' and 'proof'.

The most likely explanation of Doubler's visit was that through the underworld grapevine he had indeed come to hear about plans to eliminate me, whether they were Charlie Dane's or someone else's. I couldn't see how this situation could have arisen directly from the Danny Carter case, but if Dane was involved it might be an ominous sign that Lance Benny was a factor in it given that Charlie had been present on the night of his death. I decided I'd give Charlie a wide berth for a while until I dropped below his radar. I wasn't sure whether this was caution or cowardice on my part.

A call on Fred Fox was another matter. He might, I judged, have played a larger part in the Danny Carter saga than he admitted to, frank though he had appeared to be. Fox by name, fox by nature perhaps. Living so close to Crockendene, being one of the donors of the Lair Jaguars *and* being first on the scene to find the body, he deserved more attention than I had so far awarded him.

The best laid plans can go wrong.

The good news was that I was now officially able to drive again and my ribs agreed, so later that morning I drove over to Crockendene and parked outside Fred's home. I thought at first no one was in but eventually a woman in her sixties opened the door, obviously his wife.

'He's out,' she informed me. 'At the Lair.'

That suited me. Another look at the Jags was always welcome. Back I walked to the Lair. The double doors were open and I went straight in. I could see Fred in the alcove busy doing something in the cupboard. He closed the door in a hurry when I called out and came hurrying down to meet me.

'Morning, Fred.' He didn't look surprised at seeing me, I noted, but he was certainly not pleased. 'I called at your home and your wife told me you were here.'

'Shouldn't have bothered,' he retorted. 'Told you all I know already.'

The lack of welcome told me quite clearly that my visit was not appreciated. Tough. 'Quite a place, isn't it? Did Mr Hargreaves let you in here?'

'No, he didn't,' he said gruffly. 'I'm the custodian here now. Temporary, that is.'

'Miss Ferne didn't mention that.'

'I'm working for the Hargreaves,' he said, ill at ease. 'Someone has to do this job.'

I was curious. 'What does the job involve? That's all her memorabilia up there on the platform, isn't it?' Brandon's sergeant Judy had reported that everything she saw was related to the fifties and sixties; there was no more modern correspondence.

'I'm tidying it up. Getting things in order again,' Fox snapped. 'What do you think I'm doing?'

I wondered whether Adora knew about this. 'Want a hand?' I asked. 'I'll be seeing her shortly.'

'No need. I'll wait till I've finished.'

At that point the Lair received another visitor: Charlie Dane, the person I least wanted to see except at a time of my choosing. This wasn't one of them. I wasn't sure what was going on here. I had the impression Charlie had business with Fred but neither of them seemed keen to discuss it in my presence. To help them along, I asked: 'What's going to happen to these cars and the Lair without Danny?'

'I told you,' Fred growled. 'I'm custodian till they make up their minds what to do.'

Charlie had his say then. 'The Hargreaves have some daft idea about turning it into a trust, opening it to the public, turning the old barn into a video room and running a shop. That sort of stuff.'

'Does Adora know about this?' She hadn't breathed a word to me.

'She's thinking it over,' Charlie said gloomily. 'Probably come up with some daft idea of her own. Meanwhile, Fred here's aiming to be her chauffeur again, aren't you, Fred? Nice one.'

'So what?' he flared back. 'I own one of them anyway.'

'*Did* own it. And Adora bought it for you, didn't she?'

A shrug from Fred. 'Maybe. Then I sold it back to her for the collection.'

Not much sign of the 'old countryman' act now, I thought. 'I wanted to ask you, Fred, if there were any cars parked in the road leading up to the rear entrance on the night Carter was killed.' His home was well placed to spot anything unusual.

Fred considered this. 'Might have been one further along the lane.'

'Was it a Honda Buffalo?'

'Could have been.'

For a man aiming to be custodian of a car museum this wasn't a clever reply. There's no such car as a Honda Buffalo. That proved nothing unfortunately, as ignorance of cars is not a crime – except to car lovers – but why lie?

I was going to get no further with Fred while Charlie was here, although I would dearly have loved to know what his 'tidying' had consisted of. If I read Adora rightly, every scrap of paper kept in that cupboard would be sacred to her. I could do no better than ask her, and so I left Fred and Charlie to their discussion and began to walk back to the farmhouse. I didn't get very far before Charlie caught me up. One might almost have thought he didn't want me talking to Adora alone if he could help it.

'You going to see Adora?' he shot at me without bothering with preliminary courtesies.

'I hope so.'

'You and me both,' he said.

Really? That was a surprise. 'You know Fred Fox well?'

A scathing look at me. 'We go back a long way. Fox was Adora's fancy man and gardener when we bought the place. I'm keeping an eye on the Lair for Adora. Seems to me the Hargreaves have got their hooks into it.'

Walking was slow going with Charlie but he was determined to come with me. I hoped this was merely for the exercise and not because the woodland provided excellent cover for disposing of unwanted investigators.

'Heard you were looking into the Lance Benny case,' he remarked casually.

'There's the matter of the memorial fund Danny Carter was running – you were a subscriber.'

'So I was, Jack. Taken for a ride, weren't we?'

'*We* being all the former members of the Three Parrots?'

'Not me, mate. My dad owned and ran the place, and I was his foot soldier. That doesn't put you on the same footing as the posh twerps.'

'You were there the night Lance Benny died, though, and that does put you on the same footing as them.'

'Sure I was, and that's why I paid a few grand each year into that fund. What's that in the great scheme of things?'

'Did you suspect that it was going to Danny Carter alone and not Adora?'

'Had a fair idea but that would have made the old lady happy too. That made it OK with me.'

'Even though you're divorced?'

'Once a wife they think they're always a wife. Ask Adora. Charlie this, Charlie that, just do this, just do that. I do it. There's Melinda to think of, so it's OK by me. The farm's her home too and she's devoted to it so I try to keep Adora on side. Now, anything more you'd like to know, Sniffer Dog? What do you want with Fred Fox anyway? It's the twerps you need, the Earl of Rubbish, Sir Rex Stuffy, Noel "I'm British" Brandon-Wright and Mr Can't Make My Mind Which Sex I Go For Valentine, only he don't count. Never did and doesn't now.'

I thought of Monty's loving grief for his ex-partner but held my peace.

'You were one of the group at Gatsford House.'

He wasn't pleased. 'That was over the fund. Money counts. Flash your dosh and even the highest gentlemen in the land pay respect to you.'

'There was more at stake than that. You helped get the dead body of Lance Benny into Soho Square.'

I heard a muttered oath. 'Water under the bridge. Which of us split or are you guessing?'

'Immaterial as it's true.'

'Depends on what you were told, don't it?'

I couldn't see any harm by telling him so I ran through the story as I knew it. He reluctantly nodded. 'About right, I suppose. All you have to do now is work out which of those bastards did it.'

'Killed Lance or killed Danny?'

'Or both,' he said mockingly. 'Knowing those posh Three Parrots gents they'll say it was one of the staff, meaning me.'

'But why would any of them want to kill Danny?'

'Take your choice, Jack. Either because he'd found out too much about what went on that night or because he was blackmailing them. Probably it was both.'

'You don't seem too concerned about your own involvement,' I pointed out. 'What applies to them also applies to you.'

He stopped and turned to me. 'Look, chum, do you see any of those toffee-nosed blokes keeping mum about a murder for fifty years if they thought they could pin it on me or my dad? No, it was one of them. Old school tie and all that. They kept mum.'

He had a point there. 'That could have been partly for Adora's sake.'

He stiffened. 'What the hell do you mean by that?'

'You all loved her and wouldn't want her upset thinking that someone close to her had killed her fiancé.'

'Anyone ever pop round to assess your love life, Jack?'

'No, but then I'm not involved as a witness in two murder investigations.'

'You'll be involved as a bloody victim if you don't belt up,' he told me amiably.

So that was it. Position clear. Grasp nettles firmly. 'You're in touch with Doubler then?'

That seemed to shake him. 'You know him?'

'Everyone in the car trade in these parts knows of Doubler and his reputation.'

'Then you'll know how to watch your back. I'd take note if I were you, Jack.'

That finished that conversation and we arrived at the farmhouse in silence. Here we both had a setback. Adora opened the door but a truculent Harry Gale appeared at her side as if to protect his future bride. Sparks immediately began to crackle.

'What the hell are you doing here, Charlie?' Harry kicked off.

'About to write a cheque for Adora. Something you've never done in your life.'

'Boys, boys,' murmured Adora happily, not a whit ruffled.

'Get out,' quoth Harry with great originality.

'I *am* out but now I'm coming in,' Charlie announced belligerently.

'Adora's my wife. I decide whether you come in or not.'

'We're merely engaged, Harry,' Adora said sharply. 'You shouldn't speak to darling Charlie like that.'

'I'll speak to him any way I want, baby puss. After the way he treated you, you need my protection,' Harry purred.

I could see 'darling Charlie' was about to explode but Adora was well in control.

'Charlie is being most generous to me,' she said. 'Of course he can come in. Why don't you return tomorrow, Harry? And you too, dear Jack,' she added. 'I do need to talk to you, but not now.'

The outcome of this rearrangement of plans was that a smiling Charlie, seeing himself as the winner, strode inside, planting a smacking kiss on Adora's face, while Harry joined me on the rejection side of the door. Not to be outdone, however, Harry turned around (once Charlie had relinquished his hold on Adora), entwined her in his arms, kissed her lovingly and then quickly withdrew before Charlie could plant a punch on his face.

As for 'dear Jack', just before the door closed on me she popped her head out: 'Tomorrow, Jack.'

Tomorrow I did indeed return to see her, but once again fate changed the plan.

The first ominous sign I saw was the police car on the drive up to Crockendene Farm. There was no reply at the farmhouse door. I remembered the death threat to Adora and began to fear the worst. I pounded my way to the other places where I might find her – the Lair or the Cottage. The Lair first – and it was there that I saw the police cars and van.

There was something else I could see too. A cordon around

the Lair. Just as I reached it, Brandon walked out of the door and saw me.

'Heard about it already?' He looked surprised.

'Adora?' I asked. 'Is she dead?'

'Not her. A man. Fred Fox.'

TWELVE

'**S**till think this case is mixed up with a Soho nightclub fifty years back?' Brandon asked me.

My defences were up but I had to admit they were crumbling fast. Fred Fox lived by the gate through which any intruder on foot or by car could have entered and he was within earshot of the Lair. It was quite possible he knew exactly whom he had seen the night Danny was killed or heard a shot he suspected came from the Lair. Fox's story of his coincidental peer through the window and having spotted the body hadn't convinced me, but I was still trying to absorb the fact that the man I had been talking to yesterday was now dead.

Fred had had no connection with Danny Carter other than the fact that he had a grudge against him stemming from way back. He had not been a member of the Three Parrots; he hadn't contributed to the Lance Benny Memorial Fund; he had not received blackmail letters or sent them – to the best of my knowledge, that is.

'The jury's out,' I answered Brandon truthfully. The location of the body suggested that it had to do with Carter's death but gave no indication of how.

'What brought you here?' Brandon asked. 'Did Dave ring you?' There was a touch of suspicion in his voice that Dave Jennings's department might be stepping on his territory, good though relations between the two men were.

'I came to see Adora,' I explained. 'By appointment. No reply at the farmhouse so I thought she might be here.'

'She's at the Hargreaves' place. The daughter as well.'

'Fred Fox has left a widow. Did she find his body?'

'Yes. She's at home. We've a police officer outside and a family liaison officer with her. Fox went out about seven thirty and never came back. She thought nothing of it as he often stayed out late and they have separate rooms so she didn't miss him till this morning. The preliminary estimate is that Fox could have died not long after he'd left home.'

'What about the alarm?'

'The Hargreaves had it switched over to their home but it didn't
ring. Fox had a key.'

'So I found out yesterday,' I told him. 'He met Charlie Dane
here in the afternoon. I went to see Fred and bumped into Charlie
by chance.'

'Quite a knack of yours.'

'And useful on occasion,' I replied soberly. 'Fox and Charlie
were talking about some plan for the Lair's future masterminded
by the Hargreaves.'

'It belongs to Miss Ferne, according to her,' Brandon pointed out.

'That never stops hope.'

'Want to come inside?'

I steeled myself and nodded, and in we went once more clad in
our natty scene suits and shoes. The Jaguars themselves looked
sombre this morning, their arrangement with boots towards the
middle aisle giving the impression that they were turning their backs
on the horror forced upon them. Fred Fox's body was lying in the
turning area between the empty platform and the double doors, not
far from where Danny's body had lain.

He had been strangled. That was only too clear from the sight-
less face staring up at the roof. Had he just been performing his
caretaker duties or had he some other mission, such as finishing
his rummage through the cupboard in the alcove platform? I didn't
dwell on the sight.

'Ligature,' Brandon told me unnecessarily. 'A length of cable.'

'Found here?'

'Not that we can see so far, which means the killer came prepared.
What,' Brandon added, 'is so important about this place that it's
been the site of two murders?'

'Convenient meeting place?' was the only reason I could come
up with, and it was a feeble one.

Brandon dismissed it. 'Not officially. Adora Ferne didn't know
why Fox was here or how he'd got in. It was the son who told
us he'd given the key to him. No mention of any plans for the
place.'

'Perhaps that's because Adora doesn't know the full story about
them. When I arrived yesterday,' I said, 'Fred seemed to be looking
through stuff in the cupboard up there.' I indicated the alcove.

'Should you take another look?' Anything to get away from this macabre scene.

'I was told it was full of old photos, letters and theatre programmes from her singing career.'

'You might get a different take on it than your sergeant,' I pointed out. Even if he didn't, I wanted to have a closer look.

I followed him to the alcove, steering a path as far away from the body as I could and forcing myself to concentrate on the raised platform ahead. What could Fred have been looking for, unless it was just general curiosity? I doubted that, though. I tried to put myself in Adora's shoes. What would I put there? The piano, obviously, which dominated the alcove, a small table with a sixties' record player, a stack of vinyl records and CDs, the microphone, some memorabilia on the walls and the rest in the cupboard. They would be personal memorabilia not business, and that meant it could contain mementoes of her great love, Lance Benny. Is that what Fred had been looking for? Or for mementoes of his own days with her? Those grass clippings . . . The alcove, though, seemed heavily weighted in favour of the Three Parrots, not her later life.

I couldn't touch anything here but I could look, and the cupboard door when we reached it was open. It was a curious piece of furniture, consisting of shelving and drawers but enclosed by 'walls' of heavy plush curtaining. It was hard to see that at first because the wood was dark mahogany and the curtains the same colour. I couldn't investigate further without Brandon's permission, but he pulled out one or two of the open drawers to reveal programmes and photos of her act.

I pointed the curtaining out to him but he dashed my hopes. 'The sergeant checked that,' he said. 'More of the same.'

'May I poke around?' I asked hopefully.

'When the body's gone and your Adora's up to it we'll get her to go through it. See if there's anything missing.'

'Just a glimpse now?' I pleaded.

He hesitated then called over one of the forensic team to forage behind that curtaining. It was shielding several smaller, deeper drawers with a lot of loose photos and playbills lying on the top.

'Can we take a look?' I asked.

The drawers were duly opened for inspection. My guess was right but it didn't get me too far. In the largest one there was what looked like an empty perfume bottle and framed photos. The next was full of press cuttings and books. The last drawer contained letters. Love letters? I wondered hopefully. I longed to go through them but this was apparently a step too far. Brandon needed to know whether Fred Fox had been examining them, not me.

'You'll have to wait,' he told me firmly.

'Fair enough,' I reluctantly agreed, taking a look through the photos. At a quick glance they did indeed all seem to relate to the Three Parrots era.

'Sir Rex Hargreaves said he was driving over here right away. Struck me as odd,' Brandon said. 'Beyond the call of duty if Fox was merely temporary custodian of this place and Hargreaves' son is in overall charge – or thinks he is.' Brandon paused, then added, 'Incidentally, a chap called Rob Lane. Isn't he something to do with you and Frogs Hill?'

'Was,' I said grimly. 'He's Zoe Grant's ex-boyfriend and would-be suitor of Alice Hargreaves. How did he crawl on to your radar?'

'He was at the Hargreaves' home, holding her hand. Pleasant enough but—'

'The buts are a problem,' I agreed.

Something that might have been a smile crossed his face. 'I'll bear that in mind. Any reason for his being here today? Did he know Fred Fox?'

I tried to see Rob as a murderer but failed. 'Not to my knowledge.'

'He told my team he was your deputy. Notice anything wrong with that?' He was staring at me very hard.

I mentally hit the Lair's ceiling. 'Wrong as regards this case, highly unlikely,' I replied when I'd hit earth again. After that, I didn't need to look for any handy feathers to knock me down. I was there already. 'As to being my deputy – rubbish. Wouldn't touch him with a bargepole.'

'That's good to know, Jack. Did you know he'd been phoning for days claiming that he is your number two?'

'No. Did anyone believe him?' I fumed.

'No.'

That at least was a relief. All the same, I was still silently raging as I followed Brandon out through the Lair. Then I saw Fred Fox's body once more, which put Rob Lane's peccadilloes in perspective.

Brandon had told me he would need me again later, so I decided

I'd wait to be summoned rather than return to Frogs Hill. I could see the Fox cottage to my left where the police constable stood guard outside and inside Mrs Fox wept for her lost husband, but I walked in the other direction through the woods with the ground crackling under my feet from last autumn's dead leaves and a mass of bluebells about to sleep underground for another year. I thought of the old folk song about the ash grove where past loves lie sleeping and wondered if Adora felt that way too when she walked over to the Lair.

As I made my way round to Danny's office, now silent and deserted, I could see no cordon, so I wondered if it was still locked. The office was but the adjoining barn was not. I peered inside at the vast space, empty save for a couple of old wrecks of Jaguar Mark IIs without wheels and with hardly any paint left on them, plus some ancient-looking tools lying around. Perhaps these represented Danny's venture into the restoration business, and I wondered whether Mrs Carter would be reclaiming these pathetic indications of her lost husband.

On emerging I began to fume about Rob again, then suppressed my anger and thought rationally on the subject. Was he just putting on the macho man act to impress Alice in claiming to be working with me or was there more to it? To my knowledge Rob had never been mixed up with crime, but he was just the type to get swept into any grey areas that presented themselves attractively, especially if his self-esteem had just been dashed by Zoe's throwing him out and then by Alice's making it clear that she was preparing to move on to a new life that did not include rural swains such as Rob.

I waited another half hour but there was no call from Brandon so I nipped off to the pub for a sandwich. And there, just as before, sitting in the corner looking downcast to say the least, was dear Rob himself.

'Have you been cast out of the nest too?' I kept a cheerful note in my voice – with some difficulty.

He looked up and I expected a red flush of embarrassment as he saw his so-called 'boss', but to my surprise he looked pleased to see me.

'What's happening over there?' he asked. 'I was told to go back this afternoon.'

'Me too. You know Fred Fox was found strangled in the Lair?'

'Yes.' Rob sounded wary. 'But that doesn't involve me. He was a good chap, though. Dreadful thing. Adora's very cut up about it.'

'So am I. Especially now I find out I've acquired a new deputy called Rob Lane.'

The red flush arrived in full force. 'Only once or twice,' he muttered. 'This morning I had to find something out for Alice.'

'Which was?'

'Whether it was true that Fred was dead and if so what time he died.'

'Did they tell you, Deputy Lane?' I enquired.

'No.'

'Rob, I shall put this bluntly. Very bluntly. Never, *never* do that again. Not only will Zoe never let you cross the threshold—'

'She won't anyway—'

'But I won't, the police won't and anyone who else who hears about it. That includes your parents and any stray chums you may amazingly still have left. Clear about that?'

'Yes. Sorry. Alice has been in a real state, you see.'

'Why?' I asked. '*Why* is it so important for her to know when he died?'

'I didn't ask her.'

'Fine deputy, you are,' I snarled.

It was four o'clock by the time I saw Adora. By then I had expected her to be exhausted but Brandon had texted me to say she still wanted to see me alone. I was to go to the farmhouse, not Crockendene Cottage.

A small problem arose when I reached the farmhouse. Melinda, who had also returned home, opened the door and was inclined to dispute my right to enter and also the fact that her mother had wanted to see me alone.

'I won't have her upset,' she told me sharply.

'Your mother is already upset,' I pointed out. 'Fred was an old friend of hers; his death was a terrible one and it took place on her property. Of course she's upset.'

She had no chance to reply because Adora appeared behind her and proceeded to push her out of the way. Adora and I then retreated to the small parlour, and although Melinda made a half-hearted attempt to come too, she was promptly waved away by Adora.

'The walls are thick, Jack.' Adora smiled – with some effort, I thought. 'All my past misdemeanours may be chewed over without fear of my children being shocked.'

'Was poor Fred a misdemeanour?' I asked gently.

'A pleasure,' said Adora simply. 'You should have seen him when he was younger. He rippled with health and sunshine. He was my gardener, as you know, and he flourished here like the flowers of the field and the green trees of the wood.' She caught my expression. 'Overdramatic, you may think, Jack. Perhaps, but then you never saw Fred in his prime. He was in his twenties when he came to work for Charlie and me.'

Charlie had known him well – perhaps too well if his ex-wife's affair was known to him while they were married. That didn't quite gel, however. Charlie seemed more perturbed about the plans for the Lair than finding Fred himself as custodian.

'And he stayed on as gardener when Charlie left?'

'Only as gardener at first but then – well, you know how it goes.'

I nodded sympathetically. 'Do you have any idea why he might have been killed?'

'No, just as with Danny. I feel I'm struggling through a desert with no oasis in sight. That's why I wanted to see you, Jack. I know you're working for the police but you can reach out to me, whereas they can't and shouldn't.'

I was naturally flattered. 'I'll try. Adora, the police have probably already asked you about your memorabilia in the Lair but—'

She shuddered. 'It's horrible to think of anyone touching them but me.'

'Fred was. Did Charlie tell you that? Or the police?'

'Charlie?' She seemed astonished. 'How could he know about it?'

'He went to see Fred there yesterday afternoon and found me talking to him. Fred was looking through the cupboard when I arrived.'

'I simply cannot believe that!' It was a cry from her heart. 'What could he have been looking for – something for Charlie?'

'I don't know. He stopped when he saw me.'

'Charlie would never do anything to hurt me,' she said. '*Never.* Nor Fred. He loved me. They all love me. I shall speak to Charlie.'

'I gather the Jaguar Fred donated to you was one you bought for him.'

She brushed this aside. 'Where love is concerned, what does it matter who buys what? Fred did love me. Very much. He didn't like Danny, of course, but that came in very useful.'

'In what way?'

'Freddie could drive me to places where Danny wouldn't. That was after Danny came in 1994, of course. Danny, I'm afraid, made me get rid of Fred. He didn't approve so it wouldn't have done for him to know I was still seeing him.' She managed a giggle. 'I used to tell Danny I was going out on my own and then stop in the lane for Fred to hop in the car and take over at the wheel. We had such lovely times.'

I had hitherto thought of Fred merely as having a niche in her later love life as he didn't relate to the Three Parrots days, but I was beginning to think there was more to it.

'Where were these trips to?' I asked.

'Down Memory Lane,' she said dreamily.

'The Three Parrots lane?' I held my breath. Could this be a link?

'In a way. He would drive me to see Rex and Charlie, even dear Noel. I went to see Valentine before he became so ill and Travers before he died. Danny didn't like my Memory Lane trips, although he took me to see Blake and Alan occasionally. Fred thought our trips were only to his predecessors so he didn't like it when I married Harry.'

'Did Fred also drive you to see Gabriel Allyn?' I pressed her.

'Only once,' she murmured.

'When was that?'

She pouted – a word usually associated with children, but perhaps in some ways Adora still was a child. 'That doesn't matter,' she snapped.

'Adora, it might. It just might. Please tell me. It will go no further.' I didn't add 'unless it affects the case'.

'I asked Fred to drive me over to Sussex,' she eventually said, still unwillingly. 'This was just before Danny came to live here. It was a lovely day and I wanted to remember old loves. Particularly Gabriel. The gateway to Downe Place is an old stone archway so we drove in past that and parked in front of the house in the court-yard. I didn't have the courage to go to knock so Fred went for me.

'I hoped Gabriel would answer and he did. I could see him there. Fred spoke to him and I waited for him to rush out to embrace me. He didn't come, Jack. The door was closed against us. When Fred returned I asked him what Gabriel had said. He told me that Gabriel said he was otherwise engaged.'

I could see the tears in her eyes and regretted I'd forced her to speak. Stirring old waters can be a muddy business, but in one way I was glad to have revealed the real Adora. Whether it would help in finding Fred and Danny's killers, I didn't yet know.

THIRTEEN

The death of Fred Fox, assuming it was linked to Danny's, was leading me further away from Lance Benny and the Three Parrots. Fred had no connection with the memorial fund, only with the Lair, and yet I still felt I should not abandon the Three Parrots theory, though Brandon had intimated that he most certainly could.

My formal interview with Brandon had been on Friday, the day after Fred's body had been found. Nothing of interest to him had turned up in the Lair alcove and, subject to the usual rules, I was on my own in following this line. Was it sheer obstinacy driving me forward? I couldn't even claim I had a 'hunch'. I only wished I had. My intuition being at a low level, I tried reason. I argued to myself that Fred could have been killed because he knew who Danny's killer was – and that could well be tied up with Benny's death. Otherwise, I was forced to admit that Adora's immediate circle re-entered the picture, as Brandon was himself convinced: Simon, Michael, even Alice Hargreaves and Melinda – and not forgetting Harry Gale, who might still have hopes of remarrying Adora. I wouldn't bank on that happening but Harry was a puffed-up opportunist, the sort who wouldn't ever doubt that his manly charms would win the day.

Brandon hadn't clued me on any further developments over Danny's death or now over Fred's, which I took to mean that he was either very near an arrest or a long way from it. I did know that the trace evidence for both murders was so far disappointing and nothing tangible had emerged from the DNA results for Danny's death. Given that the Lair was frequented not only by him but by all members of the family, it was early days to expect magic regarding either of the victims. It takes time and Fred had only died a few days ago.

Which brought me back to my own position.

When Doubler spoke he meant business and he'd made it clear that someone was out to get me. Was Slugger Sam still on the horizon? My best course of action, I reluctantly decided, was to meet Slugger face-to-face instead of conversing with a balaclava. That, however, brought Di Carter back into the picture.

Dartford is not a town I often visit and wouldn't be my choice for a drive on the first of June when one expects to be full of the joys of what one hopes will be a glorious summer. The road system does its best to keep drivers from the heart of the town, although that was once a major changeover point for stage coaches. One old inn is still there, the Bull, and it was here and in the former confusingly named Bull and George Inn opposite it that Jane Austen would alight to switch coaches or stay over on her visits to her brother's home in Godmersham, which is a short drive away from where I live in Pluckley.

Di Carter was no Jane Austen, however, and her charming son Sam was far removed from Mr Darcy, but she elected to meet me in the Bull. When I walked into the main bar I spotted them sitting at a table and I nearly backed right out again. Slugger looked as formidable today as he did on the evening he kindly visited my home. I conquered my doubts, however, and greeted them as normally as I could manage.

'A gin and tonic, thank you,' said Mrs Carter primly in response to my offer of drinks. The sun was not even in sight of the yard arm yet let alone over it, as it was still well before noon, and I wondered what Slugger would choose in line with his mother's choice.

'Mine's a pint,' he told me. That would be of beer, I hoped, not gin. The rippling shoulders, pugnacious face and tattoos made me uneasy, wondering whether each casualty he claimed was celebrated in the form of a new tattoo.

I duly returned with their drinks and a coffee for myself and prepared for battle. Di Carter won the toss unfortunately.

'What yer want to see us for?' she demanded, having grabbed her gin without thanks. 'What's me and my Sammy going to get from that bitch?'

'I'm no solicitor,' I said evasively, 'so I can't say, now that Miss Ferne is about to remarry.'

Mrs Carter's eyes narrowed. 'We'll see about that. My Sammy deserves something and he's going to get it.'

'Yeah,' Sammy agreed.

'The solicitors will—'

'I'll slug 'em if they don't,' her Sammy announced agreeably.

Was this man for real? I asked myself, although my ribs knew all too well that he was.

To do him justice he gave me a bashful grin, as though he recognized that turning up late at night, breaking into someone's home and slugging them was not the way to win hearts.

I seized the moment. 'You pack a good punch, Slugger, but why me? I can't see that I've done anything to offend you personally, so who are you working for?'

He didn't like that. 'Don't work for no one,' he growled. 'On benefits.'

'Really, Mr Colby,' his mother said reproachfully. 'My Sam's a respectable citizen. Of course he don't work for anyone.' Even she saw the problem with this pronouncement and hastily added, 'No one unrespectable anyway.'

'Does Doubler come under that category?' I enquired.

This stirred Slugger into action. He banged his now-empty glass on the table. 'I'd never work for him. Not ever.'

'Have you heard any rumours that he was around at the time of your father's death?'

'If he was, I'll kill him,' Slugger assured me.

That was no light threat coming from Slugger, and I decided to ignore it.

'My boy has a right to stand up for his father,' Mrs Carter contributed.

'But you haven't run into Doubler recently?' I persevered.

Slugger glanced at this mother. 'Nah.'

'In that case, why did you attack me?'

He stared at me in indignation. 'That's my business.'

'And mine,' I pointed out politely. 'I've still got the cracked ribs.'

This amused him, which made him more comradely. 'Dad told me there were folk out to get him.'

To my knowledge, Doubler never personally soiled his hands in murder cases, and when he took them on for business it was because there was a car involved. The Jaguars would fit that criterion but not, I would have thought, Danny's death. The cars themselves were a factor in that but not the reason for it. It seemed to me more likely that Slugger could be working for someone other than Doubler.

'Who was it your father thought was after him?' I asked.

'A big bloke Miss Ferne fancied.'

'Harry Gale? Was that the name?'

He thought about this. 'Wouldn't know. Heard you were pally with Miss Ferne and reckoned you were the bloke Dad meant.'

I groaned. 'I'm *not* Harry Gale! Who hired you to bash me?' I couldn't believe he had thought this up on his own.

He looked very upset, even when another pint was placed before him. 'I did it for Dad.'

'Did you do for Fred Fox for the same reason?'

'Who's he?' He looked, I thought, genuinely blank.

'He was found murdered last Thursday in the same place as your father.'

'You did him in as well as my dad?' Slugger roared.

'I didn't do anyone in,' I said patiently. 'I work for the police.'

He didn't take kindly to this and slammed a fist down on the table. 'Best get going, Mum,' he said darkly.

'Another pint?' I offered in desperation.

'Nah. Come on, Mum. Let's go.'

'Just tell me whether you and Doubler *ever* work together or if you know of anyone else he works with?'

He stopped power walking towards the door and faced me with such menace that I nearly ducked.

'See here,' he said, 'me and Doubler don't mix and Doubler don't work with anyone. He's the boss, all right?'

I risked my all on one last throw. 'He takes commissions. Your father might have hired him.'

Silence. Then he delivered his parting punch: 'You tell me when you know who done him in, eh?'

If they came face-to-face, I wondered which of the two I would back: Slugger with his physical power or Doubler with his cunning. I just hoped I wouldn't be the punchbag in between.

I was still shaking with the effort I'd put into that rendezvous when I reached my Polo. What had it availed me? I'd learned that it was probably not Doubler who had sent him to duff me up. In that case who had sent Doubler? I'd learned that Sam thought – whether correctly or not – that he was acting alone. What I hadn't learned was who might have been whispering in his ear.

Glancing into the Pits as I thankfully drove into Frogs Hill, I thought at first sight that we had a visitor. All I could see was a girl with bright blue hair standing with her back to me. It took a moment or two to realize that I was wrong because the visitor was attacking a Reliant with zest. The face that glared up at me as I called out was Zoe's.

'What have you done to your hair?' I yelped.

'What does it look like?' she retorted. 'You don't have employer's rights over my hair.'

'Drastic, isn't it?'

'Not as drastic as blue murder.'

'Very droll,' I retorted, a tiny part of my brain wondering how that phrase had ever come about. 'I take it something's gone wrong with your life,' I added cautiously.

'The Minx's clutch is slipping,' Len shouted irritably over to us. 'Get moving, Zoe. He's coming in for it tomorrow.'

An even surer sign that Len was annoyed. Normally deadlines are irrelevant in the greater interests of perfecting the last detail of the job in hand.

I exercised employer's privilege. 'Rob?' I asked her sympathetically.

She climbed down off her high horse. 'He had the nerve to come crawling and ask me to take him back.'

'So you dyed your hair blue. Wouldn't saying yes or no be easier?'

That did it. I should have known better. A furious Zoe stood up, spanner in hand, which she waved in my direction.

'I told him,' she informed me, 'that relationships are like classics: you can go on restoring them, even repairing them, till the cows come home, but if they're rubbish in the first place why go on bothering with them?'

'And he took this comparison how?' I asked politely.

'Don't know. Don't care. I slammed the door in his face.'

'And then dyed your hair in a constructive move to deal with the situation?'

She had the grace to blush. 'It will wash out.'

'So may the trouble between you and Rob,' I said seriously.

'As I said, the hair will wash out of my life. This trouble won't.'

'What about love?' I asked mildly.

She stared at me aghast as though I had muttered a profanity.

Even Len stopped work at this question from me of all people, not one of Rob's admirers.

'In for a penny in for a pound,' I continued. 'You love the cars you're working on, however hard you have to struggle. Maybe you still love Rob.'

Still silence. Will she hit me or cry? I wondered.

Neither. 'How the hell do I know?' was her eventual answer.

'You know because you coloured your hair blue.'

'I'll do it purple next time!' she yelled and stalked back to the Reliant.

After further contemplation on the encounter with Slugger I still came to the conclusion that, whether or not Slugger was involved in these cases, Doubler was. The question was whether he was simply warning me from the goodness of his heart as he claimed or whether this was a paid mission for him. Who would hire Doubler? Charlie Dane was the obvious choice although he was closely followed by Rex Hargreaves, knight of this realm. He was the sort of person always to go for the best in town and in his own line that was Doubler. I couldn't see Rex as a double killer, but then I wouldn't have put the notorious Dr Crippen down as first choice for wife murderer. Harry Gale figured high on my Doubler list, though.

The hitch about the link to the Three Parrots was that the death of Fred Fox didn't fit in – unless he was following Danny's example with blackmail. Nevertheless, I took a mental jump into hunch territory and decided to stick with the Three Parrots line. There were two candidates who linked with Brandon's family line – Rex and Charlie. By Brandon's rules I had to stick to the Three Parrots, but it was intriguing that these two straddled both lines of enquiry.

Charlie was not amused when I contacted him. I thought he was going to turn me down flat, but then he seemed to think again. He said he'd come back to me about the time we could meet, and somewhat to my surprise he did so. Three days later I was in his comfortable office but I wasn't the only visitor. The reason for his change of heart was now clear. I thought I'd recognized Rex Hargreaves' Bentley in the car park – and sure enough here he was. Nevertheless, it was hardly a picture of domestic bliss between the two ex-husbands. The atmosphere was not cordial, although my presence might account for that. Rex was apparently relaxed in an armchair, one leg elegantly crossing the other. Charlie's hands were clasped together on the desk in front of him and he was looking at me earnestly as though we were about to negotiate a tricky deal.

The ball was in my court to commence play, although there was nothing very playful about this meeting.

'Fred Fox,' I played for openers. 'He was temporarily custodian of the Lair, where Charlie and I met him on the afternoon he died.'

Charlie laughed. 'What about it? That was hours before the man was killed and I was nowhere near Crockendene by then. As the police know,' he added meaningfully.

'Fred was looking through a cupboard when I arrived. I wondered if he talked to you about it after I left, Charlie?'

'What's all this about?' Rex turned to Charlie sharply.

'No idea, and no, I've got better things to do than chat about Adora's vanity junk. Jack's fishing, Rex. Trouble is that there's no bait. No fish either. I went to talk to Fred about this custodian business,' Charlie said casually, though I noticed that his hands were even more tightly clenched. 'Fred was expecting to be made permanent custodian. Seemed a good idea to me. He and I had our differences but he was solid enough. I wanted to know what your family's up to, Rex. Fair enough?'

'Up to?' Rex said stiffly. 'I can't see why it should interest you, Charlie, but Simon and Michael are planning to run it on a business footing. It's the obvious answer.'

Was it? I wondered. I couldn't see Simon getting much of a look in if Michael took it into his head to take it over. 'Is Adora to have a role?' I asked.

'That's hardly your business,' Rex said pointedly.

'True, but the Three Parrots and Lance Benny are, and so the Lair and its contents are therefore very much my business. And, apart from his custodian role, not Fred's.'

Charlie scowled. 'When you left Fred couldn't wait to get rid of me. Nattered on about some personal photos he'd given Adora. She probably made him pose in the nude. She always went for the Greek god type.'

'I find this offensive,' Rex informed us both. 'In any case, Fox wouldn't have been killed for a photo, and it's very unlikely that the cupboard would have contained photos of Adora's later life

anyway. It was devoted to mementoes of the Three Parrots. A time,'
he added, tight-lipped, 'when Adora was young and so were we.
What happened then is now immaterial.'

'And yet you were both contributing to a memorial fund,' I
pointed out.

'Charlie,' Rex said grimly, 'he's harking back to Lance Benny
again. The trouble with auxiliary police staff is their inexperience.
Let me explain this fund to you, Jack, as it seems to obsess you.
We paid into it because we admired Lance and we once loved
Adora.'

'Let's switch to the timetable for the evening he died,' I suggested
without implying choice.

Caught off-balance, two inscrutable faces stared at me. Rex recovered first. 'The police took us through that at the time. And I'm
sure you have already picked up every detail you require.'

'Indulge me – and you won't have to send another thug round
to beat me up.'

The split-second silence told me I'd hit a bullseye, although it
was hard to tell on whose dartboard it had landed. Charlie gave
a hearty laugh. 'Talk about imagination, Jack. You're not that
important.'

'That's a slanderous accusation,' Rex weighed in simultaneously.

'Which of you feels slandered?' I asked.

Rex fired another shot. 'His Lordship the Earl of Storrington has
already explained to you, I believe, that none of us at the Three
Parrots had any reason to wish Lance dead.'

'He has,' I replied, 'and yet you went to great lengths to ensure
the body was found nowhere near the club.'

That hit both of them and neither replied, one looking ashen and
the other as though I wouldn't stand much chance if Slugger paid
another visit to me.

'While we're on the subject,' I continued, 'let's talk about the
group of you who moved it.'

Rex had regained his composure. 'None of us murdered him. We
moved it for the sake of the club. Isn't that so, Charlie?'

'It is, Rex. My dad Tony had spent years building the place up and
he didn't want the rozzers in, poking their noses into everything.'

I decided to feed him a red herring. 'Such as drugs?'

He leapt eagerly on to it. 'Sure. Not gangs, individual dealers.

And only what you'd now call recreational drugs. Happening every-where, it was. Dad tried to keep it low key but the minute he pushed off one dealer another would pop up. If the police had thought Lance was a dealer and the club used for that purpose we'd have been closed for sure.'

'You closed anyway.'

'Yes. Couldn't keep it at bay.'

Back to the battlefield. 'Where was Adora while you were walking the body to the square?' I asked them.

'I'm sure Storrington will have told you that,' Rex replied smoothly. 'She was on stage.'

'He also told me that Lance informed you that evening that he no longer wished to marry Adora, although they had been very close.'

Charlie chortled. 'Anyone who has ever met Adora knows that she's close to everyone she fancies and wants to marry them. Currently it's that chump Harry Gale.'

'It's all or nothing for Adora,' Rex contributed, obviously relieved at the direction Charlie was leading them. 'The truth of it is that she and Lance had a fling in 1963 when he bought the 1956 D-type in which he'd had many of his racing successes. He modified it for the road and Adora fell in love with it and with him. Then it cooled, as evidenced by the fact that Adora and I were married late in 1964.'

'She was also close to Gabriel Allyn,' I threw in, interested to see where it would lead.

'Yes, he fell for her, poor chap. Can't blame him. After all, so did Charlie and I.' Rex gave what stage directions would once have termed 'a careless laugh'.

'Adora said the announcement of their engagement was to be made at midnight. Is that so?'

'Who can ever know?' Rex replied. 'Adora may have expected it. There was a rumour going round to that effect, but she might have started it – which is why Lance said he was going to leave early, just in case. It didn't happen anyway, for obvious reasons. Do you recall the exact story, Charlie?'

Oddly enough, Charlie didn't. 'Don't ask me,' he said. 'I was only Dad's skivvy, remember?'

Nice one, Charlie, I thought. 'I'll ask Noel Brandon-Wright,' I said.

'You'll get the same story,' Rex snapped.

'Gentlemen never split on each other?'

'You're offensive, Mr Colby.'

'What I find offensive is that two men have died – both connected with Adora, one at least connected with the Three Parrots and both with the Jaguars in the Lair – and yet because of some pact none of you will tell us the truth, or least not *all* the truth. I can only presume that's because one if not all of you is implicated in the murders of these two men *and* that of Lance Benny.'

'Think what you like, Jack,' Charlie snarled.

'It's what the police think that should worry you.'

Rex took the lead again. 'As we told you, Mr Colby, we none of us had any reason to want Lance dead. Therefore, what could we have to hide?'

'Nothing – unless you thought that one of you was involved in his death? Can you guarantee that one of you did not kill Benny before you all got together to move the body away? Moving it does imply that one at least of you was involved, regardless of your fine moral attitude towards saving the club's reputation.'

Rex blanched then rallied again. 'Let me tell you again. Adora finished one session at eleven o'clock. We were taking refreshments at our tables waiting for her to sing again, and it was during that period that I recall that Lance came to tell us he was going to slip away. We saw no more of him, but it would have been very quick work on any of our parts to follow him out, kill him and be back again for Adora's next session at eleven thirty. I don't recall anyone being missing from that – although I speak of fifty years ago. Except, of course, you, Charlie. You weren't present.'

'Thanks, Rex, old sport. Wondered if you'd include me among your recollections. I was up with Dad in his office at first and then down again listening to Adora. Can't be sure of exact times, but I was up there when the whistle blew over Lance's body being found. Then the gentlemen members found they had a use for me: helping to move the body.'

'You all listened to Adora from eleven thirty onwards then? No one slipped out to the loo?'

Rex sighed. 'That's possible. How could we remember now? Nevertheless, we saw no one return covered in blood. Does that reassure you?'

'Not entirely, particularly since you – the group – took the precaution of covering the body with a coat.'

'You're correct, but the point is still valid,' Rex snapped.

'How about filling in the gaps between Lance's body being discovered, your deciding to remove all suspicion from the club and what you then talked about. If the gaps don't get filled in I shall continue bullying you and the others involved, including Adora, until I get to the truth. It may be fifty years ago but evenings such as that one do not get forgotten.'

Charlie and Rex exchanged glances and Charlie shrugged. 'I'll do it, Rex. There's nothing to hide, after all. There was what you might call a bit of a shindig that evening, Jack. Adora was set on Lance announcing their engagement at midnight. She told us all about it – not to everyone's pleasure – before her ten-thirty session started. Lance wasn't present so she had the floor to herself. Full of it, she was. Off she goes at ten thirty, Lance comes in and we congratulate him and all that. Thought he was a bit silent, and then, blow me down, he disappears for a bit, comes back half an hour later, maybe ten minutes or so after she'd finished her session at eleven o'clock, and tells us he don't feel well. Not up to announcing anything, he said. He wanted to leave marriage for a while but didn't want to tell her, so he was going to do a runner. That put a cat among the pigeons. You never knew with Adora how she'd take things. Big blow to her self-esteem. No reason for that, because she had several of us on a string at the time and we used to lay bets on who she'd choose. Sometimes Rex was in the lead, sometimes Gabriel, sometimes one of the rest of us. Lance was among the also-rans, we'd thought, but for some reason she'd had it in her head for a month or two that he was the one she really wanted. You know what women are like.'

I kept silent. Who does, after all?

'So she caused a bit of a rumpus when Lance didn't appear at midnight to do his stuff. Screaming out and all that. She stomped off to try to find him and goes to see my dad to say she won't appear until he's found. Dad persuaded her otherwise and tells her to go back to her dressing room. While she was there one of the waiters finds the body, and this plan was hatched up. She, not knowing about that, goes on stage again at twelve thirty, singing songs of betrayal – 'Smoke Gets in Your Eyes' and all that stuff. After the session ended she starts sobbing that Lance had broken her heart. As if.'

I seized on the omission. 'She didn't know about Lance's body being found, then?'

'I don't recall,' Rex intervened quickly. 'She was – is – an artist and entitled to drama. Her signs of distress were at Lance's betrayal.'

'A right drama queen.' Charlie backed him up. 'We should know,' he added. 'But I lasted longer than you did in the marriage bed, Rex.'

This was ignored and Charlie continued, 'We'd got back from the square for the end of that session but some of us weren't feeling too hot and went home right away. Can't say who stayed and who went. I can't say when Adora found out Lance was dead but she had been going on like a tragedy queen at his desertion and then, typically Adora, she told Gabriel – or was it you, Rex? – that it was really him she loved. I was nowhere in the stakes then.'

'And so it all ended happily – except for Lance Benny,' I commented.

'You ask the rest of them. Ask Noel, or Valentine if he's having a good day. Or that chum of yours, Monty Greene. They'll all tell you the same.'

Which of them had hired Doubler to warn me off, I still didn't know, but then I had hardly expected to find out. What I wanted was the truth about the Three Parrots. What I had been told, I was sure, was yet another version of it.

FOURTEEN

London is a city of many parts and Soho is an area with a colourful history. Its centre is its garden, which has had all sorts of different features over the ages. It looks so peaceful now with its Tudor building in the centre, its statue of Charles II and its paved terrace boasting outdoor table tennis facilities. Beneath it, however, was once an electricity substation and then a World War II bomb shelter, and it was currently heading for yet another big change.

The Danny Carter case reminded me of the square in some ways. At ground level was Danny's death, while beneath it lay the surviving memories and repercussions of Lance Benny's death. What I needed was the staircase linking them, I thought fancifully as I strolled through the garden. Many were the possibilities but only one mattered – the right one. Wondering which of the many doorways surrounding it had been the one where Benny's body had been dumped, I crossed the road to walk down Hall Street to the former home of the Three Parrots. The building was now a jaunty Italian restaurant, but between it and its neighbour I saw the side alley in which Lance's body had first been found.

I walked down it, past a side door into the building – the one from which Lance had probably emerged. If he'd used the front door to the club into Hall Street he would have risked Adora seeing him from the stage, assuming the current restaurant area had then been the main club room. The kitchen – again judging by its present position – faced on to the alleyway, but Lance might have escaped notice from the staff if he had come through this side door. But how come he had met a killer here? Was his murderer hard on his footsteps or out here waiting for him? The latter was possible, although from the story I had heard Lance had come out more or less on the spur of the moment.

I followed the alleyway to its end, where it ran into a T-junction with a somewhat wider alley which contained waste bins both to the left and to the right. Nothing else of interest presented itself – or so I thought at first. Then I saw there was or had been another doorway, perhaps a fire exit. Could Lance have used this door – or had his killer done so? Was it another staff entrance? It didn't look in use now. I wondered whether the staff as well as the members had been interviewed by the police and whether they might have seen Lance's killer. It hadn't yet been possible for Brandon to unearth the evidence taken by the Met in 1964, and in any case I was aware that I was sticking my neck out in continuing to pursue the Three Parrots line. I still had not found a definite link, save for the Lance Benny fund. Was that enough? Brandon clearly didn't think so. I was wandering round a maze of tangled stories without even a glimpse of the centre.

Dejected, I walked down Charing Cross Road to the Embankment and took the underground to Kensington. At least seeing Monty would raise my spirits if nothing else, and Kensington was another country from Soho. London, west of Temple Bar, was once a series of separate villages each with its own individual character, and even today most parts of London keep some of that atmosphere. Kensington is no exception. A rural retreat in the eighteenth and early nineteenth centuries, it had gradually increased the numbers of estates and grand houses and became integrated into the massive sprawl of the capital.

Monty was eagerly awaiting me. 'Dear boy, how may I help you?' he asked excitedly as he led me into his exotic living room. Nevertheless, his eagerness was edged with a sharp curiosity and I was fully aware that he would try to worm every last detail out of me. Fair enough. That's why I intended to do some worming myself.

'I hear,' he observed casually, pressing coffee on me, 'that there's been another murder.'

'It may not be anything to do with Danny Carter's.' I'd start from this position anyway.

'Tut, tut. Come now, Jack. Body found in the same place? Unlikely to be a mauling by a passing jaguar, don't you think?'

'Nor linked to the Three Parrots murder.'

'I do believe you're holding out on me,' he complained querulously. 'I must be fully in the picture if I'm to help.'

'You've helped me greatly already.'

He beamed. 'So what more? And do try these delicious butter biscuits. I take some to Valentine every month because he loves them so.'

'I've been told,' I said, munching a biscuit – it was indeed delicious, 'that Adora's great love was Lance Benny. I've been told that to her Lance was merely one of a crowd of lovers. I've been told that he was backing out of a commitment to marry. I've been told that Adora didn't mind a bit. I've been told she was very upset. I've been told that the gentlemen who grouped together to walk Lance Benny's body out to Soho Square knew perfectly well that he was backing out and therefore had no motive of jealousy to wish to murder Lance themselves. I've been told that they all greatly loved Adora, which would suggest that they might at least have remonstrated with Lance at his ungentlemanly behaviour. I've been told that they took the body to the square for the good of the club.'

Monty regarded me thoughtfully. 'And which statements do you consider correct?'

'At the moment, none of them.'

'Do tell me, Jack,' he murmured, 'whom you personally think murdered poor Lance? Could it, for instance, be myself?'

'Don't sidetrack, Monty.'

'I stand reproved. Very well, dear boy. But suppose my darling Valentine had taken a shine to Lance, then my blood might be up, my gorge might rise, my hand might tremble on a knife.'

'You're as bad as the rest of them, Monty. You are guarding the truth in the best way you can.'

He chuckled. 'Perhaps.'

'Do you believe that one of them killed Lance and that they're all singing from the same hymn sheet to protect him?'

'Or perhaps they did not know which one of them killed him but feared to risk betraying him,' he commented.

'They would have worked it out long since and the protection would have stopped.'

'Some things do not pass with time. You are still circling the barricade, Jack. Ask yourself why the barricade is there.'

A barricade? I realized that Monty was right. One *had* been erected and I had been circling it for far too long. That seemed blindingly obvious now. 'Could it be, Monty, that they're protecting—'

He looked at me enquiringly, as even now I hesitated.

'—protecting Adora?'

Relief spread through me as I pushed through that barricade. I was there now. I should have been there weeks ago. She was always at the heart of this story. She told me Lance had been the love of her life. I had believed her. I had been sidetracked – not least because it appeared that Lance had backed off and therefore none of her other swains would have jealousy as a motive. Well, not over Lance, anyway. But there was another far more chilling reason for their protection.

'They thought – think,' I said slowly, 'that *she* killed Lance.'

Monty smiled. 'Perhaps.'

'She told me that everyone at the Three Parrots loved her.' I was struggling to get to grips with this.

'Pray do not include me, dear boy,' Monty murmured. 'Valentine, perhaps. He was led astray by her charm campaign.'

'They knew she had killed him,' I said, working through it. 'They knew he was backing out. They knew how badly she would take the news. They're deliberately vague and economical on details. She found out Lance was leaving. She was between sessions, she followed him, they had a row and she killed him.'

There were flaws in this. I could see that immediately, but broadly speaking that's what must have happened. It was the only reason they would have herded together to remove the body and save her. The first flaw was that Adora would have had to have moved smartly to catch Lance in that alleyway. He would have been at the Hall Street end of it long before she had reached the door herself. Unless, of course . . . I remembered that disused entrance at the rear.

'Was there a third exit to the club?' I asked Monty. 'The main and side entrances, plus one at the rear?'

'No – ah. Oh, my dear Jack, the Gentlemen's Retreat. How *clever* of you to think of that.'

'And what, may I ask, was the Gentlemen's Retreat?' I asked, fuming with frustration. *Now* he remembered it.

'Tony Dane's diplomatic means of retreat for members in the event of a police raid. Never used to my knowledge. It led from his first-floor office down to the ground floor but behind the club rooms and thus into the back alleyway.'

'So with Tony's permission, Lance could have used that and anyone, including Adora, might have been able to cut him off in the side alley.'

'True, Jack. Do take another biscuit, my dear sir.'

'There's another flaw.' I obediently munched away. 'Why should they then pay money into the Lance Benny Memorial Fund?'

'I really cannot say. Perhaps – if you are correct in your theory – they felt they were so far compromised by moving Lance's body that they had no choice. I do recall your telling me that it was Danny who sent those threatening letters, not Adora herself. Perhaps she is too cunning to let her hand be seen.'

I remembered the hostility that some of them now showed towards her. Once they had loved her but now turned against her because of Danny Carter's threats. Adora had not even noticed that they no longer adored her. She put their infrequent appearances in her life down to passing time.

'Of course she would not notice,' Monty said after I had expounded on this theory. 'Adora sees only her own image wherever she looks.'

'Nevertheless, she is a murderer even if it was a *crime passionnel* committed in the heat of the moment.' I still could not get my head round it. Step by step it was possible, but knowing Adora I could not believe it. And yet, did I know her? Like so many of her men friends, I had fallen for her charm.

'I suppose it makes sense, Monty,' I continued reluctantly. 'The reunion at Gatsford House was because they were considering whether she had killed Danny Carter because he might have been blackmailing her, or whether one of their own number had done so. Could that be? And yet the amount of money that they paid into the fund didn't seem exorbitant in terms of each man's wealth. It was still coercion, however.'

'Do remember that I am *slightly* prejudiced against the wonderful Adora Ferne on account of her seducing my dear Valentine,' Monty commented. 'However, it is certainly an explanation that holds water, and one that I have reached myself over the years.'

That made me feel better. 'Who else would they guard so zealously?' I agreed. 'They removed the body and muddied the police investigation; then, having done all that they submitted to a form of blackmail for Danny Carter's pension fund.'

'Or Adora's,' Monty murmured.

He was right, of course. Cash withdrawals could easily have gone to her rather than Danny or the Lair. That didn't tally with her being guilty of murder, however. Surely she would want to lie low, not incur her suitors' rage. Adora might think otherwise, however. She believed they all loved her – as indeed in a way they might – and would never give her away.

'Was there any evidence that Adora killed him?' I asked, not sure whether I hoped for a yes or a no.

'It was fifty years ago, Jack. I've no idea whether anybody looked at that angle.'

'Was there gossip?'

'Very, very low key, and that centred on the fact that the answer to his murder might be found within club circles. Rumours spread that drug gangs were mixed up with it and no one outside Adora's immediate circle would ever have conceived the idea that she or any of her admirers killed him. Only myself, of course.'

'It holds some water, Jack,' Brandon said on Monday when I reported in. 'It still seems leaky to me, though. I don't go with their paying into Carter's fund because of what they did in the past or that they handed over their cars for love of Adora Ferne. What about the one who refused to hand it over? Is that because he didn't approve of what he and his chums had done to Lance Benny?'

That was a good point. Gabriel Allyn might well have taken that view, but his refusal could equally well be because Adora had rejected him in favour of Lance. Or – another thought – was it because Adora was threatening them? If so, why? I was getting increasingly frustrated. It was true that once having embarked on a code of silence it's hard to break it, much as you resent it. Did they resent it each time they got a request for money and finally something had snapped? I wasn't happy with that line either.

'Even so,' Brandon continued, 'her being mixed up with the Benny murder is the best answer yet, Jack. What it doesn't do is provide a single clue to the murders of Danny Carter and Fred Fox. I don't see her traipsing around behind either with a gun or with a length of cable.'

I could see no way round this. All I could do was cling on to the one firm foundation I had: that Lance Benny's murder was linked to those of Danny and Fred. 'OK if I go ahead and check again through the stuff in the Lair where Fox was rummaging?'

'You're welcome. It's still there. As I told you, nothing to it. No signed confession to the Benny murder, unfortunately. You might do better.'

I'd do my best. It had been hard to persuade Adora to come to the Lair with me later that day and I wasn't sure I understood her reluctance. It couldn't be that she didn't want to see photos with Lance in them as she had been perfectly happy to pass the huge portrait of them both by the D-type. I could only presume that the memories that all her mementoes brought were hard to take at the moment.

'There are no ghosts here,' I said gently as we walked up to the alcove. It was hard to see this extraordinary woman as a killer, even now.

'You're wrong, Jack. My ghosts are all here. All but one.'

That thirteenth car again. Did that tie in with her being a killer or was it all put on to impress me?

'What is it that you want me to look at in particular?' she asked wearily.

'The mementoes of 1964.'

'Why?' She was alert now.

'To find something that Fred Fox might have been hunting for.' And, I had to bear in mind, might have found. This could all be in vain.

'Darling Freddie,' she murmured. 'I wonder what it could have been.'

'Perhaps nothing, or nothing relevant to his death. Perhaps he was just afraid there would be something about his relationship with you – something intimate perhaps.'

That cheered her up. 'Photos of us in action?' she asked. 'That would be fun. Straight as a die was Freddie when I first met him. He was shocked when I even suggested rolling in the hay. He wasn't even married then. No, there's only stuff from the Three Parrots days here. Rex, Charlie – you know them all by now. Some of Tony, Charlie's father, perhaps, and—'

'And?'

'Lance.'

I didn't think that's what she had intended to say, but whatever that was she had thought better of it.

We began to look through the piles of photos and programmes, although she seemed reluctant. Perhaps there were indeed ghosts from her past or perhaps she knew what we might find. Perhaps she had guessed what Fred had been looking for. I ploughed on through the heaps with her making the occasional comment. There were endless pictures of Adora, of the young Rex, even of the young Charlie, the musicians, the bar, the staff – a complete record of the Three Parrots, but nothing that I could see to help me.

'Satisfied?' she asked me, with what seemed like some relief.

I had reached the end of the last drawer and we began to walk down through the hall with those Jaguars silently looking on. If they could speak, what a tale they would tell of past and present, I fantasized. As for my being satisfied – far from it. I had an impression that I had seen a face I half recognized amongst those photos but had passed by. I couldn't pinpoint it, however. Someone who should not have been there.

While my brain was still computing all the possibilities, Simon Hargreaves unexpectedly arrived together with Melinda. Neither looked pleased. 'What on earth are you doing here?' Melinda demanded. 'We thought vandals had broken in.'

'It is really too bad of you, mother,' Simon chimed in.

Adora looked flabbergasted. 'Do remember this is my property,' she pointed out.

'You shouldn't upset yourself by coming here,' Melinda persisted.

'Jack's far more upset than I am. He's here to do his Poirot act.' Adora had decided to treat this as a joke and laughed. 'He'd just got to the point of revealing The Truth' – mock heavy tones – 'when you barged in here.'

Simon and Melinda were not amused. 'Leave it to the real police,' he ordered me.

'Come along, Mother,' Melinda contributed. 'I'll get tea ready for you.' Somehow I didn't think I was invited.

Adora quivered with annoyance. 'I will not *come along*, Melinda. I may be over eighty but thankfully I'm in full possession of both my wits and Crockendene Farm. I love you both dearly but you are not your mother's keeper, and just at the moment I'd prefer to be alone. Jack,' she added as she turned back towards the alcove and I began to follow her, 'I said *alone.*'

That was my comeuppance and I was left with Simon and Melinda, with no invitation to tea.

'It's not safe for her to be here on her own,' Simon said anxiously. 'There was a threat to kill her and the police aren't providing any protection – only you, and that's no good.'

'The first threat came from Danny, who is now dead. Have there been more?' I enquired. That threat, I reasoned, could have been a blind sent by him in the hope that she would rush off for help from the Three Parrots group and they would feel the need to pay up at the higher rates.

'No more so far,' Melinda admitted. 'But there could be.'

'Have you finished your work on the Carter case?' Simon asked coldly.

'Still one or two loose ends.' That was putting it mildly. 'The Lair might help.'

'I fail to see how.'

I spelled it out for him. 'Danny was its custodian and Fred was its temporary guardian. And Fox was one of the twelve car donors.'

'An insignificant contribution,' Simon argued. 'My mother was merely kind to him – she gave him the XJ 12 in the first place.'

'His interest seems to have gone beyond that. He was checking your mother's memorabilia.'

'What in particular?' Melinda immediately asked. 'I collected much of the material together when I came back here to live. I was born here and I love it. I know it better than Simon.'

That caught him on the raw. 'That's not fair,' he hurled at her, pink in the face with fury. 'I wasn't born here but it's my home too. You've only lived here as an adult for five years. We've been here a quarter of a century.'

They then seemed to realize that I was still here, somewhat bemused at this adult childishness coming from a grey-haired man in his fifties and a dowdy woman in her forties. I wondered how Adora's new will would provide for them, especially if – when – she married again. The old one had left it all to Danny and I was sure that these two would anxiously be pleading their own causes in the new circumstances. Certainly they wouldn't be pleading Mrs Diane Carter's cause.

In self-defence, Simon quickly changed the subject to a querulous whine: 'I don't understand what Fox could have been looking for.' He stared at the stage where Adora was sitting at the piano, playing softly.

'Evidence of who killed Lance Benny,' I said. That this could well be herself was an angle I found hard to think about.

'That old chestnut again,' Melinda said. 'Why on earth would Fox be interested?'

'It's fairly obvious,' Simon said superciliously. 'Nothing to do with Lance Benny. He either killed Carter himself and was checking he hadn't left any evidence or he knew who did.'

Melinda struggled for the upper hand again. 'Mother wouldn't have left anything here about Lance Benny. Why would she? She knew who killed him.'

For a moment I thought I'd misheard, but the look on Simon's face made me realize I hadn't. We were both goggling at her.

'Are you sure?' I asked. 'Who?'

'Of course I'm sure. That's why she's so cagey about it.' Melinda looked smug. 'It was one of the members of the Three Parrots, but she thinks they are all still her sweethearts and she doesn't want to betray them. And now I think, Simon,' she added, in case I had any intention of questioning her further, 'you and I should join Mother and help her home. Goodbye, Jack.'

No sooner had I reached Frogs Hill again than I had a call from Adora. Everyone, I thought, somewhat depressed, seemed very eager to impart information and I needed time to assess it. I wasn't going to get it.

'Simon and Melinda tell me you didn't believe them when they told you of my conviction that one of those dear men at the club killed my Lance.' Her voice was sharp and extremely cross.

'*Do* you think that?' It was true that one of the first statements she had made to me was that one of them had killed Danny, but I hadn't taken that seriously.

'Of course.' She sounded surprised. 'They all loved me very much and jealousy is a very powerful emotion. When they heard he was going to marry me, their blood was up. No doubt about it.'

'I am afraid there is, Adora. There are different accounts of what happened that evening.' I couldn't go further than that. 'Do you know which one of them killed him?'

'I don't know, dear Jack. I truly don't. That's why I never mentioned it to you. You do understand?'

I only wished I did. There's an old rhyme beginning 'Here we

go round the mulberry bush'. I was currently being led right round
it without being allowed to grasp the fruit. I was faced with two
theories: the first that Adora killed Lance and the second that one
of her Three Parrot lovers had. I mentally clutched my head.
Which of them was the truth and how on earth – assuming it was
relevant to Brandon's case – could the evidence now be found?

'What's the matter, Jack?' Louise asked. She had returned from
Canterbury after beginning a short run at the Albion Theatre, but
that was not until eleven o'clock. It wasn't until she had eaten that
she realized I had not, and that therefore something was amiss.

'It's like this.' I spelled out the basic problem. 'Was it Adora or
her admirers who killed Lance and was Fred Fox looking for
evidence of that? Where do I go from here?'

She considered this. 'Bed?'

'Very funny.'

'I'm serious. Let the brain cells chew it over while you're asleep.'

'I could try that, I suppose,' I said grudgingly.

'Good. I will too and we can confer at breakfast. Much more
civilized than midnight oil.'

'I was thinking more of a midnight whisky.'

'Not if I'm sharing a bed with you. You'd trumpet like Nellie the
Elephant.'

I was most indignant. 'I do not snore! However, would you permit
me a slice of toast and a hot chocolate?'

'Done.'

I awoke refreshed. 'How are your brains?' I asked her cautiously
the next morning.

'Still asleep,' she mumbled.

'Mine aren't.'

She groaned. 'Tell me over breakfast.'

This I did. 'I've decided both Adora and the Three Parrots group
think they're right in what they believe. Adora genuinely *thinks* one
or all of them killed Lance. They *think* she did. Hence the natural
tension, and hence the blackmail money paid into the memorial
fund.'

'So who did kill Lance? Hamlet the Dane?'

'I don't know.'

'Can't make your mind up. Just like Hamlet.' She drank some coffee and shook herself fully awake. 'Seriously, can I help?'

'Only by cheering me on.'

'On to what?'

'The missing factor.'

'Whereabouts is that?'

'Possibly in a photo of the Three Parrots club. A familiar face but I couldn't remember whose it was.'

'And now you have?'

'Yes. All night I dreamed of him.'

'That was helpful. Where did that lead you?'

'Straight back to that photo. There was a young waiter all dolled up in evening clothes grinning. I swear it was a young Danny Carter.'

FIFTEEN

How could it be Danny? I had a sudden doubt. My imagination must surely be working overtime. And yet if I was right and Danny *had* known who had killed Lance, then that would explain not only the blackmail more convincingly but the reason for his murder. There was only one way to be sure: find that photograph again. As this was a Saturday and I had no intention of waiting until I could get hold of Brandon or his team, I made an appointment with Simon who grudgingly agreed to let me into the Lair after I had laid out the possible consequences of his refusal.

I had hoped that the door would be left unlocked for me but Michael was there, eyeing me with suspicion. He greeted me civilly enough, however, and my company was evidently interesting enough for him to insist on accompanying me to the alcove.

'Does Gran know about this?' he asked.

'No, but she came with me yesterday. I'm simply rechecking the photos we looked at then.'

'Plenty here. Look at what you like but don't take all day about it. I've other plans.'

'I'll endeavour to fit in with them.'

He did manage a grin at that and watched curiously as I delved into the cupboard for the drawers of photos I remembered seeing earlier.

It was in vain. The photo wasn't there. At first I thought I must have got the wrong drawer, but another feverish search made me realize I hadn't. Was it merely out of place? I searched again but with no different result. It couldn't be sheer coincidence that the very photo I was after had vanished. It had been removed and there would be little use in demanding its return.

I debated how much I needed to see it again. I was sure enough that I was right about Danny, and if I could establish that he had indeed worked there it would give Brandon the link to Lance Benny that he needed.

I couldn't wait to get started. My ignition was on; my handbrake was off. I was ready to go.

Michael must have sensed my change of mood. 'What's wrong?' he asked.

'Nothing,' I said jubilantly. 'Nothing at all.'

Back at Frogs Hill, I began my campaign. A call to Diane Carter proved unhelpful, though. She had no idea what Danny had done in his youth, although she did confirm that the ages would fit. In 1964 Danny would have been fifteen or sixteen and perhaps working part-time or even full-time at the Three Parrots. Mrs Carter was quite sure that her darling Sam wouldn't know about his father's career either. So that was that.

I wasn't downhearted, though. I pressed on. *Someone* must know about Danny and the Three Parrots because that photo had gone missing. Adora? Would she have recognized him from the youth she had known in the sixties when he appeared at her door wanting a job thirty years later? She was unlikely to have known junior or part-time staff. The photo might have been taken at any time, before or after the fatal night when Lance was killed. When Danny applied for a job with her, however, he would have known exactly who Adora was, although whether he would have mentioned it was a moot point. He might already have had his plans for the memorial fund, or, it occurred to me with a sickening thud, he might have blackmailed her into giving him the job, the cottage – and, worse, the inheritance. After all, if I was wrong about Danny's working at the club or if Adora didn't remember him there, why had that photograph vanished?

I considered my next move carefully. I wouldn't ask Adora about it yet, nor her family, nor Monty. There was one member of the Three Parrots whom I trusted, though – the Earl of Storrington.

He sounded surprised when I told him why I'd called, but agreed that there had indeed been very young waiters at the club. He couldn't remember their names but one of them was very much on the short side and he thought that he did have a name beginning with D. He had no idea what their surnames were.

I paced around the garden for so long contemplating this that Louise came out to see if I was OK.

'I'm thinking,' I informed her.

'Not OK then. I'll make some coffee.'

Thinking worked. Assuming the waiter in the photo was Danny

Carter, was he the one who had found Lance's body? If so, this could have been Danny's secret weapon over the group who moved the body.

By the end of the day I felt secure enough about this diagnosis to risk ringing Brandon on his mobile. 'How sure are you about this photo being of Carter?' he said after listening to my spiel. I'd tried to keep the excitement out of my voice – Brandon doesn't do excitement.

'I'd say I'm at ninety-five per cent.'

'The same for its relevance to his murder?'

I tried to be cautious. 'It opens up one hell of a lot of possibilities. It suggests that Danny might have known exactly who killed Benny. It explains the blackmail, it explains his putting the thumbscrews on them, it explains why they might have snapped and killed him.'

'Why should it surface all these years later? No, delete that. Carter's blackmailing efforts were going too high.' A pause. 'But we're near making an arrest, Jack. Come to HQ on Monday, eight o'clock.'

That set me rocking on my heels. Who would he be arresting? There's no way he could tell me over the phone. I had to wait.

I presented myself at Charing promptly at eight, my former excitement tempered with the feeling that I wasn't going to like what Brandon was about to tell me. And I didn't.

'Simon Hargreaves, Jack,' he said as soon as we were alone. 'That young tearaway Michael has done his best to muddy the waters and his father's been playing the dark horse. It was his gun used that night, his DNA.'

'Natural enough if it's his gun.'

'We're aware of that, thanks. And it's legally registered,' Brandon retorted, 'but there's more. Not enough to make it watertight but enough to push it forward.'

'Is that for Carter or Fox's murder?'

'We've got more on him for Fox than Carter, but we'll get him for both. Our line is that Fox knew Hargreaves had killed Carter and was pressurizing him into making him a partner in the Lair business. That's important to Hargreaves – he sees that as his baby, the glory he didn't get from his earlier career. He wants to turn the

Lair into a non-profit organization and join up with that car museum near Canterbury, Treasure Island.'

I knew it well, for one of my earlier cases had centred on it. 'Not a bad idea,' I said.

'Nevertheless,' Brandon added, 'this line on Carter at the club is worth following up. We need confirmation, though.'

'Can I tackle the Three Parrots members and Adora on that?'

Brandon thought for a moment. 'Yes, but move carefully.'

I was once again mentally rocking on my heels. Simon? Brandon didn't often make mistakes, but Simon didn't seem to me the type to strangle someone *and* shoot another. It was unusual for a murderer to change methods.

And then I remembered Alice, who had been pestering Rob Lane for exact information on when Fred Fox had died. Is that because Simon had been absent from the house, an absence she couldn't otherwise explain?

Was Brandon right on this one and I on the wrong course? Whether I was or not, I had to move quickly. If Simon was on the point of being arrested, I needed to speak to Rex before that happened or I would get precious little cooperation. He agreed reluctantly to see me the next morning, but I was already too late by then. Brandon, too, had moved quickly.

'Come to arrest *me*, have you?' Rex greeted me. 'Another cock-eyed story you've dreamed up?'

'Not cockeyed, Sir Rex. The Three Parrots club.'

'I've more pressing things on my mind,' he said drily. 'My son has been taken in for questioning in respect to the Danny Carter case. You seem to be on your own in doggedly pursuing theories about Lance Benny.'

'A terrible time for you,' I said sincerely. 'I *am* here, on behalf of the police, to talk about Lance Benny and also the club staff.'

He stared at me in utter amazement. 'What, might I ask, has my former wife been telling you now?'

'Nothing as far as I know.'

'That's some relief. Simon is our son yet all she can say in response to the trouble that has come upon us is that neither Carter nor Fred Fox would do anything to hurt her. Simon is being accused of *murder*. Now you come jabbering about domestic arrangements in a club that has long since closed down.'

'What I want to ask you might possibly provide the clue to who did commit the murders. It could help your son.'

He calmed down a little. 'I appreciate that, Jack, but I can't see how. They seem convinced that Simon was after the inheritance that my former wife had unjustly bequeathed to Carter in her will. Ridiculous thinking, because Simon knows I'd look after him and his family if he were in financial straits. It's true he has this great attachment to Crockendene but there are other houses. They seem to think that Simon killed Fox on the unsubstantiated basis that Fox knew Simon had killed Carter. Rubbish.'

I could hardly point out that Rex himself might be a suspect for Danny's murder if there were a link with the Lance Benny case, but he was astute enough to see that for himself. Luckily he was so dispirited that in order to get rid of me he just told me to go ahead with whatever questions I had. I took him at his word, explaining Danny's possible role at the Three Parrots.

He listened carefully and frowned. 'I remember that it was one of the waiters who found the body in the alley outside the club. Can't say I recall much about him. You think it was Danny Carter? Someone suggested we take one of the coats hanging by the club entrance, put it round the body and move Lance as though he were merely drunk into the square so that Adora would not be connected with the crime and nor would the club. I remember that waiter following Tony Dane down the stairs when he came rushing from his office to fetch Travers Winton. Tony thought the club was doomed but we were more worried about Adora. She had been behaving like a maniac, yelling that Lance had deserted her, and then of course she became worse once she knew of Lance's death. The waiter intimated that he knew who had done it and I understand from Monty that you are aware we realized it might have been Adora herself, who had heard his plans to leave, caught him outside to remonstrate with him and then killed him.

'I recall,' he continued, 'that Travers told us that Lance could have been killed by one of the knives used in the club; there was a buffet supper laid out in an anteroom to the club hall. If so, we never saw such a weapon. We were all out of our depth in this situation. When Carter began his so-called memorial fund for Lance we decided not to take any chances. We would be involved in an enquiry that could lead anywhere and would certainly bring Adora into the matter. It seems to me now that Carter must have been blackmailing Adora too, and that's the reason that she left the whole estate to him, cutting out her own family.'

That made sense, I thought. Adora was the one person he could blackmail on a grand scale into giving him a job, a house and finally all she had. Perhaps the marriage to Harry had been a last shot to get him off her back. And yet she believed that one of them had killed Danny? Self-delusion on her part? Quite possibly.

'There are angles I don't understand,' I told him. 'You married Adora despite knowing that she had in all probability killed Lance.'

He managed a smile. 'The answer is quite simple, Jack. I married Adora because I did indeed adore her. In a way, I still do.'

Charlie Dane was my next hope for pinning down the connection between Danny and the Three Parrots.

'Back again?' Charlie commented grimly. 'I thought I'd seen the last of you now that Simon's under the microscope. Talk about loving families, eh? So what's this photo Rex tells me you want to talk about? No problem about it. No one's going to reopen the Benny case now.'

It didn't take a Miss Marple to work out that the grapevine had been busy. The extended family was closing ranks.

'That might happen if it connects to Danny Carter's death.'

'You're stuck in a groove, Jack. Find a new track. Take up embroidery. Let's see this photo, though.'

'It's gone missing. It showed several of you at the club with a young man behind you, obviously a waiter, and I think it was Danny Carter.'

'You've got a bee in your bonnet and no mistake, Jack. You *think*? And the photo's missing? You're doing your damnedest to dream up so-called evidence that will prove nothing. Carter's dead. I can't say whether it was him or not in a photo you can't show me but which is over fifty years old. If his widow and son can't help then how can I? Expect me to have staff records for the Three Parrots going back that far?'

'No, but there's something you would remember: the Gentlemen's Retreat.'

'Eh?' Charlie looked blank, then laughed. 'Good grief, yes. Dad was proud of that.'

'Could Lance Benny have used that way out to make his escape unseen by Adora?'

He considered this. 'Might have. Adora might have seen him if he'd gone out of the side entrance because the corridor that led to it also led to her dressing room. If he'd nipped upstairs to Dad's office and down that way, he'd be safe. Dad was upstairs with me when Adora finished her act at midnight and someone came rushing up a bit later to say his body was out there. I hadn't been up with Dad that long, though, so Lance could well have been up there during her act. He certainly wasn't there when she finished. I was still downstairs then – quite a hullabaloo it was when someone told her he'd scarpered. I went up to Dad then to see if Lance was in the office, but he wasn't, of course. No sign of him. That waiter . . .' He stopped.

'Danny?'

'Could have been him, I suppose. Anyway, he came dashing up and told us Lance Benny was dead outside. Dad went bananas – it would have been maybe twenty minutes after Adora finished her session – and went to grab Doctor Winton. A group of us followed.'

'Where was Adora then?'

'Couldn't say. She wasn't with us. In her dressing room probably.' He looked at me. 'That help?'

'It does, but Adora—'

'Make your mind up who to believe, Jack. You're a big boy now. Don't get led up the garden path by her. She's a great lady but a blooming jaguar herself. Sorts out her prey and devours it, no help required from the rest of the pack.'

I was beginning to wonder whether I was indeed being led, and if so, by whom? It was true that Brandon was still negative over the Lance Benny theory, but as Danny Carter's murderer was in custody, as far as Brandon was concerned I couldn't be accused of butting into his territory. Ten to one that photograph had been destroyed, however, which meant Adora still sat firmly in the centre of this maze.

Possible murderer, possible deceiver and one of the greatest cabaret stars of all time. Had I jumped to conclusions too quickly? If Danny had been that waiter, it could be argued both ways: Danny knew Adora was Lance's killer or that he knew which of the six men (including Valentine and Travers) had really killed Benny. The scene was still too murky, however. The more I pushed the veils aside the more they seemed to be muffling me. This might be inevitable in a mystery as old as this one, but I was going to do my best to tear down that final veil.

Physical fear is something I have had to face in my line of work, but just as bad is the psychological fear that throws up bogies not only at night but whenever it fancies. One of my current ones was Doubler, who traded on creating psychological fear to do his dirty work as much as his thugs did on the physical side. Now I was facing another: Adora. Fear can be created by the unknown, in which the known – or what I sincerely hoped was the known – might be entirely at odds with the truth.

However much one imagines what a meeting might be like, the reality can usually be guaranteed to be completely different. As now. Once I had been admitted to Crockendene Farmhouse on Wednesday morning by a hostile Melinda, I discovered that this was not going to be a one-to-one with Adora. Melinda and, surprise, surprise, Harry Gale were also present, and this time Adora clearly had no intention of dismissing them. She looked weary and the sober trousers and top she wore made her bear little resemblance to the tango dancer I had first met.

'I hear you've been throwing your weight around, Jack,' Harry informed me ponderously. Adora didn't even remonstrate with him and I felt some compunction about what I had come to do. Better me than Brandon, I reasoned.

'Adora, a photograph I saw in the Lair has disappeared – one of the Three Parrots, a group of members and a young waiter.'

Silence. At least I didn't have to battle with fruitless denials, however. Melinda stared at me blankly. Harry folded his arms as a prelude to battle, but Adora finally answered me.

'You want to know who that young waiter was,' she said quietly. 'It was Danny.'

'He worked there full-time?' It was clear she was going to make me do all the running – perhaps through sheer exhaustion.

'Occasionally. He was only fifteen in that photo.'

'You knew him before he came to work there?'

'I did.'

I noticed that this didn't appear to be news to her daughter or to her prospective husband. 'That's why you gave him a job here with a cottage?'

'Yes.'

Harry decided he was being ignored. 'Where's all this leading, Colby?'

'To the solution of his murder,' I replied.

'That's ridiculous, Jack,' Adora said without conviction. 'How could it?'

'Not so ridiculous, considering he was later blackmailing some of those in the photograph. So we come back to the question of whether that was on your behalf?'

'Oh, Jack, you can't really believe that!' She looked so appalled that I very nearly threw my hand in, but I had to press on.

'Do you want Mr Gale and your daughter to hear what I have to say next?'

Hostility really crackled in the air now.

Adora remained calm, however. 'I do.'

Harry preened himself. 'You'll have me to deal with if you upset her, Colby.'

I ignored him and took a gamble. 'Adora, Danny was working there the night Lance died, wasn't he? He was the one who discovered Lance's body in the alleyway?'

'Yes. He had overheard Lance telling my friends he wasn't ready to make our engagement public and was going to slip away. Danny told me that when I finished my session at midnight and I had to go to my dressing room to get over the shock. Danny found the body shortly afterwards, realized how horrified I would be and suggested to my friends that it would be in everybody's interests to move it to Soho Square.'

'Even though the murderer was almost certainly someone in the club at the time?'

'Yes.'

'They all wanted to protect you?'

'Of course. They all loved me.'

I took a deep breath and faced the bogies within me, one of which was how Brandon would react if he were here. 'You could have killed Lance yourself, Adora. Is that why they wanted to protect you?'

I hardly got the last word out before Harry was out of his chair and lunging towards me. Melinda was sobbing.

'Harry, *no*.' Adora was still calm.

He stopped in his tracks. 'Didn't you hear what this asshole said about you, pet?'

'I don't blame him, Harry. That's what it looks like. Danny *was* protecting me. I assumed he was protecting Rex or Charlie or Valentine. Even Gabriel. One of them must have killed him but not me.'

I subdued a surge of panic. Was I on the wrong track after all? 'How can the police be sure of that?'

I thought she hadn't heard me but she did answer. 'I could never, ever have killed darling Lance.'

'You must have been furious when you learned he wasn't going to honour the arrangement you'd made with him.'

'Yes, I was. I don't deny that. Danny knew it. Everyone knew it. What no one could have seen me do is kill him, because I didn't. After Danny told me Lance had left early, I was very upset indeed. But then I went to my dressing room and calmed down. I realized I had nearly made a terrible mistake and that I was relieved that he was dodging the marriage question. Lance wasn't the great love of my life. We'd had such fun, it was so exciting, so glamorous, but no one who treated me as badly as Lance did by running out on me could have been the hero I had thought he was. I heard some commotion going on in the corridor and people running up and down the stairs, so I went out to see what had happened. It was then Danny told me that Lance was dead. I thought Rex or Charlie might have killed him, or even Gabriel or Noel, especially when I was told that they had managed to get the body to Soho Square, pretending they were helping a drunken man. That was Danny's suggestion.'

'Did Danny blackmail you into giving him a job here?'

'*Blackmail?*' Adora looked astounded. 'No, 'course not. He *loved* me.'

'Danny? But he was only fifteen at the time!' I said incredulously.

She managed a smile as she saw my expression. 'Danny wasn't my lover. Danny was my son.'

The room swam around me, or maybe it was upside down. I couldn't tell. I must have misheard. Melinda didn't look surprised,

I noticed, but Harry looked as if the news had socked him in the face as effectively as I would have liked to have done. He was already uttering incoherent questions.

I'd get mine in first. 'An illegitimate son?'

'Nothing so dramatic, Jack. Danny was my son by my first husband, Ron.'

'Does his ex-wife know that?'

'I doubt it. Danny was always secretive.'

'That means' – I was still grappling with the implications – 'that Slugger Sam is your grandson.'

'So I am told. He's a sweet lad really.'

'When he's not slugging people,' I said.

Harry seemed to have given up the struggle to understand. Having a rival slugger in the family he hoped to join could hardly be pleasing news for him.

'Simon presumably knows about this?' I asked.

'Danny told Melinda and Simon himself quite recently. Very naughty of him, wasn't it, Melinda?'

'He was a nasty man,' Melinda cried.

'He'd had a hard life, darling,' her mother pointed out. 'My life with my first husband was up and down, I'm afraid, and Danny must have felt insecure. He was a clingy child, especially after Ron walked out on us. I brought Danny up and we were close, but when I began my cabaret work Danny became very jealous of my admirers, so he left home after Lance's death and I didn't see him again until he came here in 1994. He always wanted to be close to me and he didn't like it when I was friendly with other people. Crockendene was his home because it is my home, just as it is for Simon and Melinda. I'd always felt bad about Danny having no home of his own; Charlie would look after Melinda, I reasoned, and Rex after Simon, but Danny had nothing, which is why we had the little upset over my will.'

'That wasn't fair, Mummy,' Melinda said. 'You just said it is my home and I suppose Simon's.'

Adora just gave her a vague smile and then it was Harry's turn. He was still looking stupefied at the turn of events.

'And that, darling Harry,' Adora explained, 'is why I really can't marry you again. It would upset too many people. And Jack, I hope you see now that Danny might have feared that I killed Lance, but

I didn't. Someone else did. As to who that was, you and the police must settle the matter. There is no evidence that I killed him.'

'The photograph,' I said, 'would be a help. Have you destroyed it?'

Adora rose and went to her desk, opened it, extracted the photo and handed it to me. 'How could I destroy a photo of my darling son?'

Those veils were *still* in place over this case. Should I tell Brandon right away that Danny Carter was Adora's son? I should have done but I didn't. I had one last line to follow up.

Gabriel Allyn didn't seem surprised to hear from me.

'Lance Benny again?' he enquired when I called him.

'Broader than that. Danny Carter was the waiter at the Three Parrots on the night Benny died. Did you know Danny was Adora's son?'

A long pause. 'I did not. That perhaps explains many things. A sad life.'

Should I say more? I was undecided but he was still listening, so I continued. 'Adora denies killing Lance. She says that after Danny told her Lance was running out on her she was naturally upset, but then she realized that she had made a mistake in wanting to marry him.'

There was another silence. 'This has gone on long enough,' he said eventually. 'It's time to distil the truth.'

SIXTEEN

Today I would drive my Lagonda. On a sunny day in mid-June the English countryside is at its green and luxuriant best and the sight of picturesque villages combined with the Lagonda itself would reassure me that there would always be an England – murder or not.

Gabriel had asked me to join him at Downe Place for a gathering of the clan. The clan would be the former Three Parrots members and Charlie Dane and the purpose, I hoped, was to bring all the years of silence to an end.

As Danny Carter must lie at the heart of the matter, I had brought Brandon up to date with the developments and told him where I was going. To my surprise, he had not been thrown by the revelations and, indeed, seemed pleased. He had had to release Simon without charge but I knew he was hoping that the new information might give him extra ammunition.

'With Carter being his half-brother,' he had said on the phone, 'it makes Hargreaves' motive all the stronger. Before his death they might have had a case for contesting the will but with Carter being Miss Ferne's son that route would be closed.'

'A financial motive despite his father rolling in wealth?' I asked, sure that Brandon was on the wrong track.

'Despite that. Simon Hargreaves is after the Lair and he wants to be sure he's keeping Crockendene Cottage. So unless you come up with something dramatic, Jack, that's the line I'm going with.'

Driving the Lagonda was a good tonic for getting over my frustration. It said it all. Even though it dated from roughly the same time as Gabriel's SS 100, it seemed to sum up Adora's world of the fifties and sixties, by which time the Lagonda itself was well on the way to being a classic. I'd thought earlier that I might have brought the Packard today, my other thirties' treasure, but today required a convertible. It was one of those rare days in England when one has no hesitation in driving with the top down and what better car in which to appreciate that than the Lagonda?

As I drove through the massive gateway of Downe Place I thought of Adora's memory of sitting outside the house, the rejection that followed and of Gabriel's story of rejection by her. All so long ago, but so vivid in their memories and all could have changed so quickly if the pattern of events had been different. Would today change anything? Would it give a big push forward for the Carter case? I was up against time with Simon still in Brandon's sights, and excitement combined with trepidation churned inside me as I parked and walked up to the door.

There was no rejection there today as Gabriel escorted me to a large former orangery leading on to the terrace. Even though I was five minutes early the gathering seemed already complete, suggesting that there'd been an earlier pow-wow. I was surprised to see Monty with them until I realized this must be a kindness on Gabriel's part so that Monty and Valentine could be together. Gabriel was a kind and thoughtful man. The noise of animated conversation stopped abruptly when I came in and Charlie started the ball rolling.

'This news about Danny Carter, Jack. Casts a different light on things. I was married to that woman for ten years and she never mentioned anything about another son, only Simon.'

'Nor did she to me,' Rex chimed in immediately. 'Does it affect anything?'

'I'd say it makes a hell of a difference,' Noel declared, glaring at me as though I were personally responsible for Danny Carter's parentage. 'This fund we've been paying into like blasted lambs and then Adora has the cheek to tell us she's had threats to the collection if we refused to up the amount we paid—'

'Hold on!' I said. 'She knew about the fund?' I was horrified as once more the case turned on its head.

'Must have. She told us about the threats at the same time as Carter's annual request for payment told us the rates were shooting up. The nerve of the woman. After all we'd done for her.' The looks he received from his fellow Parroters quickly stopped him from going any further.

'But she didn't actually mention the fund?' I said.

Noel looked at the others, now perplexed.

'Maybe not,' Rex said at last. 'We may have assumed that. Everyone agree?' There were doubtful nods, to my relief. Another Carter trick, and it explained the reason for the letters.

'But Adora could have told Carter to do the dirty work,' Noel pointed out.

'No,' Gabriel said. 'Adora tends to speak the truth.'

'Let's give her the benefit of the doubt,' I suggested.

'She's used to that,' Charlie muttered.

'We're wasting time,' Rex pointed out impatiently. 'We're here to talk about 1964, not the fund.'

'And Jack,' Gabriel assured me, 'whatever you have heard before, this has to be the truth. *Our* truth, at any rate. We're all verging on or in our eighties. We need to come to terms with the past and be at peace. May I speak for us all?' He looked round his former comrades.

'Please yourself.' Charlie shrugged. 'We can chip in if we disagree.'

Gabriel nodded. 'Very well, then. Do we all agree that Danny's parentage was not known to us until now?'

There were nods all round. 'Such fun,' I heard Monty murmur.

'Do we also agree, gentlemen, that much earlier that evening – I recall it being about ten o'clock – Adora had told us with great excitement that Lance was going to announce their engagement at midnight?'

Most present nodded, although Charlie denied being present. 'Not being a member,' he added ironically.

'Do we all agree,' Gabriel continued, 'that sometime between her sessions, between perhaps eleven and half past when she was not present, Lance confessed to us that he was backing out and intended to slip away home?'

A unanimous yes to this, save for Charlie for the same reason. 'I've been thinking. I may have passed him on the stairs up to my dad's office a bit later. I reckon, as Jack suggested, that he was making for the Gentlemen's Retreat in case Adora saw him. Her dressing room opened on to the corridor leading to the side alley. We thought at the time she'd seen him going out of the door, nipped out to stop him leaving, grabbed a knife to threaten him, he tried to take it from her and it went in while they were struggling. None of us could believe she did it on purpose.'

There was a full round of nods to this.

'Do we all agree,' Gabriel continued, 'that no announcement was made at midnight, that we heard Adora screaming shortly afterwards, that we pretended to be searching for him in the building and that not long afterwards, perhaps fifteen or twenty minutes later, a young waiter, probably Danny Carter, told us and Tony Dane that he had found Lance's body? Tony then asked Travers Winton to check whether he was still alive.'

Nods all round.

'Then where were we all during that vital period of, say, eleven thirty to twelve twenty? Travers told us Lance had only very recently died, between, say, eleven forty-five and twelve fifteen, and the noise from the band alone would have drowned any cries from outside.'

'We were in the hall listening to Adora,' Rex said impatiently. 'After that, as you described.'

'But were we listening to her? Was none of us missing? Can we be sure?' Gabriel looked round. 'This wasn't a concert, after all. The Three Parrots was a nightclub. We moved around, helped ourselves to the food in the anteroom, drinks were being served.'

There was general agreement that no one could be certain and my hopes began to dwindle. No significant new ground so far.

'Then let's cut to Danny Carter's – assuming that he was that waiter – suggestion about taking the body to Soho Square. Are we agreed it was the waiter who did so?' Gabriel said.

A majority of nods.

'I took my coat from the peg at someone's suggestion because of the blood,' he continued steadily. 'I believe Travers suggested it but it might have been Danny.'

We had to move on to the more contentious areas, I realized, so I took over the lead. 'Was your reason for this plan to protect yourselves or Adora or the club?' I asked.

'Motivation tends to be thought about in hindsight,' Gabriel pointed out. 'Tony was concerned about his club but at the time we were more occupied with how to cope with the ghastly horror in the alleyway.'

'Is all this really necessary?' Noel asked crossly.

'Yes,' Gabriel said. 'Go on, Jack.'

'What was the exact order of events after Travers confirmed Lance was dead?' I asked.

'Dad and me were downstairs,' Charlie replied, 'when he came back in. You lot' – he indicated the group – 'crowded round. Travers had his say, Danny did his piece and we all got moving.'

'Did Danny go with you to the square?'

'He must have done,' Rex said. 'When we walked back to the club the band was still playing for Adora's twelve thirty to one slot, so we went up to Tony's office to cool down. We were very shaken.'

'Did you discuss calling the police?'

'I can't recall,' Rex said. 'Does anyone?'

A general shaking of heads, but Noel answered: 'I think we asked the waiter – Danny – if he'd seen anyone else in the alley. And—'

'Go on,' I said grimly when he halted.

Noel looked around for back-up. 'I'm pretty sure that he said yes. He'd seen Adora.' There was an uneasy stirring. 'He told us he'd seen her rush out into the alley just before her session began at eleven thirty and then again just after twelve, shortly before he found the body. We presumed she had attacked him earlier and then after her session ended she ran out to see whether he had recovered. But he hadn't. As Danny couldn't be positive Adora had killed him, taking the body to the square was best for everyone.' Noel stopped, perhaps aware of how this sounded. 'We all agreed,' he ended uncertainly.

'We all loved Adora,' Rex said. 'Some of us wanted to marry her. Lance had behaved badly to her. He was a rotter of the first order. I can only say in our defence that we were young. It seems weak now but we didn't see it that way. We thought we were being gallant in protecting the woman we loved.'

'And as a result it's hung over you all these years,' I pointed out.

'Can't say it has.' Charlie was getting pugnacious. 'Big mistake at the time, but the police case was closed.'

'We convinced ourselves that we could not be sure it was Adora,' Gabriel said. 'Even the waiter wasn't certain about what he'd seen. But we all believed she was guilty. Now we know that Danny was there, what was a mere seed of doubt in our minds has to be re-examined.'

'Very well, then,' I said. 'Adora truly believes it was one of you. You truly believe it was her. Who's right and who's wrong?'

'She produces a different story every day,' Charlie said dismissively.

'No.' Gabriel seemed puzzled. 'She always spoke the truth.'

Perhaps the truth as she saw it, I thought to myself, and did she speak the whole truth? My brain was signalling so fast that my speech couldn't keep up with it, and so I tried to take it step by step.

'Danny might have told her he'd seen one of you kill him or indeed all of you do so. Perhaps that's why she has acted the way she has. She believes she is protecting you.'

Their faces changed but with varying responses. Anger, enlightenment, bewilderment?

'So that she could blackmail us, you mean,' Noel snapped.

'No, you're wrong there, Noel,' Charlie said. 'We didn't hear a peep out of her for thirty years. Only when Carter came to live at Crockendene.'

'But you and Rex were married to her,' I pointed out. 'Didn't either of you know Danny was her son? Wasn't the murder of Lance Benny discussed between you?'

'Not with me,' Rex answered promptly. 'She never mentioned she had a son. And, speaking for myself, Jack, I believe we each explained Lance's death away to ourselves. Marriage is principally a matter of every day; it's the present, not the past. I think I did once try to talk about it but she just ignored me.'

'She would,' I pointed out. 'She thought it might have been you who killed Lance and she didn't want to know.'

'That,' Rex said coldly, 'is quite ridiculous.' He turned to Charlie. 'Did that happen to you?'

'Least said soonest mended in my view,' he replied. 'When I decided to get out of the marriage it was just one more reason. I didn't fancy thinking about her past and I loved that woman, but she decided one man wasn't enough for her so I pulled the plug on it.'

'Jack,' Gabriel said quietly, 'you've listened to us enough. Are you any nearer learning who killed Lance?'

My feet seemed to be getting as restless as my mind and I stood up. As I had been listening to them an idea had been forming, one so unexpected that I must have been under the impression that if I stood up I might shake it into form. I couldn't. I stood there dumbly for a minute or two while their comments and theories swirled helplessly around in my mind in search of a whole.

'Yes,' I blurted out, still not sure, but just the sound of that word confirmed it like the final click of a key turning in its lock. 'Lance's murderer wasn't any of you – it wasn't Adora either. It was Danny Carter himself.'

A silence, then a flat: 'You're bonkers, Jack,' from Gabriel. 'He was only fifteen years old. Why would he have killed Lance? Lance was a successful racing driver at the time, a hero to all teenage boys. Think of Mike Hawthorn; think of Stirling Moss and Graham Hill. He was up there with them.'

My mind went blank. I'd been a fool speaking out so soon. Reason can only take one so far, and after that there's a need to think round the issue. I tried hard. 'Imagine,' I said, 'the emotions of a fifteen-year-old boy who had lived with Adora all his life. His father had left them years earlier. He was fiercely protective of his mother and looking forward to having a father figure in his life again, especially a hero.

'And then,' I was gathering speed now, 'he hears Lance telling you all that he doesn't want to marry Adora after all. He's running away. He's a coward. Not only does Danny himself feel rejected but he's furious that his mother will suffer again.'

Dead silence now.

Then: 'My word, Jack, haven't you done well?' Monty said approvingly. 'Even I had not thought of that solution. But you're quite right. He would have resented Lance's defection.'

'Wrong, Monty. Jack, you must be mistaken,' Rex said, 'much as I'd like to think you're right, and so I'm sure would we all. But he definitely implied that Adora was the killer. That doesn't sound like the filial love that you refer to.'

I was stumped but Gabriel rescued me.

'We know, gentlemen,' he said, 'that Carter was a cunning operator. After all, he does not seem to have baulked at sending threatening letters to his mother. In 1964 the same cool operator might not have baulked at blaming Adora for Lance's murder, relying on the near certainty that we would not betray her if he accused her of the murder. That would deflect suspicion from himself. Perhaps he even saw it as the greater good: his beloved mother would be protected by a group of her admirers for the rest of her life.'

While we were struggling to absorb this, Adora herself came on stage. In person, and right on cue, at Downe Place. For a moment I thought she was an apparition conjured up out of the past, but she was real enough. She was clinging to the doorway to the terrace, dressed in a figure-hugging scarlet full-length dress as though she were on stage at the Three Parrots, with make-up and an exotic wig – but with tears running down her face. She looked wonderful, she looked a fright, and my heart bled for her.

'Thank you, Gabriel,' she whispered. 'Thank you, Jack.' She still clung to the doorpost though she was looking round pleadingly at us all.

'I'm sorry, gentlemen.' She made an attempt at a smile. 'I thought I would gatecrash your little party and find out which one of you gentlemen had killed Lance. Instead I find out it was my own son, my darling Danny.'

I thought she would fall and immediately rushed to help her but Gabriel was first, supporting her inside to an armchair.

'"The dog it was that died,"' she murmured to herself, her head drooping. 'The dog wasn't Danny, it was me.'

'We don't know—' Rex began.

'Yes, we do.' Charlie overruled him. 'You've got it right, Jack. You got it right, Gabriel. It's the only logical conclusion.'

Adora raised her head. 'I thought it was you, Gabriel,' she whispered, 'or sometimes I thought it was Rex or Charlie or any of you – all so jealous of one another.'

No one said a word, not even Monty.

'My Danny,' she sobbed. 'He loved me so much. He'd have done anything for me. Even murder.'

'One is nearer to God in a garden,' the old poem goes, 'than anywhere else on earth.' And never had that felt truer than that evening.

'Can we help her?' Louise asked when I told her the story.

'We could try. She's a strong woman, though, and she has her family.'

'Does she?' Louise said. 'What about that man she was going to marry and what about Simon Hargreaves being under suspicion?'

I'd been so busy with Lance Benny that I had put the killer of Danny Carter to the back of my mind. Not to mention . . .

'Fred Fox,' I groaned, probably inexplicably to Louise. There were still two murders to be solved (in my humble opinion, even if not in Brandon's). In theory one of the Three Parrots group could still be involved in one or both of them. And then there was Doubler.

Louise was prodding me into facing unwelcome truths. I could ring Brandon and tell him that the murder of Lance Benny was all but solved and relay my new belief about that and Danny's connection with it leading to the consequent blackmail. But Fred Fox had no reason to fear either side.

I burdened poor Louise with these findings, with the result that she produced her own line: 'You've got it the wrong way round.'

'Tell me, do.'

'Fred was blackmailing Danny Carter's killer. He was around. He saw who killed him.'

I stared at her. That was where we had begun and in all the concentration on Lance Benny I had left the simple explanation behind. Now Louise had brought me full circle. 'Blessings upon you, dearest woman.'

'It was obvious, dear man.'

'But who did kill Danny? Louise, do you think there's the slightest possibility that Brandon is right? That these two murders are set in the present and not in the past?'

She couldn't answer me, of course. I was still missing something and the answer must surely lie in the Lair.

This time it was easier. I had rung the farmhouse to see how Adora was after yesterday's scene and Melinda had told me curtly that she was quite well, thank you and goodbye. It had been Harry who had driven her to Sussex the day before, and when I reached the Lair I saw that his Land Rover was sitting outside it, although luckily there was no sign of him inside. I had no wish to meet a killer and he was fitting that role all too comfortably. The double doors were open, however, and I saw that the XJ 8 was missing, so perhaps he had been commandeered to take Adora for another ride.

The Lair seemed sinister today, almost as though the Jaguars were licking their lips for their dinner. I studied the photograph of Fred and Adora picnicking and could see what had attracted her to him. I wondered whether on one of those rides with him she had let slip the secret that she had kept from her family – that Danny was her son – and Fred had been looking for evidence of that in the Lair.

I was standing with my back to the empty space and looking up at the platform that the thirteenth car had never graced when I realized that the noise behind me meant the incoming car hadn't yet braked.

I turned my head and froze. It was making straight for me. There was nowhere to leap out of its path. Gale was out to kill me and there wasn't a damn thing I could do about it. Except, I realized in desperation, to make a grab for the large cream board on the platform above me. I jumped and the flimsy structure gave way, collapsing with me on to the bonnet of the car. That and the fact that at the last moment the brakes jerked to a stop saved my life. As I lay sprawled on the bonnet, I raised my head and looked in at my would-be murderer. It wasn't Gale at the wheel; it wasn't Doubler or any of his men. It was Charlie Dane.

'I couldn't bloody do it,' he muttered as I half fell, half climbed off the bonnet. 'I couldn't do it, damn you, Colby.'

I felt like a hypnotized rabbit caught by the headlights. 'You were going to kill me?'

He pounded the steering wheel in fury. 'I should have done it, I *should.*'

They say that when you're near to death by drowning your whole life flashes by you. Mine hadn't, but then I wasn't drowning. The whole case flashed by me, however. '*You* killed Fred Fox,' I said flatly.

'Had to,' he muttered.

'Because he knew you'd killed Danny Carter. He saw you that night.'

He slumped over the wheel, seemingly unable to move, for which I was grateful. I didn't want to end up strangled.

'Yeah,' he said at last. 'I reckon that's the long and the short and size of it. That little runt Danny. The runt of Adora's family, eh? He was no good – never was. Nor that Fred Fox; I hated him from the moment Adora took him on but she fancied him like crazy. He was trash. Why choose rubbish like him?' He gave a grim laugh. 'That's what Rex said of me when Adora told him she was going to hitch up with me.

'I knew you'd get there,' he rambled on. 'Thought I'd work out whether you were on track. I reckoned yesterday it wouldn't be too long before you were on to me. I'd taken precautions. If you want a job done properly bring in Doubler, that's what the word is. But he didn't want nothing to do with it, so it's just you and me, Jack. You going to call Brandon or shall I? It was this way. You were right. Fox was blackmailing me over Danny. Saw me come in the gates, then after the alarm went off go into the Lair with Danny.

Heard the shot, saw me come out. Families, eh?' he concluded. 'Got a wife and kids, have you?'

'Had a wife, and have a daughter.'

'Brandon won't have any trouble fixing both jobs on me. I'll plead guilty and DNA should sort it out. You take care of that family of yours, Jack. Do anything for them.'

He was really rambling now. Getting desperate to have it over and done with. I thought of my ex-wife, Eva, and Cara. My daughter, yes, but Eva? Would I do anything for her? Then I remembered I had once tried my best to save her when she was in trouble, just as Charlie had Adora.

'Families, eh?' I heard Charlie repeat as I rang Brandon.

Brandon had been right all along. The family line. Not Simon, though, but the ex-husband Charlie, out to save Adora from her own son. In a way, however, I had been right too. Charlie had killed Danny because he was threatening them over Lance Benny and Fox knew he had. And yet something didn't quite add up . . .

Brandon came to see me at Frogs Hill that evening. Louise and I had just returned from a walk when he drew up. He wanted to put me in the picture, he said.

'You did a good job, Jack. Thanks. Dane's been no trouble. Any comments?'

'How would "it doesn't feel right" sound to you?' I asked him reluctantly. 'Or, correction, "not completely right"?'

'That fits my thinking like a glove,' Brandon replied, surprising me yet again. 'There's certainly trace evidence to tie him in with Fox's murder but on Carter's it's less convincing. It was Hargreaves' gun but Dane could have had access to it as he was on friendly terms with the Hargreaves, particularly young Michael. With Hargreaves we don't have enough on him for either death, apart from motive. With Dane the motive's the weaker side. Suppose neither of them killed Danny?' We contemplated the garden in the dusk, neither speaking for a while, perhaps because neither of us could put our thoughts into words.

Brandon at last put my own thoughts into words: 'Excluding Adora herself, there's only one person who could have killed him.'

I had remembered Charlie's disjointed words about families: *Do anything for them.* Did that include a false confession over Danny?

'*Melinda*,' I said, all doubts now gone.

'The daughter,' Brandon said simultaneously. 'I'll put through a check on the DNA. Why, though? The inheritance money?'

More than that, I thought. 'She'd recently learned not only that Danny was her half-brother but that he was going to scoop every penny her mother had and that meant losing her home. Sibling jealousy with a vengeance.'

I thought this through as the dusk began to turn into night. Night sometimes provides a clarity that the clean light of day makes invisible.

'Perhaps,' I said to him, 'it all goes back to childhood. Melinda lost a mother figure, Danny a father. Adora therefore becomes all important to both of them. In Melinda's case, that will of Adora's would see her lose her family home for the second time. She saw Danny as a dangerous leech, the cuckoo in the cosy nest. He would have taken Crockendene away from her. He had to go. Charlie knew very well who had killed Danny because Fox was blackmailing her, not him. He'd seen who had followed Danny into the Lair that evening after she set the alarm off.'

Brandon wasn't my only visitor that evening. Louise had gone to bed early and I heard that whistle again. This time I was too tired even to be scared. Doubler came through that gate just as he had before.

'Told you to be careful,' he said. 'Heard Charlie Dane's been taken in.'

'He turned up a mild case of trumps. He didn't kill me.'

'Tut, tut, Jack. Didn't say it was you he was after, did I? I don't remember that. Only joking,' he added. 'I didn't like that other fellow he had it in for – Fox. I never do dirty work, as you know. I wouldn't let any of my lads touch it. Nor you. Told him it wasn't safe. Safe? In this world? I ask you. Who is? I just didn't like the smell of it. I owed you and now I've paid you.'

'I'll look on it that way,' I assured him.

'You do that, Jack. We're even now. Be seeing you.'

'I hope not,' I murmured – once he'd gone.

Zoe. I'd forgotten about my trusty employee in all the turmoil. Brandon had called early that morning to tell me that Melinda was now in custody too and that Charlie was about to be charged with Fred Fox's murder. Knowing that life was proceeding as normal, the Pits was a welcome diversion from yesterday's drama and I forced myself back to it. The first thing I noticed was that Zoe's hair was back to its usual red and I cautiously congratulated her, not knowing her latest Rob Lane situation.

'Hair looks good,' I said brightly.

'I've told him to get lost,' she replied. 'That's what you wanted to know, isn't it?'

'Do you mean it?'

'Yes.'

'Miss him?'

'Yes, but so what? Better miss him now than divorce him later on.'

That's my Zoe, I thought. She too was back to normal.

I went to see Adora after the news of the arrests had been made public. Melinda had been charged with Danny's murder, having readily admitted that she had killed him – indeed, she seemed proud of the fact, Brandon had told me, and it seemed immaterial to her that it had led to her father killing Fred. She had to do it to protect her home, she had explained.

Today it was Alice who opened the farmhouse door and I feared she might slam it in my face, but she didn't.

'Grandora will be pleased to see you.' She managed a smile. 'She's over the worst now.'

'Are you staying here with her?'

'For a while.'

'You're still going to London, though?'

'Gran insists on it. She's very brave. But she might have some surprising news.'

'Good news?' She deserved it.

'Very good.'

'She's marrying again?' I joked.

'Oh.' She looked disappointed and I realized I'd hit the jackpot unawares.

'Not darling Harry?' I asked in resignation.

She laughed. 'It's not my business to tell you.'

'What's happened to Rob?'

Alice grinned. 'Who?'

She took me along to the small room overlooking the garden where Adora was sitting – in a defiant bright blue dress with a rose in her hair.

'That looks a good remedy,' I said.

'A brave face, Jack, that's all. What is it with me, Jack? They all love me, my daughter, my son, poor Charlie, Melinda, poor Rex, Lance, Danny – and yet such terrible things happen.'

'Will you go on living here?' I asked.

'It's my home. That's what it was all about. Melinda thought it was hers; Danny taunted her that it would be his. Home is a volatile concept, Jack. But they all love me. That's what brought about Lance's death. Isn't that scary?'

'They did love you, but sometimes not sensibly.'

'You're right, Jack. I see that now. Now do come with me. I've something to show you.' She took my arm and we walked outside, across the courtyard to the path through the woods and thence to the Lair. At each step she seemed to grow stronger, brighter, much more her old self. As the Lair came in sight, she stopped and pointed.

'Look,' she said.

The blinds were up and I could see the cars inside. But something was different . . . *yes*!

It was the beautiful, unique shape of the SS 100 Jaguar: gleaming, glorious and inimitable, occupying the platform that had been awaiting it so long.

'It was always Jaguars after I first rode in that car with Gabriel,' Adora said. 'Always Gabriel. He just went away and left me when he did his National Service. I thought he didn't care, so I always insisted on my admirers buying Jaguars after that and then I accepted them when they chose to give them to me. I just had to show Gabriel that I didn't care either. Then he came back – and by that time I'd met Noel and Lance. Gabriel showed no signs of fighting back and Lance was so very, very exciting to be with. And Rex too. Gabriel had assumed I still felt the same, which I did. Deep down I still loved him just as much but I'd been so hurt when he left without saying a word about the future that I'd tried to convince myself that I didn't care a jot and that plenty of other men wanted me. With Lance it was different. I really did think that we were made for each other and that my affair with Gabriel was over. Only for a short time, though. Then on that dreadful night I knew what a fool

I'd been but it was too late. Gabriel never spoke to me after that and Rex was so very charming. I couldn't believe that Gabriel didn't care any more, but when he kept refusing my request for the car I knew I was right. He did care but his wretched pride wasn't going to let him admit it. He told me yesterday that he'd come to realize that the Jaguars are like us. However much the cars developed and grew with the years, and however much we tried to ignore what had once lain between us, the bedrock remained firm. And look, Jack, there it is. The bedrock. The SS 100.'

'The thirteenth car,' I breathed in awe.

'A gift delivered in person,' Adora said. 'With love.'

The Car's the Star
James Myers

The Starring Jaguar Cars in Adora Ferne's Lair

1949 XK 120 sports car donated by Valentine Paston in 1964

1956 Jaguar D-type racing sports car bought from Lance Benny's estate in 1965

1957 XK 150 sports car donated by Sir Rex Hargreaves in 1969

1958 XK 150 sports car donated in 1963 by Travers Winton (deceased)

1959 Mark II saloon donated in 1968 by Patrick O'Hara (deceased)

1962 E-type sports car donated in 1969 by Noel Brandon-Wright

1969 XJ 6 saloon donated by Charlie Dane in 1972

1971 E-type sports car donated by Blake Bishop in 1980

1975 E-type sports car donated by Alan Reeve in 1984

1975 XJ 6 saloon donated in 1977 by Ivan Cole (deceased)

1975 XJ 12 saloon 'donated' by Fred Fox in 1994

1994 XJ 8 saloon 'donated' by Harry Gale in 2007 (Ford had now taken over Jaguar)

Plus the thirteenth car:

1937 SS 100 2.5 litre owned by the Earl of Storrington

Jack Colby's own classic cars

Jack's 1965 Gordon Keeble
Ninety-nine of these fabulous supercars were built between 1963 and '66 with over ninety units surviving around the globe, mostly in the UK. Designed by John Gordon and Jim Keeble using current racing car principles with the bodyshell designed by twenty-one-year-old Giorgetto Giugiaro at Bertone, the cars were an instant success but the company was ruined by supply-side

industrial action with ultimately only ninety-nine units completed even after the company was relaunched in May 1965 as Keeble Cars Ltd. Final closure came in February 1966 when the factory at Sholing closed and Jim Keeble moved to Keewest. The hundredth car was completed in 1971 with leftover components. The Gordon Keeble's emblem is a yellow and green tortoise.

Jack's 1938 Lagonda V-12 Drophead
The Lagonda company won its attractive name from a creek near the home of the American-born founder Wilbur Gunn in Springfield, Ohio. The name given to it by the American Indians was Ough Ohonda. The V-12 Drophead was a car to compete with the very best in the world, with a sporting twelve-cylinder engine which would power the two 1939 Le Mans cars. Its designer was the famous W.O. Bentley. Sadly, many fine pre-war saloons have been cut down to look like Le Mans replicas. The V-12 cars are very similar externally to the earlier six-cylinder versions; both types were available with open or closed bodywork in a number of different styles. The Lagonda also featured in Jack's earlier case, *Classic in the Barn.*

Jack's 1935 Packard Series 120 Sedan (Saloon)
The Packard One-Twenty (or '120') was produced by the Packard Motor Car Company of Detroit from 1935 to 1941. The One-Twenty model designation was replaced by the Packard Eight model name during model years 1938 to 1942. The '120' was an important car in Packard's history because it signified that Packard had for the first time entered into the competitive mid-priced eight-cylinder car market. It is probable that the '120' saved Packard's bacon back in the mid-thirties – the Great Depression years. Otherwise, this theory goes, Packard would most likely have been defunct by 1940, as were Duesenberg, Cord, Marmon, Peerless and Pierce-Arrow. The Packard featured in Jack's earlier case, *Classic Cashes In.*